Mortal Choice

David Shactman

BookLocker
Trenton, Georgia

Paperback ISBN: 978-1-959622-55-0
Hardcover ISBN: 978-1-959622-56-7
Ebook ISBN: 979-8-88531-960-7

Published by BookLocker.com, Inc., Trenton, Georgia.

BookLocker.com, Inc.
2025

First Edition

Library of Congress Cataloging in Publication Data
Shactman, David
Mortal Choice by David Shactman
Library of Congress Control Number: 2025901119

Dedication

In loving memory of my father, Samuel Shactman

Prologue

Cassandra

The most unlikely event can shake the ground beneath you and change how you see the world. It can compel you to make choices that might otherwise seem distasteful or immoral— especially if such an event involves the life of your child. I know, for that is how my story begins.

I had taken my daughter, Keri, to visit her grandmother in rural Alabama. My mother still lived out in the country in her old cottage with the faded asphalt shingles and sagging front porch. The double hung windows, crooked and halfway open in the summer heat, were the same ones that used to rattle as I slept in my little girl's bed. The kitchen had one of those wooden screen doors with a rusty metal spring that closed like a slap in the face. It was that noise I heard when Keri scampered in from the back yard yelling, "Mommy, I have to go potty."

I led her to the bathroom and watched as the little girl sat on the old wooden toilet seat. Her tiny tush was not wide enough to stretch across, so she held herself up with both hands on the sides of the seat. I can still see her in my mind, my precious six-year-old; pastel blue shorts bunched around her ankles; big brown eyes set over a little snub nose; tawny brown hair falling in tangled curls down the sides of her cheeks. When she smiled, the corners of her mouth turned up, revealing tiny, white teeth. Her laugh was an innocent, joyous giggle. Less than four feet tall, she weighed only forty-two pounds, but my happy little girl was a bundle of energy.

In her tinny, high-pitched voice, she was singing a song from *Sesame Street*. Neither of us had looked down into the toilet bowl. We hadn't noticed the black head of a pit viper just below the surface of the

water. It must have slithered into the old, galvanized pipe from the septic tank in the back yard. Yes, it happens. There was an episode from *Inside Edition*, the television program, about a North Carolina man who found six snakes in his toilet over a four-year period.

The snake—a long, skinny, black, water moccasin—had wriggled all the way from the back yard to the toilet. The heat-sensitive pits between its eyes must have detected warmth from Keri's behind. Its pea-sized brain would have registered danger; a threat looming inches above its head. But the serpent was probably hungry, foraging for food, and not about to go away.

Innocent of the danger, I left the door open and went into the adjacent room to make the bed. I have played it through my mind a thousand times, imagining what happened next. The tip of its snout must have quietly broken the surface of the water. Then, uncoiling, rising through the space between the basin and Keri's behind, the serpent's head would have emerged above the toilet seat pausing midway between my little girl's thighs.

Keri was sitting on the seat singing, her head bobbing up and down with the melody. Suddenly, she must have looked down and spotted the triangular head of the black snake, its upper body coiled like a backward "s," its beady eyes, vertical like a cat, staring at her naked belly. Sensing danger, the snake would have opened its jaws displaying its bright white "Cotton" mouth. That must have been when Keri screamed and jumped off the seat. But the sudden movement would have spooked the snake, who could thrust its head much quicker than my tiny girl could rise off the seat. It struck her in the belly, penetrating her skin, injecting its poisonous venom into her abdomen. "Snake, Snake, Mommy! The snake bit me," she cried.

When Keri screamed "snake," I figured it was the child's imagination. Maybe she was stung by a wasp or bitten by an insect. But when I ran into the bathroom, I saw the long, black tube halfway in the

toilet and half wriggling on the tile floor. I screamed and snatched Keri away and laid her down on the half-made bed in the next room. Keri pointed to her stomach where I saw two puncture marks. Her skin was turning red and starting to swell.

I was terrified. Would she have convulsions? Stop breathing? Lose consciousness? Die before I could get help? I had no idea. All I knew was that I had to get her to the hospital. Hoisting her in my arms, with my mother hurrying behind, I raced out to the car. They say it's best to extract the venom within five minutes of the bite, but no way that was happening. The nearest hospital was a twenty-minute ride, and I drove like a maniac, pulling up and leaving the car right in front of the entrance to the emergency room.

A couple of patients were lined up at the intake window and looked askance as I cut in front of them. I was frantic and must have looked like a crazy person. "My daughter was bitten by a poisonous snake," I blurted out to the intake nurse. Fortunately, the nurse reacted quickly. They rushed Keri to a trauma room and injected her with antivenin. "How long has it been since she was bitten?" the doctor asked.

"About a half hour."

The doctor was reassuring. "Usually, the antivenin is sufficient to counteract the poison," he said. "In all likelihood, she will be fine. However, she's small and the poison has been in her body for quite a while, so we'll run some routine tests and keep her for observation."

They brought Keri upstairs to a hospital room, and I breathed a sigh of relief, thinking everything was going to be okay. But two hours later, when the doctor came in, I could tell by the look on his face that something was wrong.

"I'm sorry to give you bad news," he began in his formal doctor speak, "but Keri has sustained damage to her kidneys. Her urine indicates severe kidney injury, and there's been no additional urine output since a catheter was placed in her bladder. In a small number of

snakebite cases, patients develop tissue necrosis—dead tissue, resulting from the poisonous venom, blocks the tubes in the kidneys and can cause acute renal failure. It will take a few days for us to determine whether her kidney function will recover. A kidney biopsy may be necessary to provide a definitive answer."

The next few days, my mother and I lived at the hospital, staying by Keri's bedside, meeting with her doctors, checking and re-checking her urine bag. But there was virtually no output. The doctor decided to perform a biopsy. When he entered the room to report the results, I searched his face for any sign of reassurance, a pleasurable look, a smile, some eye contact. But his face was impassive, stony, his lips tight together, his forehead wrinkled. He looked like a state trooper making a traffic stop. But to me, he was not just a state trooper. He was a god who carried the fate of my only child. What he was about to say could change both of our lives forever.

The doctor asked me to step out of the room. I was shaking. If the results were positive, he would have greeted me happily, smiling, blurting out the good news. He had done nothing of the kind. He led me to an empty room down the hall.

"I'm sorry Ms. Crawford. I regret to tell you that the biopsy confirmed our diagnosis. Aside from her kidney function, Keri is a healthy little girl. However, she has sustained irreversible kidney damage. Because her kidneys aren't working, she will need renal dialysis to replace the kidneys' function.

"What does that mean, Doctor? Will she ever recover?

"Not until we can find her a new kidney. Meanwhile she will have to undergo dialysis. The procedure is not painful, but she will likely need three treatments per week, each of which will last about four hours. Aside from that, she can enjoy a relatively normal life. When they find her a new kidney, she can undergo a transplant. The operation

has become quite routine, and your medical centers in Boston are among the best."

Chapter 1 – Two Years Later

Cassandra

I enter the corner office and feel my body stiffen as Donaldson drapes his arm around my shoulder. He is the director of operations for the Boston office of the FBI, and I am a senior investigator. Twenty years ago, I was hired as a lone, black woman in a white man's job. I got little respect. Had to start working undercover, insinuating myself into places a white person couldn't go, sometimes doing shitty things with dirty men. I reported directly to Donaldson before he became the director. I couldn't stand the man. He was always putting his hands on me. Somehow, I persevered and gradually moved up through the bureaucracy. Now my work is mostly supervisory and administrative, which is why I was surprised to be summoned to his office.

I look at Donaldson and think he is typical FBI. A tall, white guy with a crew cut, blue eyes, and thin nose. Graduated from Choate and Princeton. Fits the Bureau like an old pair of slippers—a comfort I will never have. He's in his late fifties but still thinks younger women find him hot. I've heard rumors about the way he treats other women on his staff. Apparently, he hasn't outgrown that frat-boy mentality from when the Bureau was all white and male.

With his hand on my back, he steers me over to a chair. I want to shove it off, but I can't. My job depends on him. And my health insurance. As a single mother with a health compromised daughter, I can ill afford to be unemployed.

Donaldson sits facing me, and I cross my legs, glad I'm not wearing a short skirt. Fortunately, I dressed conservatively this morning in a high-necked cotton blouse and a blue suit. "Cassandra," he says (not Agent Crawford), "I got an ugly case and need your help. Last week, I

got a call from our people in Mexico. A local hunter was walking through the woods when his dog got excited and began digging in the earth. The dog uncovered a body in a shallow grave. He notified the authorities who took the body to the coroner for examination. The report was gruesome. The young man no longer had his liver, pancreas, or kidneys, and his eyes were hollowed out."

"Was he one of ours?" I ask, wondering why I should be involved.

"No, not connected. He was a twentyish, Hispanic male, five foot nine, with numerous tattoos. Turns out, police had a bulletin on a missing Hispanic American with a similar description. His name was Miguel Sanchez, and he came from Fall River."

"What was he doing in Mexico?"

"Apparently, the kid's father had prostate cancer and needed an operation before it metastasized. But he was undocumented with no health insurance and couldn't afford the operation. The family was desperate to raise money, and Miguel told them he made a deal in Mexico to get the money. They thought it must be a drug deal and begged him not to go. That's the last they heard from him and reported him missing."

"Do his parents know they took his organs?"

"No, they already blame themselves for his death. That would only make them feel worse. Besides, on top of losing their son, they now could be subject to deportation."

"Yuck! You think he went to Mexico to deal drugs or to sell a kidney?"

"Could be either, but the Bureau has been investigating rumors about trade in illegal organs in the Fall River and New Bedford areas. Organ traders find people who are desperate for cash. They offer five to ten thousand for kidneys and have the operations performed in countries where authorities look the other way. We think the kid might have agreed to sell a kidney to raise money for his father's operation.

Whether they botched the operation or always intended to kill him for his organs, we don't know."

"If they were only after his organs, why did they gouge out his eyes?"

"Corneas. Good corneas, especially young ones, go for about $25,000."

"Nice."

"Cassandra, this isn't the only case of organ trading we're hearing about. I understand there have been some suspicious cases in New Bedford. This could involve an international criminal ring. We think the best way to penetrate it is to go undercover. I hesitate to ask you this, but I know your daughter, Keri, has kidney failure. You would be the ideal agent for a sting; a mother whose daughter needs a new kidney. I know you haven't worked undercover for a long time, but the Bureau needs you here."

"You're not serious!" I tell him. I'm shocked he would even suggest involving my daughter in an FBI operation. "You expect me to involve Keri?"

"I'm afraid so. I know it's asking a lot, but lives are at stake. These people are vicious and will kill more people for their organs."

"No, I won't do that to her. Besides, involving my daughter is totally against regulations. You have no right to ask me that."

"Cassandra, sometimes, under extraordinary circumstances, regulations have to be waived. This is a matter of national security. Foreign criminal organizations are killing American citizens for their organs."

"You're asking me to endanger my daughter's life."

"We'll protect her. You'll have plenty of backup. We all take risks in this job."

"With all due respect, sir, I've taken plenty of risks for the Bureau. No way I'm involving my daughter. That's going way too far."

"We need you, Cassandra. Go down to Fall River tomorrow and interview the parents. Then, think about your future. This could be a prominent case. You've come a long way in this organization, and there's a directorship coming up. Some people would like a person like you in that position. Perhaps we can a have a drink sometime and strategize about it," he says, rising dismissively from his chair and letting me know the conversation is over. He stands near me as I get up, and then leads me to the door with his hand resting embarrassingly low on my back.

Conniving son-of-a-bitch is all I can think when I leave his office. I know perfectly well what he meant by "a person like you" and didn't miss his impish grin when he suggested a drink. He has no right to involve Keri, but he will step on anyone to get the big score. "It's for the good of the country," he told me. But, in the end, it would be good for him. Meanwhile, if I refuse, it will be a cloud on my record. In the Bureau, it's not good to turn down an assignment. The bastard is making me choose between my daughter and my career. What's in it for me? Putting my daughter at risk. Involving her in this shitty business. If it works out? Maybe I get the promotion and the raise. And all the fucking guilt that goes with it.

Chapter 2

Martin

Looks like every other murder scene. Squad cars askew. Blue lights flashing. Cops barking into cell phones. Yellow tape. A body leakin' blood on the pavement. When I started out, the sight of a dead body gave me stomach acid; burned the back of my throat. Dreamt about it at night. Now, it's just another day, though nothin' like this should ever seem normal. I duck under the yellow tape with my partner, Tony D'Angelo. In homicide, detectives are in charge of their own cases, but they always have partners. Tony made detective three years ago and been with me ever since. We spot the Chief, Mike O'Donnell, standin' off to the side.

"'Bout time you guys got here. Couple more Big Macs, Moishe, you won't be able to limbo under that tape."

I'm used to it by now. The old Boston precincts have always been the home of Irish and Italians. Never had a Jewish detective before, 'specially one with a name like Martin Goldberg. Had a hard time fittin' in. Didn't help that I'm a big lunk of a guy who's a little clumsy. Still take a lotta shit, but most of it's good-natured. We're here 'cause detectives gotta be called if there's suspicion of homicide, and by the looks of things, this guy didn't die of natural causes.

"Whaddya got, Chief?" I ask, ignorin' his attempt at humor.

"Poor bastard was shot in the back of the head and thrown in the dumpster. Might have never found him, except for the asshole driving the garbage truck. Got one of those mechanical arms that picks up the dumpster and empties it into the truck. Except this guy was talking on his cell not paying attention. Not only that, had a half empty six pack in the cab."

"9:00 a.m., a little early for drinkin'," Tony says.

"Guy must put beer in his corn flakes. Anyway, half the shit in the dumpster missed the truck and splattered on the ground. He got out to look at the mess and saw a dead body in the middle of the garbage. Must have wanted to drive away, him drinking and all, but it's his route, and he'd have some explaining to do if he left."

"ID?" I ask.

"Neal Jensen, fifty-six-year-old white male according to his license. No priors. Lives in Quincy. A few credit cards, normal amount of cash, set of keys. That's all we got. Shot right through the back of the head. Unless the guy crawled into the dumpster and shot himself, you guys got another murder to solve. Some poor bastards gotta sift through the garbage to look for a weapon. Maybe that's detective work?"

"Funny guy. Maybe there's a suicide note scrawled on a piece a cabbage. Surprised if you find anythin'. I'll take a look at the body before forensics takes him away."

Seen my share of gruesome corpses, but this one's bad. With a day or two decomposin' in the garbage, the smell is overpowerin'. I choke back a surge of nausea and breathe through my mouth like I'm in a roadside outhouse. Ugly wound shows on the back a the guy's head. A few hungry flies feast on the area of missing flesh. Obvious he was shot at close range, maybe point blank, but not a suicide. They shoot themselves in the side of the head, or the temple, or stick the barrel in their mouth. Nobody reaches round to their back. Only one shot, so the attacker may have come up from behind and shot him execution style. More likely a planned homicide than a random shooting.

"Better check out the guy's house," I tell the Chief. "Trail's already a couple days cold." Tony takes the keys from the Chief, and we get a detail to accompany us to Jensen's and secure his place. Problem is, I gotta pee and won't be able to hold it 'til we get to Quincy.

"Hey guys, gotta stop at the gas station and take a whizz."

See a few smiles as I cross the street. They're young and don't worry about their prostate. I always gotta go at the worst times. Doc said I could take that Flomax, but once you start, you gotta take it for the duration.

Traffic on Boston's Southeast Expressway is like the supermarket the day before Thanksgivin'. After a half-hour of stop-and-go, we get off at the Quincy down ramp. Green suburbs are a change from Boston's gray, dirty streets. Neighborhood approachin' Jensen's mid-rise condo is clean and well kept, but the racket from the gardener's leaf blowers sounds like a fleet a 747s.

The name Jensen is halfway down the directory. I buzz his unit, hopin' for no answer. Nobody's reported him missin', and I'd rather not be the one to tell his wife or girlfriend he ain't comin' back. No one answers, so we use the set of keys to enter the unit. Front door opens into the livin' room, and things looks in order. Nicely furnished, soft leather sofa, fifty-inch flat screen, Bose soundbar, zero gravity recliner. Kitchen is orderly, half-filled coffee cup in the sink, fridge nearly empty. "Not much in here, Tony. Guy musta lived on take-out."

D'Angelo searches through the cabinets. "Nothin' unusual here, Martin, 'cept the place is dry. Don't see any booze."

I check out the master bedroom, wonderin' if Jensen lived alone. Got two closets. One full of men's clothes. Labels from Polo and Armani. Dozen pair of shoes lined up on the closet floor. Guy wasn't hurtin' for dough. Other closet's got women's clothes. Might belong to Jensen's wife, but the place seems small. Lacks that homey feel you get from a family. Kinda feels like a temporary rental. Two pictures sit on the dresser: Jensen with his arm around a younger man dressed in jeans and a T-shirt; next to it, a picture of Jensen holdin' hands with a good-lookin', middle-aged woman.

Master bath is off the bedroom. First thing that hits me are medicines stacked on the counter. Guy could open his own Walgreens.

Gotta have ‘em checked out at the lab. Medicine cabinet’s got female cosmetics; make-up, nail polish, eye liner. Shampoos and conditioners in the shower. Drawer in the vanity got a box half-full a condoms. At least the poor bastard was gettin’ *shtupped.*

Second bedroom’s furnished like an office. Big desk. Coupla framed degrees on the wall. Filin’ cabinets filled with colored folders. I glance at some papers on top a the desk. Statements from brokerage houses. Stack of notices from Medicare. What’s unusual? Lotsa drugs, pile a medical bills, no alcohol—not even a bottle of wine or a can of beer. Gotta check out the guy’s medical records.

Chapter 3

Cassandra

The morning after my meeting with Donaldson, I drive an unmarked FBI car on Route 24, heading for Fall River and an interview with Miguel Sanchez's parents. I'm dressed in a black FBI uniform with heavy makeup and a wig because the Director wants to preserve my identity to go undercover. Leaving his office, I was livid. I couldn't believe he would even think of involving my child in some dangerous operation. Even worse, trying to bribe me by holding out a promotion. But after I got home, I had second thoughts. Keri has been on the kidney waiting list for over two years. If she doesn't get one, she will die. And the chances of a successful transplant get worse the longer she waits. People have told me there is a black-market for kidneys. I never considered it. Seemed like a desperate and crazy thing to do; like the cancer patients who go to Mexico to get blood transfusions from guinea pigs. Now, the possibility seems more real. What if I could use this investigation to learn how to find a black-market kidney? It would be a last resort, but I would do almost anything to save my daughter's life.

My thoughts are interrupted by the exit sign for Fall River. Turning off the highway, I enter a sorry downtown. It was once the largest textile manufacturing center in the country and employed thousands of mill workers. Since then, it has become familiar territory for the FBI because of poverty, crime, and drug trafficking from the nearby port of New Bedford. Some neighborhoods are still packed with old, wood-frame three-deckers that used to house cheap foreign labor for the mills. That is where I find the home of Miguel's parents, Angel and Maria Sanchez.

I park on the pot-holed street among cars that look like they belong in Havana. The old three-decker has peeling paint and sagging porches. Wooden stairs, concave in the center, their edges worn by steel-toed work boots, lead to the Sanchez's' second-floor apartment. Angel and Maria Sanchez have agreed to meet, even though they are busy with funeral arrangements. Despite their grief, they want to know who murdered their only son.

Not knowing what to expect when I knock on the door, I am pleasantly surprised. Angel and Maria greet me warmly and invite me in. The furnishings in the apartment are old and worn, but the place is immaculate and homey. I offer them my condolences and apologize for having to question them at such a difficult time. It is important to earn their trust, especially since they are undocumented and must be terrified talking to the FBI. I have several things going for me: I'm a woman, a person of color, and much more socially adept than the first agent who contacted them. I begin by asking about Miguel.

"He was such a good boy," Maria says. "Miguel never had no trouble. He did well in school and got him a job working the construction. His friends, they shared apartments and had wild parties. Miguel, he stay home and help with the rent. He never did drugs or…." But she breaks down crying. Angel brings her a tissue box and talks more about his son.

I let them go on before asking questions. "Can you tell me about Miguel's friends? I need their names and how I can contact them. Also, his employer. Anyone who recently spent time with him may have information that will help us find his assailant."

I need to ask them about his trip to get money, but raising the issue will be difficult. They don't know about the missing organs. The bureau has kept it out of the news, so it can better pursue the case. I can't tell them their son's body was ripped apart, and his organs were stolen.

Then, they might suspect he was selling his kidney to raise money for his father's operation. They would never forgive themselves.

"You told my associate that Miguel went to Mexico to raise money. If you have any knowledge about his trip, and how he was going to get the money, it may help us solve the case."

"He would tell us nothing," Angel replies. "Over and over again, we beg him not to go. We say, 'Don't do nothing foolish. Don't get trouble.' We be okay, don't worry. We find ways to raise the money. We shouldn't never have told him about the cancer. We killed our only son." They both start to cry, and it is all I can do not to join them.

Chapter 4

Martin

5:30 a.m., I drag myself outta bed. Third time I gotta pee, and no way I'm fallin' back to sleep. Stuff my pajamas in the hamper that's so full, the top won't close. Even in the dim light, I see the mess in the bedroom. Pick up a dirty sock and notice a few kernels of popcorn on the floor. Florence hated it when I brought snacks up to bed. "Damn it, Martin, you got chocolate on the sheets again. I just washed them yesterday." Her voice stuck in my head, though she's been gone over a year. What I wouldn't give to hear those complaints again. We had twenty years together, but she died a tragic death, and I'm still not used to livin' alone. She'd be pissed at the way I keep the house. Cleanin' lady comes every other week, but it's still a mess.

After Florence died, my daughter, Melissa, moved back in the house and helped out. Now she's away at college. When I wake up, the house is empty. Quiet. Lonely. Down in the kitchen, I defrost a frozen bagel and take out some cream cheese. There's green around the edges a the container, but it passes the smell test.

9:00 a.m., I'm back at my desk thinkin' about Jensen. Like to start with a motive. Why does a rich guy with a nice condo and attractive wife or girlfriend get murdered? Usually, it's money or drugs. Sometimes a crime of passion. Could be drugs, but there's no evidence. Could be gamblin', but the guy looked well-off. Inheritance? Money issues with a kid? Gotta check out his will. Could be the woman he was seein' belonged to somebody else, or maybe he had a jealous wife. Gotta check those out too.

I look through the medical records D'Angelo dropped off last night. A folder labeled "Health Insurance" got a stack of those notices sayin'

"Explanation of Benefits." Paperwork in perfect order, just like D'Angelo said. Guy musta been a little compulsive—compared to me anyway—but that ain't sayin' much.

First notices are five years old. All about "end-stage renal disease," which I guess means kidney failure. A year after they begin, there's insurance payments for dialysis. Those continue every month—first from private insurance, then from Medicare. After three and a half years, they stop. Then, they start again three months later. I miss somethin'? I page through again to see if any notices are outta place. Why would payments for dialysis stop for three months and then start up again? My friend, Cassandra Crawford, has a daughter on dialysis and I know once you begin, you can't just stop and start.

I go downstairs to visit Charley Fredricks, the coroner. He's a tall, thin man, who towers over me and makes me feel shitty about my weight. His office is off a basement corridor, far from the racket in the rest a the buildin'. Guy's helped me on a number a cases.

"Hey, Moishe," Fredricks says. "What brings you down to the dungeon? Could it be death by dumpster?"

"Good a guy in your field gotta sense of humor, Charley. How you been?"

"I've had more pleasant tasks than examining someone who decomposed in a dumpster. Other than that, no complaints. How's Meredith?"

"Doin' fine, thank God. Workin' on her degree, livin' in her own place. I'm happy for her but miss havin' her around."

"I'll bet. What can I do for you?"

"If a guy's on dialysis for three and a half years, how long can he live if he suddenly stops?"

"Not long. I'd guess a few weeks."

"So, if a guy stops for three months, he's either dead or got a new kidney, right?"

"You're on the right track, Moishe. I opened the guy up and, besides the smell, it was the first thing I noticed. The guy's got a bum kidney graft. Don't know where he got that organ, but he sure wasn't shopping at Hammond."

"You think the hospital fucked up?"

"Don't think so. Coulda been a black-market kidney. I saw an article about that stuff in one of my journals. It said 10,000 illegal kidneys were sold last year. The profit margins are huge. People pay $150,000 to $200,000 for a kidney. Donor's lucky if he gets five grand."

"Nice business. Against the law, right? Any place it's legal?"

"Iran is the only country with a legal market. They're also the only country without a waiting list. Everyplace else it's illegal, but you rarely hear about anyone getting nabbed."

"How come they get away with it, Charley? Don't the docs or the hospitals know?"

"These guys operate internationally. They get a kidney from some poor bastard who needs the money. Pay him shit. Then, they do the operation in a country where people look the other way—or tend to take a little baksheesh."

"Charley, this guy was educated and well-off. Why would he risk his life with some perp sellin' a used kidney?"

"You can't survive too long on dialysis, Martin. And the waiting list for kidneys is huge. After a few years, the guy was probably desperate, and he had the money to get an organ on the black-market. His choice may have been simple—die or buy. Can't blame the poor bastard. If I were you, I would check his passport for travel. See if he spent a pile of money around the time he stopped dialysis."

"Say you're right, Charley. Guy's desperate. Hooks up with a criminal organ gang and got no control. Buys a kidney and gets either a bum organ or a botched operation. It stops workin' a couple months later, and he's gotta go back on dialysis. Meanwhile, he complains to the perps who sold him the organ. Maybe threatens to expose 'em. Would they kill him for that?"

"I've done autopsies on guys who've been whacked for a lot less."

I leave the coroner's office with my head spinnin'. I know about crimes involvin' drugs and money but don't know shit about kidney transplants and illegal organs? It's well outta my league.

Back at my office, D'Angelo is waitin' for me. "Yo, Martin, got coffee from Dunkin," he says, bending down to put the hot cup with the cardboard sleeve on my desk. D'Angelo is six-foot-two, thin and wiry, with thick black hair he combs back with some kinda gel. Wouldn't straighten my hair if it was elephant glue. He's got olive toned skin, dark eyes, and looks younger than thirty-three. Speech still has a touch a the Italian kid who grew up in Boston's North End. Came through the ranks the hard way, workin' narcotics in the worst parts a the city. By the time he made Detective, the shit hardened him, but our partnership has been good. "Got some info on Neil Jensen," he says, sittin' backwards on a chair across from my desk.

"Save it for the ride," I tell him. "Jensen's got a wife named Sheila and house in Cohasset. Notified her last night, and she agreed to meet this mornin'. It's already 10:00. We better get our asses movin'."

I squeeze into the driver's seat with a bad feelin'. People think the worst part of policework is the risk of gettin' wounded or killed. Some think about the constant exposure to the slimier side of life. But, the toughest part for me is tellin' a wife that her husband's been killed; or worse, tellin' kids they lost a dad or mom. Rabbi or priest should do it; not me. I get nervous. Stammer and sweat. Almost as bad as questionin' family members right after a murder. I click on my seatbelt dreadin' the task.

We head out from the city on the Southeast Expressway. At 10:00 a.m., the mornin' rush hour should be over, but you'd never know it from the cars drivin' inbound. They sit at a standstill, backed up to the Dorchester gas tank.

"How come it's painted like that?" D'Angelo asks.

I ain't much for history, but I know a lot about my own city. "Lotta shit about that, Tony. They painted the tank so it looked just like the profile of Ho Chi Min."

"Ho Chi who?"

"You're so fuckin' young. He was the North Vietnamese leader durin' the war. Most people don't know he lived here in the 1920s and worked at the Parker House Hotel."

"How you know all this, Martin? You coulda been one a those tour guides."

"Maybe I'd been better off. Hey, got the report from the coroner. Cause of death was obviously the gun shot. But Jensen had a port for kidney dialysis, and a transplanted kidney that looked sick. Coulda had somethin' to do with his murder. Tell me what you got, Tony."

"Not much. Didn't turn up nothin' unusual. No weapons or illegal drugs. Not much cash. Plenty of prescription drugs like you saw yesterday, but they looked legit. I sent 'em down to the lab. No stuff about terrorism. No pornography or alcohol. I took his computer, but I.T. hasn't had time to check it out."

"Any background on the guy?"

"You already know he owned a home in Cohasset and had a wife named Sheila. My guess is they had split. Clothes in the closet belong to a woman named Cynthia Fleming. We found her paycheck stubs from the American Kidney Life Center. It was her picture on his dresser."

"Check her out?"

"Yeah, briefly. No priors. I googled her and came up empty. One of the tech guys got into her Facebook page and found pictures of her and Jensen together. The other picture on the bureau was an adult son named Blake. Did a quick check. Guy's a sleazebag. Got busted for dealing coke and is out on bail awaiting trial. Before that, he was picked up for possession and illegal carry of a firearm."

"Nice."

"We found Jensen's car two blocks from the murder scene. Two-year-old Audi A-5 convertible—nice set of wheels. Car was neat and clean. Nothin' in it of any interest."

"What'd the guy do?"

"Looks like he was retired. Had one filing cabinet filled with financial records. Stuff was neat like a drill sergeant's footlocker. Bank accounts, stocks, all his shit in neat, color-coded files. Didn't see nothin' about work. There was a pile of medical records, and I dropped 'em off last night like you asked."

"Find a cell phone?"

"No. Dumpster divers came up empty. Found some Apple chargers in the condo but no phone. He had monthly bills from Verizon. Whoever did him might of taken it."

"Ask tech to get a log of his calls from Verizon. See if they can get his contact list. What about heirs and life insurance? You find a copy of his will or anythin' about a safety deposit box?"

"Not yet. Gotta check with his bank."

"Okay, let me know. Make a list of everyone's name that comes up on his belongings. Have someone check to see if he was heavy into sports or had receipts from casinos. Look for a passport. If you don't find one, get a record from the Feds. One more thing: find out if anyone's been arrested for illegal organs. Not the music kind or the one between your legs."

Cohasset's a rich town. I look at the houses on Jerusalem Road, perched over the ocean and worth millions. Not houses for real cops, but for actors who play 'em. Jensen's former home ain't on the water but still in a rich neighborhood. Houses are big, multi-story, with brick or stone fronts, long driveways, big picture windows, manicured lawns. Audis and Beemers sit in the driveways—probably second cars. We park in front of Jensen's house. Neighbor stares as we get out of my old, unmarked Taurus. Probably figures we're from the cleanin' service.

Dreadin' the interview, I knock on the door. Sheila Jensen answers and invites us in. I flash my police ID and introduce D'Angelo. She's about five foot five and dressed in black. Got heavy make-up, eye shadow, and French manicure. Wears heels and a dress that's a little too tight, like she's tryin' to look younger than her age. I'm thinkin' she was probably an attractive younger woman, but, as Florence would say, she's grown a little *zaftig.* Just the same, she probably wouldn't look at me twice.

We walk through a large livin' room with a picture window overlookin' the front lawn. Expensively decorated, room hardly looks lived-in. I flash back to my parents' livin' room where sofas had clear, plastic slipcovers to protect 'em from people who weren't allowed to sit on 'em. Wonder if that was an immigrant Jewish thing, not somethin' people do in Cohasset.

"Would anyone like a cup of coffee or a cold drink?"

"Coffee'd be great," D'Angelo says. "Just black."

"A little milk and sugar—skim, if you got it," I tell her, always thinkin' of my weight. She leads us to a seat in the den; comfortable room with leather sofa, matching easy chair, stereo, and large TV. Pictures of a young boy sit on a glass end table, probably the son, Blake. When she returns with the coffees, I gotta express our condolences.

"Ms. Jensen, I'm so sorry about your husband," I stammer, a slight tremor in my voice. "I'm also sorry to bother you so close to the funeral. Always tell people it's the worst part a my job. Wish I didn't have to barge in and ask a lotta questions. But I'm sure you want us to find your husband's killer."

"I understand, Detective. I expected this would be necessary."

I try to calm myself with a sip of coffee, but the cup slips in my hand, and spills all over the rug. "Oh! I'm sorry. Let me wipe it up," I say, red-faced, feelin' like a *schlemiel.*

"Don't worry. I'll get it," she says, and kneels down pattin' the ugly stain with some cloth napkins.

"How can I help you, Detective?" she says, sitting back down on a chair.

"Ms. Jensen, we're at the very beginnin' of our investigation," I answer. "Any information you can provide will be helpful. I need to ask you about your relationship with your husband. Were you livin' together or separated?"

"We had been separated for a little over a month."

"How long had you been married?"

"Neal and I would have been married twenty-six years this summer."

"As you can understand, Ms. Jensen, I need to find out everything I can about your husband, includin' the reasons for your separation. I need to understand his state of mind, what he was goin' through. Did he appear worried or anxious about anythin' besides his health? Did he ever appear fearful or irrational?"

"Neal was not an irrational man, Detective. The reason he split was obvious. He was having an affair. Just the same, he was not a bad man. Our relationship had gone downhill. We fought constantly about little things. Maybe he had an affair because we were doing so badly, not the other way around. He betrayed me, and I was angry and hurt. But he didn't deserve this. We had many good years together before this happened. I prefer to remember the good times and not dwell on the recent past."

"When did you know he was havin' an affair?"

"Not until he told me he was leaving, but I suspected it. I had gone with him to the dialysis center and noticed the way that slut looked at him. Now I know what she was up to."

"Who was that Ms. Jensen?"

"Cynthia Fleming, his dialysis tech. She was after his money. She knew he had it. How much of the 200 grand for his new kidney do you think she got?"

"You say your husband paid $200,000 for a kidney?

"I assumed you already knew that, Detective."

"We knew about the kidney," I say, not wantin' her to think we don't know what we're doin'. "But not the amount. You believe that Cynthia Fleming helped arrange an illegal kidney transplant?"

"Of course. She was his dialysis tech. Worked with him twelve hours a week. Found out he had money and set him up. Maybe gave him a little on the side to seal the deal. Who are we kidding? Neal was a decent person, but he was fifteen years older than her, chained to a machine three days a week and had a shortened life expectancy. Not exactly your dream fiancé."

"They intended to get married?"

"So she said. Can't marry a corpse. Let's be real. She was his technician. She had to provide blood samples for the kidney match. She had to check him, prep him, make sure he was physically ready for the transplant. You think she wasn't involved?"

"Can't say at this point, Ms. Jensen. She's certainly a person of interest. If you got any evidence, it'd be a big help."

"All I can tell you is what I believe. Maybe she wasn't satisfied with her cut from the operation. If he was going to be healthy and rich with a new kidney, she wouldn't do bad marrying him for his money."

"Did Neal have any enemies? Fallin' out with business partners? People he might have offended?"

"No, not that I know of. He was angry as hell about the transplant, but aside from that, he got along well with people."

"What about your son, Blake?" D'Angelo interjects.

"Blake? Blake is a difficult person. For years, Neal tried to help Blake. He kept coming to his rescue, bailing him out, giving him money. But Blake didn't know from appreciation. He never gave anything back. I wanted Neal to help Blake start a business. He didn't want to do it; said it was throwing good money after bad. I suppose I badgered him, and he eventually gave in."

"What kind of business Mrs. Jensen?"

"They opened a convenience store. Neal fronted all the money. Blake could have made a good living, but he just pissed it away on drugs and booze. Blake started dealing out of the store. The police busted him and then arrested Neal because he was listed as a partner. Neal convinced them he wasn't involved, and he made bail for Blake. But that was the last straw. The business was going badly and Blake needed more money, but Neal shut him off. They had a huge fight. Blake threatened him, but Neal had finally reached his limit. He refused to help."

"Could Blake have killed him?" D'Angelo asks.

"No way. He doesn't have the courage. And deep down, I believe he loved his father."

"When did you find out that Neal was goin' to get a kidney?" I ask, gettin' back to the transplant.

"He told me a few weeks before it happened."

"Did you know it was illegal?"

"Yes, and I was worried. We argued about it. I warned him it was dangerous. He had no idea who those people were. But he had been on dialysis for over three years and was afraid this was his last chance. I did all I could to discourage him."

"But he went ahead anyway?"

"Yes. When he returned from the operation, he thought his health problems were over. He was feeling renewed, triumphant. That's when he told me he wanted a divorce."

"You know who arranged the transplant? Who he talked to? Where he went?"

"No. He wouldn't talk about it. Wouldn't tell me anything. After the operation, we were hardly speaking."

"Ms. Jensen, I assume you were the chief beneficiary of your husband's will. Did he ever indicate that he might change it?"

"What are you implying, Detective? Of course, I was the chief beneficiary. We were married for twenty-six years. If Neal wanted a divorce, he would have to work out all the terms of a divorce settlement. Who do you think would have the sympathy of the court?"

"I get your point, Ms. Jensen, but he was involved with someone else. Can I ask you a personal question? Are you currently in a relationship?"

"Is that relevant, Detective?"

"Won't know unless I ask."

"Well, yeah. Neal dumped me for another woman. I was lonely. I knew a nice guy."

"Would you mind tellin' us his name?"

"Derrick, Derrick Hanson."

"How long have you known him?"

"A few years. We work out at the same health club, Bay State Fitness. He was just kind of a workout buddy, but I guess you could say we became more than friends after Neal split."

"Would you mind givin' us Mr. Hanson's contact information? I'm sure you know we gotta interview anyone related to the case. Did Mr. Hanson know Neal? He ever talk to him?"

"No, Derrick had nothing to do with Neal. Look, detective, I don't know what you're getting at, but you can't compare my relationship with Neal's affair. I was alone and my friend Derrick gave me some support. Not like my husband who fell for some slut who was after his money and got him killed."

"I understand, Ms. Jensen. I think that's all for now, but we may have to talk with you again as the case develops. Thanks for speakin' with us today. You've been most helpful. I'm sure you want to see us solve this case. If you think of anything, even somethin' you don't think is important, please let us know. We'll do everything we can to find Neal's assailant. And I'm sorry about the rug. Can I pay to get it cleaned?"

"No, of course not. It's just a little spill. Don't worry about it. Good day, detectives."

We get back in the Taurus headin' back to Boston. "Guess we better check out this Fleming woman," D'Angelo says. "And Hanson too."

"Damn right. Case just got more complicated. Fredricks was right on about the kidney. Can you get the computer guys to do some research? Have 'em get the contact info for Fleming and the dialysis center. Find out about funeral arrangements. Want to see who shows up. Have 'em do a background on Hanson. Get everything they can on the son; where he works, lives, credit history. Hopefully, there's a will in a safety deposit box. See if they can get hold of Jensen's tax returns. Also, anythin' else they can find out about Fleming."

"By the way, what made you think Sheila had a boyfriend"

"On the end table beside the sofa there were copies of FLEX, a weightlifter's magazine. She didn't look like the type."

"Thought you'd press the issue?"

"Yeah, it weighed on my mind."

Chapter 5

Cassandra

I try to peer over his desk as the doctor studies Keri's lab results. He makes a few notes in her thick folder. He examines the dialysis graft in her left arm. Why isn't he saying anything? What is he thinking? I'm afraid he has found something wrong. My hands grip the arms of the chair like I'm at the dentist.

"You're doing great," He finally says to Keri. "You won't have to see me for another month. You can wait outside while I have a word or two with your mom, and then you'll be good to go."

Why does he want to talk to me alone? I know how much can go wrong. Keri's blood pressure might be off. She could have an infection or anemia. A chemical imbalance. Her health is so precarious, like she's on a tightrope, and there's no net. It's more than two years since she started dialysis. Three times a week, she goes to the clinic where she sits in a chair for four hours while the machine cleans her blood. Without the treatments, she would die, but she can't survive on dialysis forever. She needs a new kidney.

Sitting in front of Dr. Green's big desk, I feel like a kid in the principal's office. The doctor leans back in his chair with that self-assured, condescending manner common to so many physicians. Not many people intimidate me. I've seen those looks as a black kid in the Deep South. Now, I'm a seasoned FBI agent. I've worked undercover, arrested murderers, shot criminals. But this man scares me to death because I am powerless; completely at the mercy of what he might find. He has the power of life and death over my little girl. Every time he opens his mouth, he might say what I fear most. She has an infection, a chemical imbalance, a heart condition.

"She is a delightful little girl, Mrs. Crawford."

"Thank you, doctor. How is she doing?"

"Keri is doing adequately. Her blood tests are within acceptable levels. Her other organs are still functioning satisfactorily. However, long-term dialysis exacts a toll on the body. Complications sometimes occur that are irreversible, and the chances of a successful transplant diminish over time. As I've told you before, you need to get her a kidney transplant as soon as possible."

"As you know, doctor, she has been on the waiting list for a donor, but the list is long. Doesn't wait time move her up the list?"

"Waiting time is one factor. She also has priority because of her age. However, the number of people waiting for kidneys far exceeds the supply. Last year, over 120,000 people were waiting for kidneys, but only 23,000 received them. You need to do more, Mrs. Crawford. You need to try harder."

"I have been trying, Doctor Green," I say, barely able to suppress my anger at his pompous attitude. "But I still have no prospects."

"You need to keep at it, Mrs. Crawford. Ask your friends and relatives. Make inquiries wherever you can. Use computer websites to find live donors. Register in as many areas as you can for deceased organs. You need to think of it as a full-time job."

"I'm a single mother, Doctor. I have a full-time job," I tell him, wondering if he learned his imperious attitude in medical school. Would he talk to me like this if I were a man? A white man?

"Well, I guess we all have our plates full," he says, rising dismissively behind his mahogany desk. "Don't forget to book your next appointment with my secretary on your way out."

Steam hisses through my ears like air brakes on an eighteen-wheeler, but I have to suck it up. I know enough not to diss a person who is critical to my daughter's health. Nevertheless, the man is boorish and insensitive. He does not understand how hard I've tried, or how bad I feel for not succeeding. Holding back tears, I book an appointment with the cute, blond receptionist.

Back home, I bake fudge brownies for Keri, as if to assuage my guilt. Curious as ever, Keri watches every step, asking why I do each thing. "Can I lick the bowl, Mommy?" she asks, and how can I refuse? Keri runs her finger along the inside and licks off the sugary batter—just like me when I was little. Afterward, we play a couple of card games, Old Maid and Crazy Eights, before Keri's bedtime. "Read me a story?" Keri asks, knowing that will allow her to stay up a little bit longer. I read from one of her favorite books, but before I finish, the girl is sound asleep.

Gently turning off the lamp, I take one last look at my little girl, defenseless in her sleep. I would do anything to protect her; to make her healthy again. I think about being a single mother, and what it was like for my own mom. My parents were by no means wealthy, but my father was a shop foreman for one of the big steel companies in Birmingham. It was a union shop and he made decent money. Education was paramount to my parents, and they sacrificed their own needs to put me in private schools. My father was killed in a tragic accident when I was fourteen years old, leaving my mom as an unskilled, black, single mother.

I was fortunate in many ways, and I always felt loved, but it was a difficult childhood. There were only two other black girls in my private school, so I grew up mostly with white kids. I was smart and joined in the school's activities, but it was the deep south, and I never fit in. I had few friends and little social life. Outside of school, I was lonely. I would come home in the afternoons with no one to play with, and my mother would often be out working late. I missed having my dad. So, I did my homework, sometimes crying between lessons.

My father had life insurance, so my mother could keep me in private school, but not without a struggle. Always looking for work, she took any job she could find, often cleaning the basements and toilets of white people, sometimes leaving early in the morning and not returning home until after dark. No matter how hard she worked or how tired she was, she was always there for me, providing support, urging me to do well in school, encouraging me to do my homework, talking to me late into the night. She was determined that I would go to college and escape our poor community for a better life.

Now, as I look at Keri, innocently asleep in her bed, I reflect on everything my mother did for me. I can't imagine giving anything less to my little girl. How can I even consider involving her in an FBI case with criminals who sell human organs? If I endanger her by cooperating in a sting, I could never forgive herself. I told the Director that I wouldn't do anything to expose my daughter. Yet, there are other considerations. Her welfare depends upon my career. A directorship would give me security and a healthy raise. By the time Keri goes to college, it could cost over $200,000. How would I ever afford that kind of money? There is nobody else to help her, least of all my deadbeat ex-husband who is God-knows where.

Also, there are other considerations. How can I walk away from Angel and Maria knowing that I'm the best person for the job? Where else is the FBI going to find an agent whose child needs a kidney? More importantly, there is another thought lurking in the back of my mind. Kidneys are scarce, and someday, a black-market kidney might be Keri's only chance. I'm a law enforcement officer, and I know it would be illegal, but that wouldn't stop me. I could never watch my little girl die no matter what the consequences. I would do just about anything to save her life.

Chapter 6

Martin

After Sheila Jensen's interview, I figure I gotta inform the Chief. I ring his line and he says to come right over. "Is this about the Jensen murder, Moishe? Whaddya got?"

"Might of uncovered an illegal trade in kidneys. Still diggin' up information and got people to question. It's a federal offense, so I thought you'd wanna know right away."

"This might be bigger than you think," he answers. "I had lunch the other day with the Chief over in Fall River. They recently uncovered a suspected case of organ trading. As you say, it's federal, so they turned the case over to the FBI. Don't know what happened. You know the Feds. They hate to share anything with us. Maybe you could check with Crawford, that woman you know from the FBI."

"Cassandra? That's a coincidence. Her daughter needs a kidney. Good thinkin', Chief. Will do."

I spend most of the afternoon with Google, tryin' to learn about illegal kidneys. Near the end of the day, I check in with D'Angelo. "Find anythin' on the Fleming woman?"

"Nothin' important. The techs went through Jensen's phone bills. He had lotsa calls to Fleming. I got contact info for Fleming, the dialysis center, and the son, Blake. Also got a copy of the funeral arrangements."

"Thanks Tony. Find his passport or a will?"

"Not yet. I'm waitin' on a warrant for his safety deposit box."

"How about his files? Any bank records? Any big money withdrawn in the past year?"

"How didja know? About five months ago, he took a second mortgage on his house and closed a big money market account. Couldn't find where the money went."

"Anythin' about organs?"

"Next on my playlist."

"Make a note on what you find."

Sun's goin' down as I turn into my driveway and park the old Taurus, "courtesy" of the Boston Police Department. Gettin' home before dark, I can't help but notice my yard. By this time of year, Florence would've cleaned out the flower beds, and some of the early perennials would be comin' up. I woulda lugged some heavy bags of mulch from Home Depot and scattered 'em around the shrubs. None of that's done, and brittle leaves from last winter still cover the beds and blow across the lawn, pissin' off my neighbors.

Unlockin' the front door, I'm still not used to returnin' to an empty home. No lights in the hallway, no cookin' smells in the kitchen, no Florence to complain I'm late again, and supper is getting' cold. Dirty dishes are piled in the sink and a forgotten gallon of milk sits on the counter. I smell it and pour it down the drain. I haven't eaten nothin' since lunch and take out a "Hungry Man's Fried Chicken Dinner" from the freezer. Hate eatin' dinner alone, so I turn on the TV, just for company. Afterwards, I got a headache and go to the medicine cabinet for some Tylenol. The tamper-proof bottle reminds me when I first met Florence.

It was 1982, Reagan was President, and I was a sophomore at Northeastern University. Seven people in Chicago had just died from takin' Tylenol. I was in the college bookstore lookin' for aspirin to replace my Tylenol. I took a small bottle off the shelf and stepped backward, knockin' into another student. She had a plastic tin of pushpins that fell to the floor and broke apart, scatterin' all over the aisle. Both of us were down on our knees, pickin' the little colored pins off the floor when we glanced at each other and began laughin'. Turns out, we laughed together for over twenty years. I always assumed we'd spend the rest of our lives together, but I lost Florence over a year ago, and life ain't ever been the same.

I wash down the Tylenol with a glass of water and clean up the kitchen. Then, I call Cassandra. I first met Cassandra "Cat" Crawford three years ago when we helped each other on the "Fenway" case. I had been investigatin' a drug murder and Crawford was pursuin' a possible terrorist cell fueled by drug money. It's rare when the FBI cooperates in any way with local police, but the suspects overlapped, so we helped each other out. Case got its name 'cause there was a shoot-out in Fenway Park.

Workin' together, I came to respect Cassandra. She was a black woman tryin' to succeed in a white man's job. I knew about bein' accepted in a place that sees you as the "other." Probably harder for a Black than a Jew. You had to try a little harder and be a little better to get the same respect. You had to be tough just to keep goin'. Sometimes you had to control yourself when you heard the words nigger or kike.

Crawford was tough during the Fenway case, but she had a good heart. Since Florence died, we've become friends. Every so often, we go out for lunch or dinner, or go places with her little girl. Not sure why it works. She's a Black woman who grew up poor in the south, and I'm a white, Jewish guy from New England. She's attractive and put together, and I'm big, overweight, and don't know Calvin Klein from Kevin Kline. I think about her a lot since Florence died. But I'd be a *meshugener* to think a woman like her would be attracted to a paunchy, middle-aged cop like me.

She answers the phone on the second ring. "Martin, it is so nice to hear from you," she says. "I was just thinking about you this morning. I haven't seen you in ages."

"That's why I'm callin', Cat. Thought we might get together for dinner. Be great to see you and catch up. Also, I got some business I want to discuss."

"What's going on, Martin?"

"Nothin' urgent. Tell you over dinner."

After the call, I feel better. Without Florence, my social life has been nil. I relax on the old Lazy Boy recliner in the livin' room and switch the TV to the golf channel. Tiger Woods is linin' up a fifty-foot putt on a golf course in Dubai. The fairways look strange surrounded by desert with giant skyscrapers in the distance. Woods stands over the ball prepared to make his stroke, but before the ball reaches the hole, I'm asleep on the chair. Without Florence, I sleep through too many nights with my clothes on and the TV blarin'. This time, I wake at 1:30 and gather enough energy to climb upstairs and spend the rest a the night in my own bed. Makes me feel better about myself in the mornin'.

Chapter 7

Martin

The mornin' after our visit with Neil Jensen's wife, D'Angelo and I prepare to meet his mistress. After Sheila Jensen's warnin's, we're wary about her involvement. I ring the doorbell, and when Cynthia Fleming opens the door, I flash my ID and introduce myself and D'Angelo. "Please come in," she says in a shaky and waverin' voice. I ain't surprised. She's gotta be scared talkin' to us.

I recognize her from the picture in Jensen's condo. Short and thin, she's no more than five foot two. She's gotta pretty face, hazel brown eyes, small nose, thin lips, and shortish hair—wears a conservative black dress with no makeup or eye shadow. Looks more like the grievin' widow than Sheila Jensen.

Fleming's condo is a small two-bedroom with a livin' room and a galley kitchen. It's got one a those two-level counters that provide a workspace in the kitchen and a dinin' space with bar stools on the other side. Place is immaculate. Fleming leads us to a couch in the livin' room and asks if we'd like coffee.

"Love some," I answer, and ask if I can use the bathroom. I'm embarrassed I have to go before we even talk, but it gives me a chance to snoop around. First room off the hall is a bedroom she must use as an office. It's got a computer, printer, and desk with filin' drawers. Next is the bathroom, which is spotless. After flushin' the toilet, I check out the medicine cabinet. It's a habit from so many investigations, but lately I find myself doin' it at friends' houses. Find nothin' but over-the-counter drugs, so figure the meds in Jensen's condo were all for him. I peek in the master bedroom before returnin'.

Fleming brings two cups of coffee into the livin' room, and I begin with my condolences. "I'm sorry about Neal Jensen," I say, "and I apologize for havin' to question you at such a difficult time. I don't know about your relationship, but we identified some of your stuff in his condo. We want to do everythin' we can to bring the perpetrator to justice, so we're talkin' with everyone who might be able to help."

"I understand, detective," Fleming answers with her head downcast, avoidin' eye contact.

"When did you first meet Neil Jensen?" I ask.

"I met him a little over a year ago when he became one of my dialysis patients. No one is formally assigned to a patient, but I generally took care of him when he was there. Most patients develop a routine. They keep the same schedule, sit in the same area, work with the same staff. One day, he asked me to have coffee with him when his session was over."

"That happen often?"

"It is discouraged, but I didn't intend to have a relationship with him. I was just being friendly.

"But it developed into a relationship?"

"It seemed harmless at the time. Over the next few weeks, we met several times for coffee. Neal began to confide in me. He was unhappy in his marriage and having frequent fights with his wife. I was getting divorced from my husband, living by myself, and feeling lonely. I guess we were both needy and had lots to talk about. The first time he asked me out to dinner, I refused. He was still a married man. Besides, I shouldn't have been socializing with a client. Eventually, I gave in, and we started going out. I never intended to get serious, but things clicked between us, and we fell in love."

"You discuss future plans?"

"We were both going to get divorced, and then we planned to marry. But first, Neal had to get the kidney transplant. We decided to keep our relationship secret until after the operation."

"Who knew about your relationship at that time?"

"I'm not sure anyone did. We were careful. We hid it from everyone at work. I had met Neal's wife at the dialysis center, but their troubles started well before me, and I don't think she suspected anything."

I catch a glimpse of D'Angelo looking askance. "What about friends or relatives?"

"I suppose my husband might have been suspicious. I guess I should tell you about Clayton. My marriage was a disaster. We had some serious problems, and I recently filed for divorce."

"What kinda problems?" D'Angelo asks, rarely worried about being insensitive.

"Clayton was abusive. I recognized it too late. We had dated for a year, and he seemed like the nicest guy in the world. Then, about two years after we got married, he lost his job. He became morose and angry, and it seemed like I couldn't do anything right. He would yell at me for the slightest things. He started doing drugs, and I suspected he might even be dealing on the side."

"Didja ever ask him about it?"

"I was afraid. We were having frequent arguments, and sometimes he became violent. I didn't know what to do. One night he came home at midnight smelling of alcohol. I confronted him, and he hit me in the face, giving me a black eye and a cut on my right cheek."

"Didja report it to the police?" D'Angelo asks.

"No, not at first. I moved back home with my parents and filed for divorce. I had hoped that was the end of it, but he began calling me. He kept apologizing and asking me to come back. Then he started following me. I was scared. I had to get a restraining order. I don't know if he ever saw me and Neal together."

I glance at D'Angelo. We're both thinkin' the same thing.

"What's Clayton's last name?" D'Angelo asks.

"Thurmond."

"You hear from him since?"

"He started calling again right after Neal's death, but I wouldn't talk to him."

"We'll need to talk with him," D'Angelo says. "You think it's possible Clayton killed Mr. Jensen outta jealousy?"

"No, Clayton wasn't a murderer. I loved him," she blurts out and begins to sob.

I wait for her to compose herself, thinkin' this timid woman is hardly the type to be involved in the illegal organ trade. "Sorry to put you through this," I tell her. "Is it okay if we go on?"

"Yes, I want to get this over with."

"So, Neal had his transplant and came back from the operation in bad shape. What happened then?"

"No, Neal came home feeling great. He thought all his health problems were over, and we could move on with our plans. He told his wife he was filing for divorce. We planned to marry as soon as the divorce was granted."

"Did she know that?"

"Not until then. They were already separated, so she wouldn't be surprised that he wanted a divorce. They had fought like caged animals. Maybe she was happy to see him go, but divorces are never easy. They started to fight about money. About two months after the operation, the new kidney started to fail, and Neal was in an ugly mood. They had an argument over the phone. I couldn't help but overhear. He told her he never loved her; that he had found a woman he really loved and was going to get married. I remember he said, 'I don't want to talk about money anymore. Let the lawyers argue. As far as I'm concerned, you don't deserve shit.' He slammed down the phone and told me, 'That's it. She's getting nothing. I'm not talking to her anymore.'"

"Was that true? Did he speak with her afterward?"

"I don't think so. He refused to answer her calls. Then, he started getting calls from his son, Blake. Neal's wife must have told Blake that his father was going to disown them; run off with another woman. Neal figured Blake was worried about his inheritance; worried he would leave everything to me."

"Was he?"

"He talked about changing his will, but I don't think he had done it yet. He wanted to wait until we got married. I know what it looks like, but I wasn't after his money. I loved him."

"I understand. So now Neal has separated from his wife, moved into his condominium, and has a failin' kidney. What happened next?"

"Well, I began staying at his place most nights. As soon as his symptoms started, he went to his nephrologist and found out the transplant was failing. The doctor told him he would have to go back on dialysis. Neal was furious. He contacted the people and demanded his money back or a new kidney. He wouldn't tell me who they were; said it was best I didn't know. They told him it wasn't their fault. They explained that transplants don't always work. Of course, the whole thing was illegal, so there was no recourse."

"So, what did he do?"

"Neal was violently angry. I had never seen that side of him before. I thought about Clayton and worried I was getting into the same thing all over again. Neal threatened to expose them. He told them he knew enough to get them convicted selling illegal organs. He gave them an ultimatum. If they didn't agree to his demands by June 1, he was going to the police. Of course, he never made it to June. They got to him first."

"How d'you know that?"

"I guess I don't, but who else would do this to him?"

"You sure you don't know any of the people he dealt with?"

"Absolutely. He wouldn't tell me."

"You know if Neal had any enemies? People he dealt with in business or other parts of his life. Someone who mighta held a grudge?"

"No, he got along well with almost everyone. Besides his wife and the transplant people, I never saw him angry. Well, except maybe at his son."

"Okay, let's talk about how he found a kidney. You know how he came to hear about it?"

"In the dialysis center, patients talk about it all the time. Life expectancy on dialysis is about five to ten years, and less for older patients. After a few years of dialysis, the chances of a successful transplant diminish. So, patients who have been waiting for more than a couple of years start to get desperate. Patients have asked me about the kidney trade a number of times. Often, they pretend to be joking, but behind their smiles, I know they're serious. I've heard a couple of the techs whispering about patients looking for kidneys. A few times, they stopped talking when I got near; made me feel like an outsider."

"You know of any other patients that found a kidney?"

"No, but I've heard some of the technicians talking quietly: 'So-and-so got his kidney last month,' or 'that one is getting hers next week.' There's no reason to keep it quiet if things are legit. I don't think Neal was the first one in the Center to make a connection. I asked him about it, but he told me not to go there; to stay away. It made me uncomfortable. I even thought of quitting, but I needed the job."

"Are you saying the dialysis people were involved?" D'Angelo asks.

"I don't know. I'm a little afraid of being there after this happened."

"But you are involved," D'Angelo says. "You prepped him for his operation. Wouldn't everyone in the center know where he was gettin' a kidney?"

"No—I don't know. I kept the paperwork updated. It had all the proper information about an altruistic donor. It looked perfectly legitimate."

"But you knew otherwise," D'Angelo says. "You were part of this illegal kidney deal."

I see Fleming start to tremble and then begin to sob. D'Angelo often plays the bad cop. I've seen him soften up some hardened perps. When Fleming recovers, she begins to talk.

"I don't know how all this happened to me. I come from this quiet little family. My father was a Presbyterian minister and my mother was a schoolteacher. I was religious, and I was always timid and shy. I hardly even dated very much before I met Clayton; and that was a disaster. I was like a—a wallflower. Yet, somehow, I've become an adulteress whose lover was murdered after I helped him get an illegal kidney from some criminal group of organ traders. I can't believe that this has happened to me; that this is now my life and I'm telling it to the police."

I look at this timid, nervous woman. Hard to believe she was involved with criminal organ dealers. Despite what Sheila Jensen thought, it don't ring true. If I could trust Fleming, she could possibly help us break this case. "The Center must keep medical records for all their patients," I say. "Do the techs work with the records?"

"Of course, we have to keep all the patient data up to date."

"How long would they keep the records for someone who terminated?"

"I'm not sure, but I know Medicare requires records be kept for at least five years."

"So, the Center would have records of all the patients who terminated in the past five years. I guess those patients either died or got a new kidney."

"No, not all of them. Many could have moved away or changed their dialysis provider."

"Yeah, guess that's right, but anyone who got an illegal kidney in the past five years would still be in the records."

"I guess so."

"Ms. Fleming, we don't have sufficient evidence or probable cause to demand the company's files. When it comes to people's medical records, judges are very tough. Plus, we don't want the dialysis people to know they're bein' investigated. But you have access to files that may contain names of patients who received illegal kidneys. Those files could help us find the people who killed Neal Jensen."

"No, you can't be serious. You want me to get those medical records? Neal was murdered, Detective Goldberg. I could be killed!"

I look at Fleming and know I gotta make a decision. Should I use this woman, after what she's gone through, to help my investigation? Is it fair to put her innocent life at risk? I look over at D'Angelo but know it's me that's gotta make the decision. It's one I might regret in the future. I may hate myself for doin' this, but I decide to pressure her. She could get the evidence to convict these murderers and save other people's lives.

"Ms. Fleming, you said you were in love with Neal. You were going to marry him. Whoever these people are, they killed your future husband in cold blood, and they're a threat to other patients you deal with every day. You could help us find his killers."

"I can't believe you're asking me this. No one is supposed to copy or remove medical files. I would be terrified. I'm even afraid now to go in to work. No, detective. I loved Neal, but I can't imagine doing what you're asking."

"Ms. Fleming," D'Angelo says, staring into her eyes, "I believe you. I'm sure you only intended to help Neil Jensen. But you gotta realize that this case will eventually come to trial. You helped Jensen get an illegal kidney. That makes you an accessory to a crime. You face a possible conviction and will lose your license to practice. But, if you help us break this case, no judge is going to convict you."

"What are you asking me to do?"

"Here's what I'm thinkin'," I respond. "If other illegal transplants have happened, and we can get copies of the records, we can find people who got kidneys and get 'em to talk. My partner is right. You could be charged with a crime, but this would help put you on the right side of the law."

"You're threatening me. You're asking me to put my life in danger. I want to help you get the people who killed Neal. But haven't I been through enough? I've been honest and told you everything I know."

"I appreciate that," I answer, "and I realize you're in a tough position. I won't press you for an answer right now, but think it over, and I'll get back to you. And please call me immediately if you suspect you're in any danger."

"Do you think I'm in danger, detective?"

"I think the sooner we solve this crime, the less danger you will be in."

Chapter 8

Cassandra

I park my car across the street from Spadaro's, a little trattoria in Boston's Italian North End. Martin is already there when I arrive. Just like one of my agents, he sits in a booth with his back to the wall, facing the door so he can see who comes in. That's the trouble with this line of work. You're always a cop, even when you're off duty.

Martin Goldberg is not like most cops or FBI agents. Perhaps that's why I'm so fond of him. He's a big, strong guy who grew up in a bad neighborhood. He was a street kid, city tough, rough around the edges. Still talks like he comes from the projects. But outside that hard veneer, he's soft inside. He's a *mensch* (borrowing a word I learned from him). Somehow, the years of police work haven't hardened him like so many others. We've become friends, and he's like an uncle to my daughter. Since Florence died, however, he hasn't been the same. There's a sadness that wasn't there before. I've tried to help. I've invited him numerous times for dinner. Offered a friendly ear for him to talk. But Martin is defensive. He doesn't talk much and is reluctant to express his feelings. He goes just so far before putting up a wall. At times, I've wondered if we could be closer, but I realize we are very different. Besides, Martin doesn't seem to think of me that way. Maybe because Florence's death was so recent. Maybe because I'm Black, or not Jewish. Other guys would have tried to get in my pants, but Martin has shown no interest. It's probably for the best. I value his friendship and don't want to risk losing it.

"Cat, great to see you. Been too long," Martin says, before giving me a big hug.

I am not a dainty woman but feel small in his big bear arms. “Good to see you also. I was so happy you called,” I say, noticing how Martin looks. He’s got on brown pants, black loafers, and white socks. Florence would never have let him out like that. He is so different from the dudes I’m used to, suppressing a grin.

“Martin, it’s funny you called, because my boss just told me about a case you were working on.”

“No shit. Chief told me the same thing about you. They playin’ us, or what?”

“Don’t know. The Director told me you had a case involving an illegal kidney.”

“Strange they’d put us together. The Bureau never likes to work with us. Usually just pushes us outta the way; don’t tell us shit. Tell me what you got?”

“Kid named Miguel Sanchez from Fall River. Goes to Mexico to cop money for his father’s cancer operation. Turns up dead with his organs missing.”

“That sucks. What’ve you found out?”

“I talked to the parents and got the names of his employer and close friends. One of his friends worked construction with him and knew he was going to Mexico to make a score. Miguel wouldn’t tell him anything, but he figured it was drugs. He suggested I talk to a guy named Jose Moreno; said he was Miguel’s friend. A second friend didn’t know Miguel was going anywhere, but he also mentioned Moreno. We had two people try to track down Moreno, but he ghosted. Had a steady job for two years, and the day Miguel’s death hit the news, he disappeared.”

“Where did he work?”

“Right question. The American Kidney Life Center in Fall River. He was a dialysis tech.”

"No shit! The murdered guy I'm investigatin' was getting' dialysis from the same company. If these two cases are tied together, we may have a lot to talk about. Maybe we should do it over drinks."

I like martinis with just a sniff of vermouth and a couple of olives. None of that fruity, infused stuff. Martin orders his usual J&B and water. Then he tells me about Neal Jensen: "He was separated from his wife and havin' an affair with a good-lookin', younger woman. Turns out she was his dialysis tech at the American Kidney Life Center. We interviewed her and confirmed he got a black-market kidney. She claims he wouldn't tell her who he was dealin' with."

"You believe her?"

"Think so. She was afraid; practically shakin' in her chair. My guess is she's innocent. Ttryin' to help her future husband. But Jensen's wife thinks she set the whole thing up."

"The bitter wife, abandoned for a younger woman?"

"Maybe. Can't rule it out. But this woman's got access to the medical records at the Kidney Life Center. I asked her if she could find records of other suspicious transplants."

"So, you suspect the center is involved. Will she do it?"

"Don't know. Givin' her time to think about it. She's scared. I pressured her but didn't want to push too hard. Could be puttin' an innocent life in danger. If somethin' happened to her, it'd be on me."

The waiter brings our dinner. Martin has the veal parmesan with a side of spaghetti. I get the vegetarian lasagna. The conversation slows as we begin eating, but we both have similar thoughts. "We could help each other," Martin says, trying to suck in a long strand of spaghetti hanging from his mouth. Tomato sauce drips on his shirt, but he doesn't notice. "We need to find out about these American Kidney Life Centers, get a hold of their financials and tax returns, find out about the CEO. These places gotta be regulated. Be nice to see their records. You guys are better than us at getting' that stuff."

“I can do that. But if we can’t find Moreno, the dialysis tech is your best lead. If she was living with him and working in the dialysis center, she was at least an accessory. I don’t blame you for not pushing her right after the murder, but you might have to lean on her. It’s always a dirty business with informants, but sometimes we have no choice.”

“It sucks, but you’re probably right. Maybe she’ll cooperate without too much pressure. Meanwhile, it’ll be good to work together.”

“It will, Martin, but I’m conflicted also. I don’t know what to do. The Director wants me to go undercover. Wants me to do a sting, pretending I need a kidney for Keri. I don’t want to refuse an assignment, but I don’t want to involve Keri.”

“What’d you tell him?”

“I said I would take the case, and even go undercover, but I would not involve Keri.”

“And he said, ‘That’s great, you probably won’t have to.’”

“Close enough. You been in this business too long.”

“He’s suckin’ you in. All you done over the years? You don’t owe the Bureau shit. How’s my little girl?”

She’s doing okay, but I’m worried. Keri has needed a new kidney for a long time. She can’t survive many more years without one. And the longer she does dialysis, the less likely a transplant will be successful.”

“Isn’t she on the waitin’ list for a kidney?”

“Of course. She’s on several lists. But there are not enough donors.”

“Lists? There’s more than one?”

“The system is complex. Most people think there is one waiting list, and you just put your name on it and wait your turn. But it’s not like that at all. Every hospital in the country that does transplants has its own waiting list. The more waiting lists you enter, the better your chances.”

“So, you go to every big hospital around here and get on their list?”

"No, it's more complicated. There are fifty-nine local organ areas in the country, and each one takes the lists from all the hospitals in its area and combines them. So, it doesn't help very much to be on more than one hospital list in each area, but it does help to be in many different areas."

"That mean you gotta register all over the country?"

"Yes, but distance also matters. Kidneys last about twenty-four to thirty-six hours. The quicker an organ is transplanted, the better the outcome. There are eleven separate regions in the country, and speed is important. If you can get to an area quickly, you got an advantage."

"What else do they consider?"

"Most important is a good match with the donor. They look at blood type and tissue. Everyone has these different antigens, and the number that match-up are important. They also consider body size, medical condition, and time on the waiting list. Age is important and children get some priority, but if they're 'highly sensitized,' like Keri, they're moved down the list."

"You just register everyplace and send all her information?"

"It's not that easy unless you're rich and don't have to go to work. First, you apply and wait to see if you're accepted. Then, Keri has to travel to each place with a caretaker—me, in this case—who agrees to help her through the transplant operation. Once there, she goes through a thorough physical exam. She has to see a whole team of people including a surgeon, nephrologist, transplant nurse, social worker, and psychologist, and sometimes a dietician and anesthesiologist. Each trip is expensive. Airfare, hotels, meals, and other expenses cost well over $1,000. After that, we have to pay to send blood samples to each location once every month for as long as she's on their waiting list."

"What if you don't have that kinda time and money?"

"Then you're shit out of luck. People who are poor rarely go on more than one list. Those with the most time and money go on multiple lists and have the best chance to get a kidney."

"So, the system benefits the rich."

"No kidding. I'll tell you about Steve Jobs, but let's get some coffee."

When the waiter comes, I order a decaf coffee. Despite saying he shouldn't, Martin can't resist a cannoli with his cappuccino.

"Remember Steve Jobs from Apple?" I say, resuming the conversation. "He needed a liver transplant and could afford to be on multiple lists. Jobs found a transplant center in Tennessee where the wait list was only a third as long as California's. That wasn't his only advantage. Transplant centers have different rules for accepting patients. Jobs had pancreatic cancer. Many centers won't give a liver to anyone with that condition, because the liver could provide a longer life to someone else. Jobs died two-and-a-half years after his transplant. In effect, he took a liver away from someone who could have lived much longer. But it wasn't because he was Steve Jobs, or because he cheated. He simply had the time and money to work the system. The system isn't intended that way, but the rich live longer and the poor die quicker."

"That sucks. Waiting list sounds like they're for people who have agreed to donate their kidneys when they die. What about live donors?"

"Live donors are preferable. They're the gold standard. A live kidney lasts about twice as long as one from a dead person. And, you can schedule everything perfectly so the kidney is transplanted as soon as it is removed. A few people donate kidneys to someone they don't know, but almost all live kidneys come from relatives or close friends."

"Can you give Keri one of your kidneys?"

"I would give Keri my kidney in a minute, but we're not a match. There is also something called a 'paired donation,' where I would give a matching kidney to someone's loved one who would, in turn, donate their kidney that matches Keri's."

"You musta looked."

"Sure, but I haven't been able to find one. The demand is way higher than the supply. If you could pay people to donate their kidneys, there wouldn't be such a shortage."

"But it's illegal."

"Right, but think about illegal drugs. If people want kidneys and buying them is illegal, there's going to be a black-market."

"I get it. That's why we're here. Don't know about payin' people for kidneys. Rich people wouldn't donate. Only poor people desperate for money. You want to live in a place where poor people sell body parts to the rich in order to survive?"

"You can think of it that way, but both sides could benefit. I would gladly bump up my mortgage if I could buy Keri a kidney. That money could change someone's life, get them out of poverty, provide money for medical help, send their kid to college. Donors can get along fine with one kidney. Plus, they can save a life."

"Don't like it. You'd have scams. People ripped off for their organs. People forced to pay off debts by selling their kidneys. We don't let people sell their body parts. Some things gotta be fuckin sacred; things you can't put a price on."

"Come off your high horse, Martin. We pay people for blood and hair. We pay surrogates to carry a baby for nine months and then give birth. That's a hell of a lot more difficult than donating a kidney."

"Yeah, but where does it stop? How about an eye? You can live with one eye. Would you take an eye from some poor bugger who needed the money?"

"Don't give me that holier than thou crap. White slave owners used to take my ancestor's teeth to replace their own. What if it was

Meredith? What if Meredith was dying and you could save her life by buying a kidney? Could you sit back and let her die?"

"I'd take a kidney donated from a friend or a relative but wouldn't bribe some poor fucker to cut out his organs."

"Get real, Martin. The black market is already out there, but not for your people. You don't want to know about all the other Sanchez's; brown folks getting cut up by Mexicans for some white man's kids. My people are selling their bodies all kinds of ways, but you're more comfortable pretending it's not happening."

"I'm just sayin'…"

"You're just saying what? It's not going on in your neighborhood? You're a cop. You should know better. And it's bullshit you wouldn't do it for Meredith."

"All right. Don't get so upset. Maybe I'm bein' naïve."

The waiter brings dessert and coffee, but our conversation has become strained. I know I should be able to soothe things, but I get so emotional about Keri that I just can't get past it. We depart with an awkward goodbye, leaving both of us feeling badly.

Chapter 9

Martin

First thing on my schedule the next morning is Neal Jensen's funeral. I arrive on time but make sure I ain't the first one there. An hour earlier, my men parked a van across the street. Somebody'll take pictures of everyone who enters and leaves. Glad to see a sign-in book in the lobby. It'll have names and addresses. One of my guys will photograph the pages. I sit in the rear, so I can see people's faces when they leave. About forty people attend the service. Thankfully, the casket is closed. The sight of Jensen's decomposed body hangs in my head like a bad cold.

My suit is too tight and I gotta unbutton it to sit down. Florence used to buy mosta my clothes. I gotta lose weight or get a new suit, but I hate shoppin' and have lousy taste. The service begins, and I pay attention to the three people in the front row. Sheila Jensen, dressed in black, sits between two men. Younger one must be Jensen's son, Blake. He wears a blue blazer over a black T-shirt. Hair is unkempt, long, and oily, barely coverin' a tattoo on his neck and several ear piercin's. Got that one-day beard growth that's now considered cool. Guess I'm too old to get it. Other guy is big. Must be six-four and 240. A well-worn, brown leather jacket covers a white shirt and tie. Has one arm wrapped around Sheila Jensen's shoulders. Must be Derrick Hanson. Looks like a weightlifter. Can't see his face but should get a good look on the way out.

Tryin' not to be obvious, I glance around the room. Only other person I recognize is Sheila Fleming. Dressed conservatively in black, she sits in the center of a middle row surrounded by other people. Not surprisin', she's keepin' as inconspicuous as possible.

The service is short. Neither the son nor the wife offers a eulogy. Minister asks if anyone wants to speak, but no one comes forward. He does his own eulogy, but it's impersonal. His eyes frequently checkin' his notes. Probably never even met Neal Jensen.

I watch nearly everyone file out before gettin' up to leave. A tall, well-dressed man with silver hair and an expensive suit walks in front of me. Know I've seen him somewhere but can't recall who he is. Hopefully, he signed the guest book. Few people are likely to go to the cemetery, and I don't want to go and make my presence obvious. One of my guys will be dressed as a worker and take pictures with a hidden camera. Every person we can ID will know somethin' about Neal Jensen.

Back in the car by 10 o'clock, the funeral hasn't helped my mood. Hardly slept last night thinkin' about my dinner with Cassandra. Felt like such a *schmuck.* Couldn't I tell she just needed a sympathetic ear? When Meredith was hospitalized for her drug overdose, I would have done anythin' for her. Maybe Cat was right, but did she have to get so upset?

Sometimes I forget where Cassandra comes from. Her ancestors were slaves. Didn't even own their own bodies. Her mother grew up where she could get hung for stealin' a piece a bread. Cassandra grew up in a place where black girls weren't expected to succeed. I also grew up poor, but it was different.

Although I grew up in a tough neighborhood, there were high expectations. My Jewish parents faced discrimination, but not like Cassandra where mosta the doors were shut. My family started with nothin'. My parents lived in a third-floor walk-up in one of Dorchester's wood-framed, three-deckers. With help from my mother's family, my father opened a little convenience store on Blue Hill Ave. Six days a week my parents hardly left the store in the daytime. When I was born, they had a playpen behind the counter and my mother nursed me in the back room. The store was our second home, and as customers spoke to my parents in Yiddish, I absorbed the old language.

While my father worked ungodly hours, my mother had other goals. Her family came from a more cultured background in Germany, and she was determined that her son would not be a shopkeeper on Blue Hill Ave. She read to me every day and took me to museums. She helped with my homework. She tried to send me to piano lessons, which lasted about a month; and she dragged me to dance classes, which I hated. I just wasn't that kinda kid.

In the 50s, Dorchester was safe, and there was a large Jewish community that was becomin' prosperous. But by the 60s when I was growin' up, things had changed. The richer families were gettin' out and buyin' homes in the suburbs. Neighborhoods in Dorchester were becomin' poor and Black, and it wasn't safe anymore to play ball in the streets. Playgrounds became territories for gangs, and violence was common.

One Sunday mornin', I was fourteen and helpin' my father stock cigarettes behind the counter. Two young men with dark sunglasses and hoodies entered the store and stood behind the furthest aisle as my father waited on a lone customer. My father whispered, "We got *tsouris*. Go in the back room and lock yourself in the bathroom, *Farshtayst*?"

"No, I'll stay with you," I whispered, but my father shoved me toward the doorway. I did as I was told but stood against the locked door, afraid, tremblin', listenin' to what was happenin'.

"See this gun, kike. Gimmie everything in the register or you won't live to see that kid again."

"Here's the money. Take whatever you want. I don't want no trouble. I get along with everyone."

I knew my father was being robbed, but I was scared. Didn't know what to do. What if they beat him up? What if they shot him? Should I go and try to protect him? Before I did anythin' I heard one of 'em say, "Get along with this you kike, muthafucker." Two explosions followed. I had never heard gunshots before but knew what they were. I wanted to run to my father but was afraid they would shoot me too. I stood behind the locked door shakin', not knowin' if they would come for me. Finally, I heard the shop door slam shut. I unlocked the door as quietly as I could and peeked out. As soon as I saw they were gone, I ran to my father behind the counter. It was too late. He died instantly from the shots at close range. A pool of blood lay on the floor. I remember screamin' but have no memory of what happened next. The police later said they found me lyin' on top of my father, my face, arms, and clothes covered in blood.

My mother was devastated. She tried runnin' the store by herself, but business was tough. The only way she could keep it goin' was by cuttin' off any help and workin' horrendously long hours. I helped out as much as I could and got to know the local cops who tried to keep an eye on the store.

Meanwhile, school was becomin' as tough as the neighborhood. The classroom chairs of friends whose families got out became empty. I was one of the biggest kids on the block and fought my way through high school, sometimes protectin' my few remainin' friends, but often a target 'cause of my size. More than once, I came home bloody and bleedin'. I became angry, resentful, and prejudiced. I stopped goin' to temple, not bein' able to understand a god who could be so cruel.

My mother was held up again a year later but luckily unharmed. The cops on the beat became our friends, stoppin' by the store, buyin' cigarettes and coffee. I got to know all their names. Somehow, through all her troubles, my mother always managed to give me support and encouragement. She insisted that I get good grades and go to college. But I was no student. I wasn't interested in school and hated homework. I sucked in math. About the only thing I read were Superman comic books. My mother wanted me to be a doctor or a lawyer, but that wasn't goin' to happen. I'd become a tough, streetwise kid. I hated the crime and violence all around me. I wanted some kind of justice for my father's murder and my mother's hard work. Maybe I wanted to scrub out the guilt from my father's shooting. I told my mother I wanted to go to Northeastern University and study criminal justice: to become a cop. She was so upset. She still remembered the stories my grandfather told about the cops and pogroms in Russia. "*Goyim! Goyim* become policemen!" she said. "For what have I spent all these years saving for your education? You think any of these people want a Jew in their department? Moishe the Jew, they'll call you. You're throwing your life away."

I lasted two years in college before droppin' out. Luckily, I did well enough on the police exam to become a patrolman. My mom eventually came around and was proud when I made detective. I may have grown up poor in a tough neighborhood, but there were high expectations, and I always had support. It was always taken for granted that I would live a better life than my hard-workin' parents—a far cry from what Cassandra faced growin' up in rural Alabama. Sometimes, I think Cassandra and I are similar because we came from poor families, but maybe the gulf between us is bigger than I imagine.

Chapter 10

Martin

Mornin' after the funeral, I'm sittin' in my office when D'Angelo walks in. "Hi Tony, ready to go?"

The day after my dinner with Cassandra, I had called Cynthia Fleming to arrange another meeting. Fleming was resistant, not wantin' to meet. "Detective, I'm afraid. I'm not sleeping at night. I'm sorry, you may think I'm a coward, but I'm just not the type of person who can do what you're asking. I told you all I know. Beyond that, I don't want anything more to do with this. Please don't involve me in your investigation."

Already, I'd decided what to do. I hated usin' pressure to make someone an informant. Felt like blackmail. But after meetin" with Cassandra, I knew it was the best way to do the case. I steeled myself to proceed.

"Ms. Fleming, it's not as simple as you wish," I told her. "You're heavily involved in this case whether you like it or not. You knew about Neil Jensen's kidney. That alone makes you a suspect and an accessory to a crime. I have to warn you that the FBI considers you a person of interest. You wouldn't want agents from the Bureau to show up at your place of work. I think we should meet again and talk this over."

On the drive over to Fleming's condominium, D'Angelo brings me up to date on his progress. "I checked out the will from the safety deposit box. Looks like Jensen was loaded. He left nearly all of it to his wife and a few bucks to his son. I told you the son's a low-life. Got a crappy apartment in a shitty part of town. Credit check was ugly. Guy probably can't get a credit card. Jensen's passport was in the box. Just one stamp showin' a trip to Mexico. Same time he got money from the bank. Did a rundown on Sheila Jensen. Nuthin' there. Guys from I.T. checked out her Facebook page. Lots of pictures of her with another guy. Big fucker. Must be the guy with the weightliftin' magazines."

"Had to be Derrick Hanson, the guy who was next to her at the funeral. Anythin' on arrests for organ tradin'?"

"Nada. If it's goin' on, nobody's gotten busted."

We arrive at the condo and are greeted by a reluctant Cynthia Fleming. I try to say a few comfortin' words about the funeral, but Fleming interrupts. "Detective Goldberg," she says, staring directly into my eyes. "Yesterday was a difficult day. I sat at Neal's funeral and looked around at all the people who had nothing to say about him. Not his son, not his ex-wife, not his friends. It was painful. No one expressed sadness or affection or fond memories. He was a good-hearted person. I loved him, and he deserved better. I don't know what kind of people could have done this to him, but I'm afraid they know who I am. I'm even afraid someone has seen you visit. I just can't get further involved."

Comin' from narcotics, D'Angelo has a tougher attitude than me. Playin' bad cop is easy for him. "Ms. Fleming, you're already involved," he says, movin' closer and forcing her to make direct eye contact. "We're gonna find Neal Jensen's killers and you're gonna be a witness. Their lawyer will say you broke up Jensen's marriage. He'll ask if you had sex together. When was the first time? Where? Wasn't he your patient? Your lawyer may object, but the jury will eat it up."

"That's unfair, Detective. It's sleazy," Fleming says angrily. "He had left his wife, and we intended to marry. If that comes out, it will cost me my job. Besides, it doesn't point to anything illegal."

"It's just the beginnin', lady," D'Angelo answers. "You wanna hear what some pitbull lawyer will say? 'You knew about the kidney, Ms. Fleming. You prepped him for the operation. You're an accessory. Didja know Jensen paid $200,000 for the kidney? Didja get a piece a the action? Maybe you lured Jensen into an affair, and then told him you could get him a kidney. Maybe afterwards you became afraid Jensen would expose everyone and had to be dealt with. That's conspiracy to commit murder.' That's what you're up against lady."

Fleming's facial expression droops like a vase full of week-old roses. She probably planned to be firm, but her determination seemed to evaporate with D'Angelo's warnings. She stares at the ground, averting our eyes. Strange that I can be half of this hardhearted routine when I'm doin' my job, but I'd be nervous sayin' hello to this woman in a bar.

"Detective D'Angelo is warnin' you for your own good, Ms. Fleming," I explain. "You're likely to face criminal charges. It would certainly help you to be on our side. Your assistance could be valuable. I'd advise you to cooperate in any way you can. Besides, if you're innocent, and you loved Mr. Jensen, you'll want us to find his killers."

"Fleming takes a deep breath and finally looks me in the face. What is it you want from me?" she asks.

"We briefly discussed the patient records that you work with at the center. Do you ever have the opportunity to be alone with those records?"

"Sometimes I work the evening shift. If I am the one with the most seniority, I leave last and lock up."

"What about takin' records home? Anyone ever do that?"

"It's against company rules to take patient records off-site, but it's occasionally done; especially if someone has medical or child-care issues."

"Ms. Fleming, Cynthia, is it OK. if I call you Cynthia?"

"Yes, of course."

"If AKLC (American Kidney Life Center) is involved in the black-market kidney trade, and we can get copies of patient records that show a transplant like Neil's, I'm sure we can find his killers."

"What if I get caught copying records? What if I am even suspected? If those people killed Neal they won't hesitate to come after me."

"We'll assign people to look after you and protect you. We've done many operations like this in the past, and we know how to protect our informants."

"You're threatening me with prosecution. You're asking me to put my life in danger. I want to help you get the people who killed Neal, but I'm scared, Detective Goldberg. How can I trust you to keep me safe?"

"You can trust me, Cynthia. In all my years on the force, I've never lost an informant. You'll be doin' a great service, and I'll be responsible for protectin' you."

Chapter 11

Cassandra

The finely tailored, silver-gray suit from Nieman Marcus cost $595 and is far from my usual wardrobe. The matching pumps are $195, the most expensive shoes I've ever had. I take

Keri by the hand and climb into the rented Lexus. Undercover has its perks.

Last night, I had to tell Keri we were changing dialysis centers. "Why Mommy?" the little girl asked. Kids get so used to routines. They change so fast, we picture them young and flexible, but they need structure and like the familiar. I had to lie to her. Would it be the first of many?

"I found a place that's better, honeybun. It has all new equipment and nice people. Once you get used to it, you'll like it better."

"But I won't see Mary anymore. And what about Mr. Bascombe and Mrs. Feeney. I don't want to change, Mommy."

As the only kid in the center, Keri was a bright spot for the elderly patients, and she got to know many of them. I feel like such a shit, doing this to her. "You'll meet new people, honey, and we'll go back and visit your friends at the old place."

I park the car in the AKLC lot. It is housed in a red brick office building, and by 8:00 a.m., the parking lot is full. The center occupies one large rectangular room on the ground floor. As soon as I walk in, the place strikes me as an upgrade. Artwork adorns the walls of the brightly lit room. Nurses and technicians wear clean, starched uniforms. The space is completely open with no walls or dividers. A circular nurse's station with chest high counters occupies the middle of the room. Reclining chairs are evenly spaced around the room's perimeter, each sitting next to a shiny new machine. Tethered to each machine by color-coded rubber tubes is a patient. Most are gray-haired, and a number are overweight, but no one looks uncomfortable. Curtains hang at each station for privacy, but none of them are closed. Patients sit close to one another and a few are engaged in conversation. Most, however, are resting, reading, or fingering their electronic devices. A few watch television. The whole operation is calm and organized. No one is running around. You'd think everyone is there for R&R rather than life-saving dialysis.

The woman at the front desk expects us and greets us warmly, paying special attention to Keri, who is nervous about the change. I hated to involve her but knew she would get excellent care at this center; better than where she had been. Introducing myself as Sandra Ford, my new *nom de guerre*, I tell her I am a Senior Fund Manager at Fidelity Investments in downtown Boston. The Bureau has an asset there who will confirm my employment to anyone who asks. Everything about my identity is planned to scream money. Sandra Ford looks like the kind of professional woman who can afford $200,000 for an illegal kidney.

After a brief tour of the Center, a technician takes Keri to one of the stations. The procedure is much the same as what she is used to, but the people and the machines are different, and she looks scared. Her eyes bore into me as they attach the needles to her graft. "Why did you have to bring me here?" her look beseeches. I know my little girl is doing all she can to hold back tears.

I am suffused with guilt. What right do I have to drag my daughter into this? Two people have already been killed. I can imagine what a judge would say if there was ever a custody hearing. "Your honor, this woman purposely exposed her daughter to a ring of dangerous, international criminals, risking the innocent girl's life to further her own career." At least I don't have to worry about custody. That asshole is never coming back.

I was twenty-five when I met Franklin and had just started my third year with the FBI. Back then, if you were Black, Boston was not a friendly city. I missed my home and felt guilty leaving my mother alone. Besides, the job sucked. Nobody in the Boston office of the FBI wanted to work with a Black woman. But I was a useful tool because I could go undercover and spy on my own people. It was supposed to be my dream job, but I never felt so alone. Then, a friend introduced me to Franklin. He was tall and handsome, with a bushy afro and big, brown, bedroom eyes. He grew up in the South and was also having a tough time getting used to Boston. We had a lot to talk about and would stay up late at night, drinking Mateus and watching Arsenio Hall. It was nice coming home to someone after work, having a warm body in bed, and a smile greeting me in the morning. And, it had been a long time since I had been able to let any feelings of intimacy creep into my life.

Years of therapy have helped me understand a difficult and traumatic childhood. In some ways, I grew up privileged. My parents sacrificed to send me to private schools. I received a good education and was expected to go to college. I was exposed to art and music and books and became an avid reader at a young age. Always being near the top of my class academically gave me a measure of self-confidence.

But there were many downsides. As one of the only Black girls in a Southern private school, I was very much alone. I had many acquaintances but no real friends. I was left out of parties and never had any dates. At that age, I wanted so badly to fit in.

But, although my mother loved me dearly, my home life was also barren. I missed my father, who died when I was fourteen. My mother worked such long hours that I often cooked and ate dinner by myself before she got home. Having no real friends, I spent many hours alone, coming home after school to an empty house and feeling sorry for myself.

When I was a junior in high school, desperate to be accepted, I volunteered to be a scorekeeper for the football team. One of the white players began to flirt with me. I was so excited just to gain his attention. At seventeen, those are the things that seem the most important in the world. I went home and had fantasies of us together, going to the senior prom. One night, he asked me to go out with him after the game. I was so naïve and needy; I should have known better. He took me to a deserted area, and we started to kiss. I was totally inexperienced, and I let things go until he wouldn't stop. He raped me. Forcefully. Against my will. I protested, but mostly succumbed.

After that night, he never paid any attention to me. I didn't know what to do. How could I tell anybody? I was mortified, and it would be my word against his; an unpopular black girl trying to attract a star football player. Of course, everyone found out and blamed me. Even worse, I blamed myself, feeling guilty that maybe I was the instigator. Maybe I deserved what happened. I kept my anguish bottled up inside and didn't realize the trauma that I suffered.

I used the pain and loneliness to build a wall around me. To protect me, so that nobody could hurt me or reject me or abandon me. But I only understood this later, after much therapy. When I started college in the Northeast, I was so unprepared; fiercely self-sufficient, but socially backward. I had trouble building any friendships. Growing up in private schools, I was too white for Black students who were into establishing their identity, and I was too black for many of the Whites. Besides, I avoided any intimacy. I was reasonably attractive and had a few relationships, but it was always approach and avoidance. When things got too close, I always found an excuse to pull back. It wasn't until three years out of graduate school that I began my relationship with Franklin.

It was the first time I was able to really let down my guard. Being able to share my life with another person was a new experience. It was like coming in from the cold. I trusted him and thought I had found my soul mate, my life partner. We lived together for two years before deciding to get married. Shortly afterward, we had Keri. But Franklin was a free spirit. He loved to party, stay out late, drink, dance, and smoke weed. In the beginning, we had fun times. But Franklin was not so good at family life and even less good at working. I was putting in long hours, trying to gain respect in a tough job. Franklin couldn't handle being tied down, taking care of Keri while I was working; staying home because we couldn't afford babysitters. He started to "go out with friends" after I got home. Started coming home at two or three in the morning, disheveled, and smelling of smoke and beer. God knows who he had been with. We fought often, and finally he just walked out. Up and left like he never had a wife and daughter. I was devastated. Abandoned in my most important relationship. I swore I would never get involved in another relationship.

Chapter 12

Martin

"I felt bad, pushin' her like that," I say to D'Angelo as we ride back from our interview with Cynthia Fleming.

"You're a wuss, Martin. The fuckin chick was in it up to her neck. She knew what was goin' on. Who knows? Maybe the widow was right. Woman works for a dialysis company connected to the organ trade. Spends twelve hours a week with patients and gets to know who has money. Maybe comes on to someone and gets a nice piece a the 200 grand."

"You been watchin' too many movies. Fleming's timid and innocent. Jensen was probably the only affair she ever had, and she fell for him like Russian protestors fall out of windows. I think she's naïve and gentle and very scared. She's so innocent, I'm worried she'll fuck-up as an informant. It's on us to keep her safe."

Next stop is Blake Jensen's, but I spot some golden arches and figure we have time for a quick bite. I get a Big Mac and fries, and a Diet Coke. Probably shoulda got the Southwestern salad.

Blake Jensen lives in the Wollaston Beach area of Quincy. The two-mile beach on Quincy Bay looks across Boston Harbor to the city skyline. Years ago, it was a popular beach, but now people travel to prettier, more distant places.

"How come nobody goes swimmin' here anymore?" D'Angelo asks.

"Could be 'cause the City of Boston's been dumpin' raw sewage in the harbor. Been closin' the beach 'cause of fecal bacteria."

"No shit. That explains it."

Quincy Shore Drive, the road along the beach, now got just a few clam shacks and cheap, fried food restaurants. The area off the beach has got one and two-family wood frame houses and low-rise apartments. One of those old two-families is rented to Blake Jensen.

The Taurus doesn't look outta place in front of Blake's house like it did at his mother's. His tired two-family badly needs a paint job, and half the stair treads up to the second-floor unit are torn or missin'. Blake was resistant when I called. "I got nothing to say about my father," he said, tryin' to avoid any meeting. Told him it was a murder case, and his choice was a voluntary interview or formal interrogation. I knock on the door, half expectin' he won't answer.

I'm pleased to hear a metal bolt snap back and a chain come offa the door. We hold up our police IDs, suspectin' Blake's been greeted like this before. He lets us in with a grunt and leads us into the livin' room. Dressed in jeans, a black tee shirt, and bare feet, his oily hair looks like it hasn't been washed in a week. Livin' room is grungy and smells of stale tobacco. On an old wood coffee table, cigarette butts float like dead bugs in half filled cups of leftover coffee. An empty beer can lies on the floor. Furnishin's are like student leftovers; blue couch covered by old throws, brown Barcalounger, couple of beanbag chairs. No pictures on the walls, no drapes or curtains, just some dingy window shades sittin' at different levels.

Blake sits on the Barcalounger. Leaves us little choice but to sit on the dirty couch, since we're not about to do the interview from the beanbags. Blake does not offer coffee. I gotta begin with my usual apology. "Sorry to bother you so close to your father's funeral. I know it must be a bad time, but it's a murder investigation and we gotta talk to everyone in the family." The condolence speech is much easier with Blake.

"How long will this take?" he speaks for the first time. "I got an appointment."

"It'll wait," I say, figurin' it's bullshit. "We might as well get right down to business. Before your father's kidney operation, you were in business together. Is that right?"

"Yeah, sort of."

"How often did you see your father at that time?"

"Not much. He just set me up. I ran the business, and he checked in once in a while."

"You weren't close?"

"Look, he was okay. I wasn't the easiest son. He bailed me out of trouble a few times. Gave me money to start the business. But he could be an asshole. Couldn't understand why everyone wasn't just like him."

"I understand the business was in trouble. Did your father owe any money? Anythin' about the business that could cause him trouble?"

"No, it was on me. He didn't get involved."

"Did you know of any other business difficulties he might have had? Any people who didn't like him?"

"No."

"Did you know he was gettin' the transplant?"

"My mother told me. We had a falling out and I wasn't talking to him at the time."

"What was the fallin' out about? Why weren't you talkin'?"

"C'mon, you got the story from my mother. Don't play dumb cop."

"Okay, you got busted for dealin' drugs outta the store. You gotta stand trial. You shouldn't tell us nothin' that might incriminate you, but drugs ain't our concern. We got a murder to solve. Your mother told me your father wouldn't give you any more money. Is that what the fight was about?"

"Yeah."

"You were angry. You threaten him?"

"Listen, I didn't kill my father. I said some shit I shouldn't have. I feel bad about it. Feel sorry it was the last thing I said to him. He wasn't a bad guy. He didn't deserve to get popped."

"Mr. Jensen," D'Angelo says, playin' his usual role, "Y'know you're in your father's will."

"Aw fuck! All you goddamn cops are the same. You'd love to pin this on me. I told you I had nothin' to do with it. I don't know how much money he had after payin' for the kidney, but it will all probably go to my mother. Now she's got that asshole, Hanson, who's after her money. I'll be lucky if I ever see a fuckin' dime. That's all I got to say. Why don't you people leave me the fuck alone?"

"You got court comin' up, Blake," D'Angelo warns him. "You know the score. Some judge is going to decide whether to give you a suspended sentence so you can run your business, or lock you up for a few years; let you do time with a few of your drug-dealin' buds. Maybe you'd like to tell us somethin' that might influence the judge's decision."

"What the fuck do you want me to say? I don't know who killed my father. Maybe it was the kidney people. Maybe it was the piece of shit who is after my mother's money. Maybe it was that asshole Thurmond who keeps comin' to the store lookin' for my father's girlfriend. How the fuck should I know? That's supposed to be your job."

Just like at his mother's, I exchange glances with D'Angelo. All we need is another suspect. "Are you sayin' Clayton Thurmond has been comin' to your convenience store lookin' for Cynthia Fleming?" I ask.

"Yeah, he's come around a buncha times. My father told me not to talk to him. He said to call the cops if he kept coming around."

"Did you?"

"Call the cops? Are you shittin' me? You think I wanted cops hanging around my store?"

"Did you ever talk to Thurmond? D'Angelo asks. Do you know anything about him?"

"My dad's girlfriend was his ex. Kept asking if my dad was gonna marry her."

"Was he?"

"Fuck if I know. Nosey bastard. Told me if they got married, she'd get the money. Said I'd be cut outta the will."

"You two talked about that?"

"What of it? I was shit outta luck either way. One way Hanson gets the money. The other way the girlfriend gets it. Look, I told ya, I don't know nuthin. I got an appointment. I gotta get outta here."

I stand up gettin' ready to leave and point a finger at Jensen. "Don't forget what my partner said, Blake. You're still in line to inherit. Makes you a possible suspect. We can help you. If you cooperate with us, it could influence the judge in your drug case. You best think about it."

"Thurmond. Not a popular name these days," D'Angelo says as we drive away.

"There was Strom Thurmond—Senator from South Carolina," I say.

"Yeah, and there was Nate Thurmond, Golden State Warriors," he answers.

"Can't think of any others."

"How about Thurman Munson, New York Yankees."

"Good catch, Tony."

Chapter 13

Cassandra

Keri is half asleep on the ride home from the dialysis center. The procedure isn't painful, but it's tiring on her little body. I make her a snack and give instructions to the babysitter before getting ready for work. Changing out of my Sandra Ford clothes, I consider what to wear for my late afternoon appointment with Director Donaldson. I make sure I pick an outfit that isn't tight or revealing. Why did I have to get stuck with him for a boss? He hangs around like unwanted relatives.

I get to the office and review my staff's research on AKLC. The company's CEO, Mr. Bradley Stone, is well known in the business community. His billion-dollar net worth places him in the Forbes 500. He has houses in Manchester, Massachusetts, and Palm Beach, Florida, and a condominium on the Boston waterfront. Stone has a reputation as a fierce competitor. He tries to dominate every market he enters.

I learn that AKLC's strategy is similar to other large dialysis chains. The law requires every dialysis center to have a medical director. AKLC seeks out the nephrologists with the largest caseloads and offers to hire them as medical directors. It's practically a no-show job. Their supervision requires only a couple of hours per week, and they get paid generous salaries, but the contract terms include strict non-compete agreements. The doctors can't affiliate with any competitor for a period of ten years. Although dialysis patients can go to any treatment center they choose, they almost always go to a center that's affiliated with their nephrologist. If the company can execute contracts with the largest nephrology groups in the area, they can kill the competition. In many areas, AKLC now controls over 80 percent of the market.

I had my people dig up some background on Bradley Stone. Corporate records reveal that he also owns a website called OrganMatch.com. The site matches people who need organs with people willing to donate them. Not just kidneys, but livers, pancreases, lungs, parts of intestines, and bone marrow. On their webpage, the first thing you see is a big, red, bold promotional statement:

> *We have thousands of donors waiting to provide organs. Many of our patients receive new organs within six months of registering. We can save your life.*

The site is filled with ads from people who got organs through the web site. A large notice with a picture of a policeman states:

> *Paying money for organs is strictly illegal and punishable by fines and prison. All of our organs come from living, altruistic donors who receive no financial benefit.*

Apparently, the company serves as kind of a social network, connecting donors and recipients. It doesn't offer any clinical function or any other service beyond providing names and contact information. There is a registration fee and a monthly charge as long as you use the service. I wonder whether it's legit. For every match, there could be thousands of people sending in checks every month. And the company may have no other expenses than a twenty-something running the web site. Not a bad business plan.

Could it be a scam? It would be a perfect site for illegal organ traders to identify people who need organs—kind of like Stone's other business. What better places to find people who might buy a kidney than a dialysis center or an organ matching web site?

Maybe I've become too jaded. I spent most of my adult life in the FBI suspecting everyone of being a criminal. This whole operation might simply be what it appears. Decent people willing to make personal sacrifices to help other human beings. In that case it might be real. It might save Keri's life.

The site has testimonials from patients and donors. Videos show recipients embracing donors who saved their lives. Despite the soppy nature of the ads, I find myself tearing up. Then, I wonder if I should register. Why not? But, would I be registering to get Keri a kidney or to investigate Bradley Stone and OrganMatch.com? How can I confuse the two when they could mean life or death to my daughter?

My appointment with James Donaldson is at 4:00 p.m. Entering his office, I immediately notice his eyes moving from my face down to my breasts. "Good afternoon, sir," I say in my most business-like manner.

"Good to see you, Cassandra. You're looking very nice, as usual."

Ignoring his compliment, I take a seat in one of the chairs next to a couch and coffee table. "I'm glad you decided to take on this assignment," he tells me. "I know you were hesitant, but you made the right decision. It's an important case, and I'm looking forward to working with you. Maybe you can start by giving me an update on your progress so far."

I tell him about my meeting with Angel and Maria Sanchez and the connection between Jose Moreno and AKLC. I describe how I transferred Keri's care to AKLC using my undercover persona, Sandra Ford. Also, I give him a short briefing on Bradley Stone. "He has amassed a fortune by being a super-aggressive competitor."

"Have you found any hint of a connection between AKLC, Stone, and the kidney trade?"

"I spoke with Detective Goldberg from the Boston police. Neal Jensen's girlfriend has suspicions about AKLC and may cooperate with their investigation by copying patient records and looking for suspicious kidney transplants."

"You have a close relationship with the Boston detective?"

I try not to react to his insinuating smirk. "We're just friends, sir. As you recall, we worked with him on the Fenway case."

Donaldson flashes a raised eyebrow look. "What are your next steps?"

"I plan to talk with people who knew Miguel Sanchez. My staff is trying to locate Jose Moreno. Also, I'm hoping to get more background on Bradley Stone. Beyond that, I'm hinting to people at AKLC that I am desperate to get Keri a kidney; waiting to see if anyone bites."

"Good, I think you're on the right track."

"Sir, what if someone at AKLC offers me a connection to get an illegal kidney? I have been willing to involve Keri this much, but I do not want to involve her any further."

"Hopefully, you won't have to. In all likelihood, we will have sufficient information to pursue it on our own."

At the word "hopefully," I cringe. I'm not a fool. I'm being sucked in, and there's little I can do about it. I need this job. I want the promotion. And you don't get very far if you refuse FBI assignments; even from this misogynous asshole who is claiming national security.

After a pause in our conversation I ask, "Will that be all sir?" He answers "yes" and I get up to leave. But on my way out he says, "Wait, I forgot something," and he walks over close beside me. "I forgot to tell you the new directorship job was posted, and I suggested you would be well-qualified for the position."

"Thank you, sir," I answer, moving a step away.

"I think it would be helpful if we got together to strategize. It might help your chances," he says, moving still closer, placing his hand very low on my back. I neither give him an answer nor the satisfaction that I even notice. I hold everything in, give a curt "good day sir," and walk out the door.

The whole humiliating situation has left me in a funk. I feel shitty about involving Keri. Feel bad about my dinner with Martin. Feel dumb for being sucked in by the Director. I'm so sick of taking this job home and wallowing in my own sorrow. I need to get out, to be with people, maybe to have a few drinks and let loose. A warm body wouldn't be bad either. My sex life has been as barren as those Fall River streets.

I call my friend Leon and arrange for a babysitter to be here after Keri goes to sleep. Leon is a parole officer in the city of Cambridge. We met a couple of years ago when both of us had business in the Cambridge courthouse. He's a tall, good-looking guy who happens to be single. Neither of us are looking for any kind of ongoing relationship, but we enjoy each other's company. These days you might call him a friend with benefits.

After putting Keri to bed, I shower, wash my hair, and put on a little more make-up and eye shadow than usual. I squeeze into black leather pants and throw on a short leather jacket. It feels great leaving Sandra Ford behind. Nothing like a little debauchery to raise your spirits.

I meet Leon in a crowded bar in Harvard Square. Most of the patrons are at least twenty years younger. That's the thing about college towns. You go back and visit, and everybody's stayed the same age except you. Leon is standing at the bar and has draped his leather jacket over an empty stool.

"Hey Cat, you lookin' great," he says, giving me a quick kiss on the lips. "Saved you a seat at the bar unless you want to find something quieter. What're you drinkin?"

"The bar is fine," I answer. "Vodka martini."

"Two vodka martinis," Leon tells the bartender. "Grey Goose," Leon remembers, giving me a sly look, familiar with my appetites.

We start up a conversation with another couple at the bar, and two martinis go down like a Michael Jordan jumper. Two hours later, we're on the couch at Leon's condo. He's broken out the good stuff and we both sip double shots of Hennessy's. Soft jazz plays in the background. It isn't long before my pants are on the floor. Leon is gentle and slow, kindling my desire with his tongue before doing the deed.

The afterglow has barely worn off when my cell rings. Not a good time to answer the phone, but when you're both an FBI agent and a single mother, you don't get to choose.

"Hey Cat, it's Martin. I've been meanin' to call you. Feel terrible about the other night and I wanted…"

"Martin, I appreciate your call, but I can't talk now."

"Just take a minute, Cat. I thought about what you said the other night…"

"Martin, I've got company. I'm sorry, but we need to talk later," I say, knowing it will hurt his feelings, but aware that Leon is stroking my inner thigh. Could the man possibly be ready again?

"Oh! Oh, I'm sorry Cat. Didn't realize. Call you tomorrow," Martin says, clearly embarrassed, and he quickly hangs up the phone.

Leon, my man, is already hard as a rock, and it's like the call never happened.

Chapter 14

Martin

"I can't do this again. I came this close to being caught," she tells me, holdin' her thumb and forefinger close together. We're in the basement of the police station. Practically tremblin', she hands over a folder of copied medical records. Cynthia Fleming looks at me pleadingly. "Please, Detective. I'm trying to do the right thing, but I'm just not cut out for this. I'm scared. And now I think they suspect me." Tears well up in her eyes.

I hand her a tissue, hatin' what I'm doin'. After several meetings, I've come to like this woman. I've dismissed the idea that she could be involved with illegal kidney dealers. She's more like the girl next door who lives at home and cares for an elderly parent. I know she's only doing this out of fear; fear that I caused by threatenin' her with a prosecution that probably wouldn't happen, and by playin' on her guilt over Neil Jensen's death. Wonder what she thinks of me. Doesn't fit my self-image that people are afraid of me. Most women simply ignore me; never give me a second look. Maybe I'm not as nice as I think. "Sorry you're upset, Cynthia," I say. "Why don't you tell me what happened."

"I came in early to continue going through the records. It was a half-hour before opening and I used my key. I don't like to get in too early because it might arouse suspicion. I was up to 's' in the files when I found a patient who had terminated. I took the record to the copy machine, and just when I finished copying, the nurse came in. 'You're here early,' she said. I told her I was just trying to catch up. The day before was so busy, I had no time to update the records. 'You're not copying patient files, are you?' she asked and tried to see the file in my hand. 'Those are confidential medical records. It's against the law for anyone else to see those.'"

"Whatd'd you tell her?"

"There was no reason for me to copy medical records. I had to think of something to say. 'This was just someone I used to work with,' I told her. 'A real nice guy. He stopped coming here and I wanted to get in touch with him. See how he was doing. I just needed his contact information, but you're right. I could have written it down without copying the whole page. It just seemed easier to stick it in the copier.'

"She gave me a disbelieving look. 'Let me see who that is,' she said. 'Oh, that's Mr. Silburger. You're right, he was a nice guy. I remember him well. He moved to Arizona with his wife. Wanted a warmer climate. Look, Cynthia, don't do this again. If you need information like this, you can always ask me. If someone found out that I let my staff copy medical records, I could get in a heap of trouble.'

"She let it go at that, but I'm afraid she's suspicious. I'm lucky it was a patient with a legitimate termination. I'm too afraid to do this anymore."

"Cynthia, you're already up to 's.' We're almost done. What about takin' the files home? Can you do that?"

"We're not supposed to take them out of the office, but I know a few techs who have little kids and have taken files home to catch up; people who can't stay late because of their children. But I would have to ask permission. Now, it's too suspicious."

"We've just begun to check out the files you copied. Haven't found anything yet. I hate to give up now. You're near the end of the alphabet. If you could take one batch home, that might do it."

"You're using me, Detective Goldberg. I know you want to solve this case, but you're taking risks with my safety. Sure, I want to find Neal's killer, and sure I'm going to want some judge to let me off, but

I could get killed in the process. You're pushing me too hard. I'm afraid to do anything more until I see how things go after this last incident."

"It's okay to be careful. Wait for a good opportunity. One more thing, Cynthia. Any more contact with Clayton Thurmond?"

"He called a couple of times. I just hung up."

"You know about Thurmond's background? Before he moved back here?"

"He lived in Scottsdale, Arizona. Said the place was growing like crazy. He was working for a big car dealership."

"He tell you why he returned?"

"He grew up around here. Said he wanted to move back where he came from."

"He tell you he was arrested in Scottsdale?"

"No, for what?

"Beat up his girlfriend. Put her in the hospital. Pleaded guilty to assault."

Cynthia Fleming gives me a pained look, like I'm nothin' but bad news. After the meetin', she leaves through the police garage so she can't be seen. Don't blame her for bein' scared. I'm takin' advantage of her and riskin' her safety, but I'm also bein' careful. One of my guys follows her from home and work and periodically checks her place. Would be difficult for anyone to get to her, the kidney people or Clayton Thurmond. Of course, there's always a risk. God forbid, if somethin' happens to her. I'll only have myself to blame.

I have an afternoon appointment with Sheila Jensen's boyfriend, Derrick Hanson. He was stubborn when I called, resistin' any kind of meetin'. "Whaddya want with me?" he complained. "I never even met the guy."

"Mr. Hanson, you were havin' an affair with Neil Jensen's wife, and then the guy got murdered. You must have expected the police would want to talk to you."

"You telling me I'm a suspect?"

"Not yet. The investigation just began. If we're gonna solve this murder, we need all the info we can get. We're talkin' to everyone who had any kinda relation to Neil Jensen."

"I had no relationship with Jensen. I got nothing to say to you."

"That may be the case, Mr. Hanson, but I need to meet with you. We can make it easy, or detain you for a formal interrogation. Up to you."

"Okay, okay. Can we meet in private? I don't want to talk in front of Sheila."

"No problem. You're down in Cohasset. Why don't we meet halfway?"

I told Hanson to meet at Sullivan's by Castle Island. Sullivan's is a hot dog and take-out place by Carson Beach on the southern tip of Boston Harbor. It sits near the highway, has a large parkin' lot, and walkways along the water. On the way over, I get a call from Cassandra. "Sorry I couldn't talk last night," she says. "I didn't mean to be so abrupt."

"No problem, Cat. My fault. Should've asked if you were busy." I felt like such a fool, thinkin' Cassandra was still dwellin' on our dinner the other night. She got her own life, and plenty of other guys at her disposal.

"Martin, I'm sorry I was so upset at the restaurant. Can we possibly get together tonight? I got things to tell you. There's been several developments in the case."

"Of course," I answer, hidin' my hurt feelin's and knowin' my place. We make arrangements to meet.

D'Angelo is tied up with other business, so I arrive solo for Hanson's interview. I spot a tall, muscular guy waitin' by the take-out window. He looks about six-feet-four with shoulders like an NFL fullback. Biceps, the size of my neck, bulge out of his short-sleeve, black polo shirt. Guy must live in the gym. "Mr. Hanson?" I ask.

"Derrick."

"Pleased to meet you. Thanks for drivin' up. Nice day, thought we could walk along the water and talk. Want a cup of coffee or somethin'?"

"No, I'm good."

We walk along the bay makin' small talk. Hanson says he worked for two years on the Big Dig. "I worked in the tunnels 100 feet below the street. We used to have to go down in these elevator cages, like we were working in a mine." I picture him tossin' 100-pound boulders on to a flat bed.

"We had become workout buddies," Hanson explains. "I used to show her how to use the Nautilus machines. One day, we got to talking, and she told me about her husband; how he had kidney disease and had to go on dialysis. He was angry and taking it out on her, treatin' her like shit. Then, the asshole had an affair with his nurse and dumped her like a used car. I felt bad for her, and—well—y'know, stuff happens."

"Stuff happens? Like you screw the guy's wife?"

Hanson looks at me like I'm a slug he'd like to squish on the sidewalk. "Don't play wise-ass cop," he says. "They were separated, and you know it."

Hanson could crush me with one hand tied behind his back, but I'm not goin' to go easy on him. "You're sayin' the affair didn't start 'til after he left her?"

"That's right. Listen, I'm no angel. I'm not gonna tell you I never had sex with a married woman. But Sheila wasn't like that. She wouldn't of cheated on the son-of-a-bitch until after he dumped her."

"Was she angry?"

"Yeah, of course, but mostly scared. Y'know, the guy walked out and left her on her own."

"Angry enough to want revenge?"

"Sheila? No, she ain't like that."

"You're a big guy, Derrick. She never suggested you might visit him?"

"Cut the shit, Goldberg. I told you I never met the guy. I hate to say it, but the asshole got what he deserved. I guess those kidney people play for keeps."

"What makes you think it was the kidney people?"

"Who else? Looks like she suckered him right in; pretended she loved him, hit him for 200 grand, and then had him knocked off."

"Except, she was goin' to marry him."

"Yeah, and I'm gonna marry Mother Theresa."

"Neal Jensen had a lot more money than Mother Theresa."

"Aw, fuck, I figured you'd ask me about Sheila's money."

"You knew Jensen had money?"

"Of course."

"You and Sheila were better off with Jensen dead."

"Hey, you said you wanted to talk; to get some information. Am I a suspect or what?"

"Not at this point, but you had a motive."

"Listen, I got a nice thing going with Sheila. She's a great woman. I don't care about the money."

"You never talked to her about the money?"

"Yeah, we talked about it. She was worried. But she was gonna get the money anyway. Her rich husband dumped her for his young nurse. Women make out pretty good in court. You think the judge wasn't going to be sympathetic? She didn't have to knock him off to get his dough."

"Nice situation for you, wasn't it Derrick?"

"You know what, Goldberg? If you didn't have that badge, you wouldn't have the balls to talk to me like that. I'd put a fist right down your fuckin throat."

"You threatenin' me, Derrick?"

"I'm not stupid. I don't threaten cops. But I know what you're doing. You're just trying to get under my skin. That's the way you guys work. But I didn't agree to come all the way out here to put up with this kinda shit. You wanna talk to me again, you can call my lawyer. Meanwhile, you oughta work out a little. Lose some a that belly fat. Might make you more intimidating."

Chapter 15

Cassandra

"Be careful what you wish for," the saying goes from Aesop's Fables, "lest it come true." After I decided to accept the assignment. After all my deliberations and conflicting emotions. After all my hesitations about mixing work and family. After all my fear of exposing my daughter to danger. After working undercover, confused, conflicted, and afraid I was doing the wrong thing, I finally got what I reluctantly aimed for. A whisper, a number, a contact that could break the case and solve two murders. But could further endanger my daughter.

It happened early this morning. Keri was hooked up to the dialysis machine and playing a game on her iPad. I had just come out of the lady's room when I was approached by one of the technicians—a woman named Susan Landis. She asked me to come into a small office next to the bathroom.

"Sandra, I shouldn't do this," she said in a whisper, "but I see you with that precious little girl, and I know you have been discouraged about finding a kidney. I could get in trouble for telling you this, so please don't ever let anyone know this came from me. I have a man's name and telephone number. He can find Keri a kidney. It won't be cheap, but people say he is reliable. If you're not interested, just tear it up. Forget I ever spoke to you. Whatever you decide to do, don't tell anyone where this came from. I'm just heartbroken watching you all the time with that adorable little girl, knowing you may lose her in a few years."

She handed over a little scrap of paper. All it said was "Herman – 212-465-9378." My heart was thumping so hard, I was afraid Landis could hear it. I tried to force a tear as I looked into her eyes.

"Thank you. I don't know what to say. I can't tell you what this means to me. I gave her a hug, leaning my head on her shoulder. "Don't you worry. I'll never tell anyone where this came from."

Since then, I've felt like a piece of shit. It's one thing, disguising yourself to a group of thugs who are stealing cars or dealing heroin. It's quite another to betray someone who might be trying to save your daughter's life. Of course, that might not be her motivation. She said all the right things, but she could be working for a ring of illegal organ traders who have murdered two people.

That happened this morning, and now all these thoughts are flashing through my mind while sitting at the kitchen table with Keri playing Chutes and Ladders. Keri giggles as I cry, "oh no!" landing at the top of a chute and sliding back down the board. Can she tell I'm only half-present, thinking about what happened. No way. She is so innocent. Absorbed in the game, she has no idea that her mother is going to expose both of us to danger. A danger that could imperil our lives. Or, one that could end by arresting the very people who could possibly save Keri's life.

Keri shakes a nine, the exact number she needs to land on the last square and win the game. "Can we play again mommy? Please? Please? One more time?"

How can I say no? How can I say no to this wonderful little miracle, the most important thing in my life, this treasure who I love more than anything else in the world? How can I say no to making her happy and playing another game of Chutes and Ladders? How can I say no if I actually find her an illegal kidney?

We finish two more games just as the babysitter arrives. I want to put Keri to bed before leaving for dinner with Martin. I take her upstairs and watch as she brushes her little teeth. She has to rise on her tiptoes to lean over the sink and rinse her mouth. Then, she runs over and jumps up in my arms. "I love you, mommy," she says in that squeaky little voice.

"I love you more, you little rascal, even though you beat me three times." It's all I can do to hold back tears as I tuck her into bed and kiss her goodnight. I linger at the door, worried that my newfound "connection" could further involve my little girl.

What am I going to say to Martin? I'm wondering on the drive to Spadaro's, I'm eager to tell him about the offer to buy a kidney, but first I need to repair some damage. I got angry and treated him badly at the restaurant. Then, when he called, he probably realized I was with another guy. I could hear the hurt in his voice, but what else could I have said? Men! They all have their expectations. Keri's doctor thinks I'm just a full-time mother. My boss thinks the FBI is my whole life. Martin expects me to be like the girl next door. Leon's the most real. He just thinks I'm a good fuck, which is okay, but there's nothing else there. They all want to decide who I am. Put me in a box that meets their needs. But who am I really? The problem is, even I don't always know.

So many years of therapy and I'm still confused. Will I ever have another serious relationship? Another real commitment? I seem to avoid the kind of guy where that would be possible. Take Martin, for instance. He's a nice guy, and he's great with Keri, but he's nothing like the men I'm attracted to. My shrink asks me, "Why do you think you choose these kinds of men? They don't treat you well. They don't respect the person you've become. You're still punishing yourself—choosing the kind of relationships where you can't get hurt. Building a wall around yourself so no one can discover the girl who felt guilty and dirty after being raped in high school. You're not that person anymore,

Cassandra. That's a self-image that you have grown out of; that you have left behind."

My shrink is probably right. I'm so fucked up. I never choose realistic partners. I hook up with brothers who are cool. Could I ever get off on someone who's just a nice, normal guy? But what normal guy would want me? A cop. An FBI agent who got her stripes under cover, ingratiating herself with low-life criminals.

When I arrive at the restaurant, Martin is already there, sitting in a booth, back to the wall, eyes facing the front door. He greets me with a stiff little hug. "I ordered you a drink," he says, avoiding eye contact. A martini sits on the table. There's an awkward silence that I feel the need to break.

"Martin, I'm sorry I got so angry the other night. I shouldn't have…"

"Cat, it's okay. It was my fault. I was clueless. If Meredith needed a kidney, you were right. I'd probably consider just about anythin'."

"Interesting you say that now because I just made a connection. Today, at the dialysis center, a technician gave me the phone number of a person who can sell me a kidney. I've been thinking about how this will play out. I'm so confused. So conflicted. What if I find these people are for real? What if the kidney is a good match? Am I going to turn them in, or save my daughter's life?"

"Thought about that," Martin answers. "These kidney dealers are murderers who kill people for their organs. At best, they take kidneys from desperately poor people, pay them shit, and sell 'em to the rich for a big score. But if it was Meredith who was desperate for a kidney? I'd probably be conflicted."

"You see where I'm coming from? I'm going under cover and trying to arrest the very people who could save my daughter's life."

"It sucks. They shouldn't of put you in this position. But we got two murders. One thing, sellin' a kidney for profit. But killin' people for their organs is different. You don't have to feel bad about arrestin' murderers."

No point telling him I would feel worse not getting Keri a life-saving kidney. I feel bad about the whole case, but I'm not about to repeat the argument with Martin. It's a relief to see the waiter delivering our food. Martin asks if I want another martini. Tempting, but I don't need a DUI on top of all my other worries. I opt for comfort food. A dish with a fancy name, but basically spaghetti and meatballs. Martin has veal parmesan with a side of spaghetti. The meal gives us a chance to change the subject; talk about the food, the waiter, the dessert staring at us from the next table. Martin loves food, and his appetite gradually overcomes his anxiety. He tops off his dinner with a caramel flan and a cup of cappuccino. When the waiter clears away the empty plates, it's Martin who gets down to business. "Cat, you said there were new developments in the case. What you got?"

I'm loath to dive back in to the case, even though it's the excuse for being here. How nice it would be just to sit and talk with a friend; make the rest of my life go away, if only for a few minutes. But my life is never like that. I know people who are utterly irresponsible. Their lives are a mess. They behave badly. They let other people down. Their switches don't have off positions. And sometimes they pay the price. God knows I've arrested a few of them, but not without a touch of envy. Sometimes I yearn to be less responsible, more carefree. Just let go and not care. Like the song says: "Forget about today until tomorrow."

But that isn't me. Freud would blame it on my super-ego. Martin would say I have Jewish guilt. Donaldson would tell me I have a job to do. And my shrink …

"Cat, you go away?"

"Sorry, Martin. I drifted off to martini land. I got a couple of things to tell you. First, we located Miguel's friend, Jose Moreno. He got picked up in Mexico during a drug bust. When his name hit the computer database, it rang a bell. We have a Mexican agent, Luis Rafael, who I spoke to before he questioned Moreno. Moreno admitted he knew Miguel but denied they were close friends. He said Miguel kept to himself and didn't hang out with the other Latinos. He knew Miguel needed money but didn't know anything about his going to Mexico until he read about it in the papers. Luis didn't believe him and told him so. I got the transcript on my cell. Take a look."

Rafael: Okay Moreno, let's quit the bullshit. Listen up. Miguel Sanchez is your close friend. We know that from your buddies and Miguel's parents. His father needs money for a life-saving cancer operation. Miguel is desperate to get it, but he doesn't know how. You work at AKLC as a dialysis tech. You know that kidneys sell on the black-market for $200,000. Miguel, who has never been out of the country, goes to Mexico; a place where the drug cartels are involved in the illegal organ trade. He turns up dead with his liver, pancreas, kidneys, and corneas missing. At the exact same time, you quit your job at AKLC and turn up in a Mexican jail. It's all just a coincidence, right, Jose?"

Moreno: I got nothin' to say.

Rafael: Jose, your best friend was murdered. You know what these bastards do? They kidnap people and store them in refrigerator cars until they have clients for their organs. They tie them down in the cold and keep them barely alive. Then, when they're ready to use their organs, they hollow out their eyes to sell their corneas. Then they slit them open from their neck to their belly and cut out their kidney, liver, and pancreas. That's how your best friend died. You worked for AKLC for three years. Did they do this to your best friend?

Moreno: Hey man, I'm not goin' there. Miguel was my friend, yeah. But these AKLC dudes are bad-ass mutha-fuckers. I didn't do nuthin'. I got away from there. Whatever's goin' down there got nothin' to do with me'.

"Well Cat, no hard evidence, but a source saying AKLC people are 'bad-ass mutha-fuckers.' Not the most upstandin' witness but sounds like we're on the right path. Got anythin' else?"

"I did some background on Bradley Stone. Aside from being the CEO of AKLC, he also owns a business called OrganMatch.com. They operate a website that matches people who are looking for organs with people who are willing to donate. I don't know how much they rake in for each person who registers and pays a monthly fee—whether they actually find matches or just keep the money. Of course, I'm FBI and am always expecting a scam. It could be a way to find people who might be willing to buy a kidney."

"Seems like Mr. Stone is cornerin' the market. Any background on him?"

"Yes. I told my people to use our resources to see if there's any dirt. Turns out he's having an affair with a woman who runs the Nattai Institute, a chain of training schools for dialysis technicians. Her name is Roni Cohnheim, an Israeli emigrant. The woman left Israel seven years ago under murky circumstances, possibly to avoid prosecution. I asked my people to use their connections with Mossad, the Israeli intelligence agency, to find more information. Turns out Cohnheim was a nurse at the Ben-Shmuel Medical Center in Tiberius. There was a scandal at the center having to do with illegal kidney transplants. Investigators questioned Cohnheim as well as other doctors and nurses in the hospital's nephrology department. Cohnheim insisted she knew nothing and claimed other people were trying to frame her."

"No shit! Stone is hooked-up with a woman who was connected to the organ trade. In our business there are no coincidences. How did she get here?"

"She left the country shortly after the scandal and came to the U.S. Because of the shortage of nurses, it was easy for her to get a green card. She began working in the Nephrology department of Beth Israel

Hospital in Boston. Within two years, she opened her first kidney dialysis training school. Don't know where she got the money. Now she's got locations around the country. Apparently, they place many of their graduates at AKLC."

"Guess it's time for me to have a talk with Mr. Stone."

"What about your end, Martin? Anything new?"

"Been workin' with Cynthia Fleming. She's been secretly copyin' medical records from the dialysis center, but last week she almost got caught. Worried about her. Got no right to put her in so much danger. Anything happens to her, it's my fault."

"You still think she's innocent?"

"Pretty sure. She was in the wrong place at the wrong time. Jensen's wife thinks Fleming was after her husband's money and started the affair to set him up. But Sheila Jensen is bitter. Why not, since she thinks Fleming broke up her marriage?"

"Martin, this web is getting pretty complex. See if I got this straight. In addition to Cynthia Fleming, we got her ex, Clayton Thurmond, AKLC, Susan Landis, Bradley Stone, Roni Cohnheim, Jose Moreno, Sheila Jensen, her boyfriend Derrick Hanson, and Jensen's son, Blake. Except for Moreno, they all had a possible motive to do away with Neal Jensen. But not all those people have a connection to the kidney trade. I think that's where we should focus."

"You sure, Cat? Suppose one of the suspects killed Jensen for his inheritance. Maybe the murder was about money, not kidneys. Jensen's trip to Mexico for a kidney may have had nothin' to do with his murder."

"I doubt it, Martin, but suppose you're right. Maybe Stone and Cohnheim and these kidney people are all legitimate. Maybe they are in it just to help people like me. What if I go undercover to Mexico or India or some country where I could get Keri a kidney? Would you stop me from saving my daughter's life? Would you and I arrest the people who could save her? What am I going to do Martin? What the hell am I going to do?"

Chapter 16

Martin

Early the next morning, D'Angelo and I drive to the executive offices of AKLC. They're located in a high-rise office buildin' in downtown Boston. We park in the underground garage and take the elevator to the lobby. Even though we show our police ID's, we gotta sign in and wear badges before we can enter the elevators. Security's tight.

The elevator opens on the seventh floor into a modern reception area. Deep carpet, leather furniture, artwork on the walls. We're used to police stations and courts, but this is corporate America. We're greeted by the male receptionist. "Detectives Goldberg and D'Angelo. We got an appointment with Mr. Stone."

"I'll tell him you're here. Please have a seat and make yourself comfortable. Can I get you something to drink? Coffee? Water?"

We politely refuse. Magazines from kidney associations are on the table and a brochure from OrganMatch.com. I'm halfway through the brochure when a nicely dressed woman approaches. "Mr. Stone will see you now," she says, signalin' us to follow.

Stone rises from his desk, and I immediately recognize the man from the funeral. The tall, silver-haired man leavin' the church in front of me was Bradley Stone. We shake hands, and Stone leads us to a round conference table. The CEO's corner office is impressive. Great views overlookin' Boston Harbor. Rich, dark wood furniture. Pictures of Stone with actors, athletes, and politicians. Tables adorned with glass sculptures. Everything matchin' and tasteful, yet not over the top. D'Angelo stares out the giant window like he just landed on the moon.

"I assume you're here to ask about Neal Jensen?" Stone says, hardly botherin' with the usual pleasantries.

"Yes, we are," I reply. "Did you know Mr. Jensen?"

"No, not personally."

"If I'm not mistaken, I saw you at his funeral."

"Yes, I was there."

"How come? His death wasn't caused by kidney disease."

"As I'm sure you know, detective, Mr. Jensen's case was not routine. He stopped getting dialysis and got a kidney transplant. Unfortunately, the transplant failed and he had to resume dialysis. A short time later, he was murdered. Such a chain of events is, at best, unusual. I thought it deserved my attention."

"You know where he got the kidney?"

"No."

"You have any knowledge at all about his transplant or who might have provided him a connection for the transplant?"

"Absolutely not. I examined his file knowing you would ask. All the paperwork was properly completed and appeared to be legitimate. I have had copies prepared for you. The only other information I have was about the clinical services Mr. Jensen received at the Center."

"That information would confirm Mr. Jensen had a failed kidney transplant. The Center prepped him for the transplant. Wouldn't you know the details about the provider?"

"Only the name of the hospital where he got the transplant. I told you the paperwork appeared to be legitimate. Let me be clear right up front, Detective. We run a business that saves people's lives. We have high standards. We make a fair profit. We do well by doing good. I am well aware of the black market for kidneys, but it would be foolish to jeopardize my business by any involvement with the illegal kidney trade."

"What about your employees, Mr. Stone? If someone wanted to find people who needed kidneys, your dialysis centers would be good places to look."

"I'm sure you are correct, Detective. However, we conduct background checks on all our hires. In addition, all of our nurses and technicians have completed professional training programs."

"I understand dialysis patients sometimes consider buying a kidney in the black-market and often ask their caregivers for information—not just at your center, but at all dialysis centers."

"Do you think I can stop them from asking? What would you have me do?"

"It'd be illegal to help them. I'd hope you'd actively discourage them."

"Do either of you know why I started this business?"

We both say "no."

"Well then, I'm disappointed in you. You haven't done your homework. I had a fourteen-year-old son who died waiting for a kidney. He was on dialysis for several years. I tried everything, but I could not find him a kidney. I watched him die, and it was horrible. I became clinically depressed. It broke up my marriage and nearly destroyed my life. I started this business to help people avoid a similar fate."

"I didn't know Mr. Stone. I'm sorry for your loss."

"I'm telling you this because there were thousands of people in the world who would have sold my son a kidney, but buying one was illegal. So, I lost my only son. I still wake up at night feeling guilty because I may have made the wrong choice. I make sure all my patients understand the best legal means by which they can find a kidney. But I don't condemn them to die like my son. If someone decides to save their life by buying a kidney in the illegal market, I will not help them, but I will not discourage them. I already have one death on my conscience and do not want another."

I think about my discussion with Cassandra and feel bad for Stone. D'Angelo, however, seems skeptical. He looks around at Stone's office and the signs of wealth and power that he has accumulated. Probably thinks that Stone isn't the type of guy who would be stopped by a little infraction of the law. "I hear you right?" he asks Stone. "You let your help tell people how to get illegal organs?"

"I didn't say that. I said I would not discourage a technician from answering them. I would rather patients be informed, both about the considerable risks and the actual possibility of obtaining an organ. If they have more information, they will make better decisions. The vast majority will be better off waiting for their turn on the list. They should know that. But they will hear us better if we don't pretend there is no other alternative. At the same time, there is a line that cannot be crossed. If I thought any of my people were providing a connection to the black market, I would terminate them immediately. We investigate all our technicians before hiring them. They are professionals. We recruit our staff from the very best training schools."

DeAngelo does not let him off easy. "You get most of 'em from the Nattai Institute, don't you?"

"That is correct. The school has an excellent reputation, and we have had good experience with their graduates."

"And with their CEO Mr. Stone?"

Bradley Stone's demeanor changes instantly. The room feels as if the polar vortex has suddenly blown in from Canada. Narrowing his eyes, he stares at D'Angelo. If he ever thought this was a routine, friendly interview, that notion is over.

"If you're trying to make a point, Detective, why don't you just come out and say it."

"We know you got a relationship with Roni Cohnheim. Is that why most of your people come from that school?"

"As I told you, the school has an excellent reputation. You can check that from your own sources if you haven't already done so. I was recruiting from the school before I knew Ms. Cohnheim. Her students have excellent training and perform exceptionally well. I would continue to recruit from the school regardless of my relationship."

D'Angelo does not let it go. "You ever refuse any of her people?"

"Detective, I don't like your insinuations. My relationship with Ms. Cohnheim has little bearing on my business and nothing to do with your investigation. In fact, I don't see any reason why I should tolerate the police investigating my private life. I am well-connected in this city. If any of these confidential matters become public, there will be hell to pay."

"You threatening us, Mr. Stone?"

"I am asserting my privacy rights, and my rights as a business person to hire anyone I choose."

"Even if those people come from someone who was mixed up in the kidney trade in Israel?"

Bradley Stone's face colors as he tries to control his anger. "For your information, Ms. Cohnheim is an excellent nurse and an accomplished businessperson. She was in the wrong place at the wrong time in Israel, but that is well behind her. I refuse to discuss her any further since my relationship with her is a private matter and has nothing to do with Neal Jensen. I think I have answered enough of your questions."

"Just a few more if you don't mind," I intervene, thinkin' D'Angelo has pushed hard enough. "Do you know Jose Moreno?"

"No, I never heard of him."

"He worked for your company in Fall River. He was a dialysis technician."

"We have several thousand employees, detective. I do not get a chance to know most of them."

"How about Miguel Sanchez?"

"No. Did he work for me also?"

"No, he was a twenty-two-year-old kid who was found dead with his organs missing. He was Jose Moreno's best friend."

"Why are you telling me this, Detective Goldberg?"

"Because I have two murders to solve. Both are tied to the illegal kidney trade. Both had connections to your centers, Mr. Stone. If you have any information, it would be a good idea to come forward."

"I'm going to tell you something—both of you. I don't like you or your insinuations. Neither I nor my company has anything to do with your investigation. You have no business looking into my private life. My company has a battery of lawyers that can sue you and your department if you invade my privacy and defame my reputation."

"It would be helpful if you could provide a copy of Mr. Moreno's personnel file," I say.

"Then I'm sure you can subpoena it. Good day detectives."

"Stonewalled," D'Angelo murmurs on our way out.

Chapter 17

Martin

After droppin' D'Angelo at the station, my thoughts drift back to Bradley Stone. You meet all kinds in this business, and you never stop learnin' about people. You want to categorize them, sort them accordin' to their characteristics: extrovert/introvert, confident/self-conscious, open/defensive, aggressive/passive, self-absorbed/modest, handsome/ugly, rich/poor, neat/sloppy, honest/dishonest, single/married. You want to slot them into little boxes by race, religion, gender, geography. I know that's not kosher these days. Shouldn't profile. It's not "PC." But I can't help it. Expect it's a very human tendency; the way our minds work, tryin' to make sense of the world. So, I try to fit Bradley Stone into his own little box.

Guy looks like a typical CEO. Tall, handsome, rich, smart, smooth, self-confident. Beginnin' of the interview, he was open and honest about the kidney trade. But when threatened, he lashed out; became prickly and angry. I think his behavior was defensive, coverin' up a trauma; a wounded man, driven to despair by the death of his son and the breakup of his marriage. A man who might have become stuck in depression and guilt. Instead, he became obsessed by this evil that killed his son and nearly ruined his life. Built this monument to his son by bein' single-minded and ruthlessly driven. When D'Angelo gave him a hard time, he threatened us. Wouldn't even give us Moreno's file. He's smart enough to know better.

Sometimes, when people are struck by one thing, they become fanatical believers in the opposite. Ex-smokers about smokin', obese people about dietin', non-believers about religion. Sometimes people who have lost loved ones by bein' passive become vengeful and violent. Bradley Stone bears a boatload of guilt about lettin' his son die without a kidney transplant, and his life may be driven by the need to free himself from that guilt. My gut says he's a man to watch.

My gut's also makin' hungry noises. Can't stand another TV dinner. Too late to shop in the supermarket and cook a meal. Need some easy take-out, so I go to Rubin's, my favorite Jewish deli. Rubin's has been a fixture on Harvard Street, just north of the Coolidge Corner area of Brookline. I drive down the street and notice the shops that cater to a large Jewish population; bagel stores, kosher meat markets, the Israel Book Shop, and Chinese restaurants. As usual, Maxie is behind the counter. I order my standard, the Manhattan; corned beef, hand-cut Rumanian pastrami, and chopped liver on cissel with brown mustard. I add a quarter-pound of potato salad, a half-sour pickle, and a couple of pieces of *rugelach.*

"What? You want nothing to drink?" Maxie asks.

"Sure, Max. Throw in a Dr. Brown's cream soda."

Back home, I set up a tray table in front of the TV and unwrap the sandwich. Find an old rerun of NYPD Blue. I watch the fast-paced plot, quick dialogue, split-second action, and sudden violence. It's a different world. Not like the borin' tasks that ordinarily fill my day. In my twenty plus years on the force, I've fired my weapon only twice and don't yearn to do it again.

I get down to the last few bites of my sandwich. Maxie stuffs so much meat inside, you gotta squash the bread to get your mouth around it. When you get down near the end, if you're not careful, the meat gets squeezed out the back. That's what happens: the pastrami, with an ugly glob of mustard, falls on my lap. I go to the kitchen for a towel to wipe off the stain when my cell phone rings.

Aggravated, having stained another pair of pants. I still got the plot of the TV program in the back of my mind. I'm not considerin' the possible nature of the call. Not suspectin' anythin' important. Not thinkin' another tragedy is about unfold. I pick up the phone and bark an inpatient "Goldberg!"

"Detective Goldberg, someone's been in my condo," comes the voice of a terrified Cynthia Fleming.

"How do you know?"

"I think some things have been moved."

"You sure you're not just anxious with all that's been going on?"

"No, Detective. Someone's been here. I'm scared."

"You think someone could still be there?"

"No, I looked, but I'm afraid. Someone could be coming after me."

"Okay, try to calm down, Cynthia. Tell me what happened from the time you left work."

"Today was one of the few times I had a night shift followed by a morning shift. It was a perfect time to bring patient files home, copy them, and return them before anyone would arrive in the morning. I waited until everyone left before I locked up and took the files. When I got home, the deadbolt on my door was unlocked. The doorknob was still locked, but I'm always careful. I never forget to lock the deadbolt, especially now."

"But you went into the house anyway?" I ask.

"Yes, I figured I must have forgot with all this going on. Besides, you have people watching me."

"Yes, we do. What happened next?"

"Well, I yelled 'is anyone here,' and I glanced around all the rooms. Everything seemed all right, so I went in the kitchen and made myself some chamomile tea to help me calm down. After I drank the tea, I took the files into my office and turned on the copier. The machine makes a lot of noise when it boots up, but I thought I heard a sound coming from one of the other rooms."

I'm worried listenin' to her story. Want to call this in right away and get someone over there but don't want to panic her. "What happened next, Cynthia?"

"I was scared, but I had looked all around before, so I decided to look again just to reassure myself. I started in the bedroom. Maybe something fell over. I always pile things up in my room. I looked at the far side of the bed and then under the bed. There's a master bathroom off of the bedroom. It is a small room and I could see immediately that no one was there. Then I realized I hadn't checked the bedroom closet. I jerked open the door and something moved! I must have screamed, but when nothing happened, I looked into the closet and saw a hatbox that had fallen to the floor. On my way back to the office, I checked the hall bathroom but saw nothing. I could have sworn there was a noise, but I went back to my office feeling this whole thing is doing a job on my head. I had to get a grip."

"It's okay, Cynthia," I say, trying to comfort her while hidin' my own anxiety. "What did you do next?"

"I opened my drawer to get an empty file folder for the copied records, and the files were out of place. It was clear that someone had gone through them and put them back out of order. That's when I decided to call you and—oh my god!!! I hear something again."

"Stay calm, Cynthia. I'll call this in and get a police detail to look around. Everythin' will be all right," I tell her, tryin' not to let on that I'm worried. That it might not be her imagination. She could be in danger."

"Detective, my lights just went out."

"Cynthia, are you okay?"

"EEEEE! Somebody's coming into the room"

I hear another scream, a loud noise, and the phone goes dead.

Chapter 18

Cassandra

I have a 2:00 p.m. appointment with the man who calls himself Herman. I don't know what to expect. He could be part of a sophisticated ring of international organ dealers, so I expect him to be careful. He could be watching me, so I have spent the day at home, not wanting to risk being seen leaving the FBI office. I finish my cup of afternoon coffee before dressing in my Sandra Ford persona. I consider wearing a wire but decide it is too risky.

Yesterday I called the New York telephone number scribbled on a scrap of paper. Of course, the Bureau tracked the call but couldn't get any identification. I called with my new iPhone purchased in the name of Sandra Ford with no list of contacts or chains of text messages that could reveal my identity. Location services had been turned off. I had closed the door to my office, connected the phone to an undetectable recording device, and dialed the New York number of the man called Herman. The name was unlikely to be any more reliable than my own.

"Hello," the man answered on the third ring.

"Hello," I replied. "Is this Herman?"

"Who am I speaking with?" he asked in clear English, but with a discernable accent.

"Sandra Ford. My daughter is a patient at the American Kidney Life Center."

"Ah, you must be the woman that works at Fidelity. What can I do for you, Ms. Ford?" he asked innocently, although he knew perfectly well why I was calling. I didn't like this man already.

"I think you know. My daughter needs a kidney."

"Are you calling from your cell phone, Ms. Ford?"

"Yes."

"My people are in close contact with religious Jewish people who are willing to donate kidneys. You see, in Jewish law it is a *mitzvah* to help save someone's life. You know the word *mitzvah?"*

"Yes, I do," I answered, familiar with Martin's occasional Yiddish expressions.

"*Mitzvah* literally means commandment," he explained, ignoring my answer. "But in common usage it means a good deed or an act of human kindness. In the Jewish religion, there are 620 specific *mitzvot*, some positive to do and some negative to avoid, and they are the source of all moral law."

"Didn't know that," I answered.

"So, we are in contact with people who are willing to donate kidneys purely for altruistic and religious reasons—to perform a *mitzvah*. Unfortunately, there are many more people seeking kidneys than there are altruistic donors. So, we can't help everyone, but it is possible we can help your daughter, particularly if we can find a good organ match. I happen to be in Boston now. Could you possibly meet with me tomorrow morning?"

"Yes, this is important to me. I can put everything else aside."

"Very good. Can you meet me at 10:30? I will stand by the front door of Faneuil Hall."

"Yes, 10:30 is fine. How will I recognize you?"

"Not to worry. I will recognize you, Ms. Ford. I have your photograph."

At 2:00 p.m., dressed like a wealthy hedge fund manager, I drive downtown in the Lexus. Years ago, when working undercover, I was always dressing down, trying to fit in as a tough, black woman, a street-smart dealer or petty criminal. This is a new persona, and it works its way in to my bearing. I find myself strutting more confidently and holding my head up higher, ignoring the flirtatious glances or just dismissing them with the flick of an eye. It's only an act, but it's nice to know I can still turn a few heads.

Faneuil Hall, a stately brick building by the Boston waterfront was first constructed in 1743. Famous for revolutionary speeches by Samuel Adams and others, it is often referred to as "the cradle of liberty." Alas, these days, it is part of Boston's Faneuil Hall Marketplace, where throngs of people go to shop and eat.

I park the Lexus in a nearby garage and walk to the front of Faneuil Hall. Crowds of tourists are milling around the site, but no one appears to be waiting by the entrance. Standing by the front doors, I have that eerie feeling of being watched. A few minutes pass, and I nervously check my watch. Ten minutes later, a heavy-set man dressed in slacks and a sport jacket approaches the building. He walks right up and greets me without the slightest doubt of my identity. "Good morning Ms. Ford. Herman Poleskey. Pleased to meet you."

"The pleasure is mine, Mr. Poleskey."

"The hotel around the corner has a nice coffee shop," he says. "I suggest we escape these crowds and have a quiet place to talk."

"As you wish."

We enter a posh, boutique hotel where Herman seems to know the maître d', and we are led to a booth in the far corner. Herman thanks him and gestures for me to sit down. He speaks confidently and has a gracious manner, like a man who has seen the world. He asks all about Keri. How is she doing? Is she happy? How did she contract kidney disease? How is she tolerating dialysis? Then, he tells me about the opportunities he has had to help other children. He talks about his own family back in Israel and politely asks about Keri's father, my ex-husband. Despite all my suspicions, the man is charming. Over coffee and scones, we have a pleasant, unhurried conversation.

Nearly a half hour passes before Herman says, "I apologize, Ms. Ford, but I must get down to business. First, I must sincerely apologize for being somewhat misleading in our telephone conversation. As you can imagine, I work in a very sensitive area. I didn't know who you were, and you were using a cell phone that was not secure. What I told you was partly true. We do have connections with Orthodox Jewish communities that sometimes provide altruistic kidney donors. Unfortunately, those opportunities are very rare. As you can understand, most prefer to donate within their own communities. The great majority of our kidneys come from paid donors; mostly people from other countries."

"Paid donors Mr. Poleskey? I thought it was illegal to pay for organs."

"The laws governing these transactions and their enforcement can be, as you say, fuzzy. For example, in Israel, paying for a kidney is illegal. Yet, if an Israeli citizen gets a transplant in another country, Israeli health insurance will likely cover the cost. In many countries, the operations are technically illegal if the donor has been paid, but the donor simply has to sign a paper stating that he or she did not receive remuneration. It is in no one's interest to investigate. The hospitals and doctors want to save people's lives."

"You say that the laws are 'fuzzy.' But, in fact, it is illegal. Is that right?"

"That is correct. If your daughter gets a kidney from us, it will not be legal, and you will be a party to an illegal transaction. If anything happens to your daughter, you will have no recourse. In fact, you will not even know who you are dealing with. As you might suspect, my real name is not Herman Poleskey, although everything else I have told you today is true. You will have to put your trust in me, despite the illegal nature of this deal. That is why I am not going to sugarcoat anything about this transaction. I will strive to be a completely honest broker, if that does not seem like an oxymoron."

"Pardon me for being blunt, Mr. Poleskey. You ask me to trust you, but if you are so honest, why would you be involved in this illegal business?"

"A fair question, Ms. Ford. What kind of person would be involved in such a shady business? I can tell you quite honestly that I am proud of what I do. I have saved countless lives, more than many doctors. I have brought people back from the edge of death and despair. I believe it is a moral tragedy that we do not permit people to derive a benefit from saving other people's lives. Tens of thousands die because of our imperious, self-righteous attitudes."

"A moral tragedy, Mr. Poleskey? Perhaps from the recipients' perspective, but what about the desperately poor people who need to sell their body parts? How do I know what these people have been exposed to? What diseases they may have? How do I know my daughter won't be harmed?"

"My people have an excellent track record. Can we guarantee the success of every transplant? Of course not. But neither can your Mass. General Hospital. When the time comes, you will know the hospital where the procedure will be conducted. You will know the surgeon's background and how many transplants he or she has completed. Most likely, the surgeon will be board certified in the United States."

"You must realize how frightening this whole thing sounds."

"I know this is terrifying, Ms. Ford. How can you trust your daughter's life to some criminal cabal? Many things could go wrong. Your child could die. You would never forgive yourself. It is a horrendous choice that is forced upon you. A devil's dilemma. I sympathize. I understand as well as anyone who has not confronted this situation. I have counseled many mothers through this same quandary. If you had any other alternative, I am sure you would not be here today."

"Mr. Poleskey, I can't believe I'm even here talking to you. No one should ever be forced to face this kind of decision."

"I understand. Now, I must tell you about the business side of this transaction. Assuming we can find your daughter a kidney, the cost will be $200,000 dollars. There are many people who must be paid. Unfortunately, the donor receives a relatively small sum. We must pay the lab, the hospital, the surgeon, the anesthetist, and the entire medical team. There can be considerable costs for transportation and lodging. Sometimes, there are payoffs that you don't want to know about. And, of course, I receive a commission for each client. I do not get involved in the clinical operation. I am simply a broker—an honest broker if you will. It may amaze you to know that despite all the costs and risks involved in our operation, we still charge less than the cost of a kidney transplant in the United States, which now averages about $260,000. Of course, your Medicare program covers most of that cost, so Americans are not aware of the expense."

"I am fortunate to be able to cover the cost, Mr. Poleskey. How and when do you expect to get paid?"

"If you decide to work with us, we will need a deposit of $10,000 to cover the search for the kidney and the initial lab work. The deposit is entirely non-refundable, but it does not obligate you to go ahead. If you change your mind, it's not so much to lose. You have a lot to consider, Ms. Ford. I advise you think this over carefully. Unfortunately, I will be in town for only two more days. After that, I may not be back for several weeks. You have my cell phone number and can call me at any time with your decision. Please be discreet over the phone."

Chapter 19

Martin

When the phone goes dead, I immediately fear the worst. My heart pounds, but there's no time think. Just have to react. I call headquarters, give them Fleming's address, and have the nearest patrol car dispatched immediately. I grab my car keys and am out the door. Other patrolmen will get there before me, but I'm frantic and drive like a *meshuggener*. My hands tremble as I grip the wheel.

By the time I reach the condo, a half-dozen police cars are parked outside. All too familiar yellow tape cordons off the buildin'. I pause before getting' outta the car, steelin' myself to cope with the scene. Other officers see me comin', and I can hear them murmur. By now, they know she was workin' for me. There's a bunch of subdued "hellos," but everyone has their heads down, avoidin' eye contact. I'm expectin' the worst.

The door is open to the unit and several officers are inside. I stretch a pair of blue paper booties over my shoes, like the ones you see in hospitals, so I won't disturb the scene. Several officers open a space to the office, and I see what I feared most. Cynthia Fleming's lifeless body lies crumpled on the floor. A dark brown puddle leaks from her head, a combination of brains, skin, bone, and blood. Then somethin' happens that hasn't occurred since I was a rookie. Bile rises up in my throat, and I know I'm gonna puke. Barely makin' it to the bathroom in time, I lurch toward the toilet. An ugly combination of undigested corn beef and pastrami finds the bowl, but some splatters on my leg, matchin' the earlier stain from Max's sandwich. I wash up and prepare to go back out, knowin' I'm gonna be embarrassed. The other guys feel bad for me and try to avert their eyes.

I get a quick briefin' from the officer in charge of the scene. "The first patrol car got here within two minutes of your call. We're not sure how he gained entrance, but the forensic guys will look for clues. The back door was open, so we assume that's how he left. We found the woman dead on the floor just like you see her. Shot in the back of the head. I called it in and got a call back from the Chief. He wants to see you after you get finished here. Sorry, Martin. It must be tough."

I thank the officer and force myself to examine the scene. There's no evidence of a physical struggle. Killer musta been hidin', waitin' for her or surprised by her return. Musta come up from behind and shot her at close range without a struggle. Cynthia had said there were things outta place, includin' her files. Perp may have been here for a while. Probably lookin' for somethin' specific. Whatever it was, Cynthia Fleming paid for it with her life.

Reluctantly, I go back to the bedroom-slash-office where the body lies undisturbed on the floor waiting for forensics. Against the wall is a desk with a laptop computer and a combination printer/copier. Above the desk, the wall is splattered with blood. Fleming's briefcase is on the floor, lyin' open and empty. I know she took the remainin' medical files home to be copied, but they're not in her briefcase. I try to picture the scene. Fleming sittin' at her desk, talkin' to me on the phone, when her assailant, who had possibly been hidin' in a closet, rushes up behind her. Probably never touched her. Just shot point blank at the back of her head. Thank God, she must have died instantly, never havin' known what happened. Small consolation for a wasted life.

On my way outta the room, I happen to notice a tiny sliver of paper visible under the cover of the copy machine. Liftin' the cover with the tip of my fingernail, not wantin' to mar any evidence, I call over one of the investigators who is gloved. He finds a medical record for a patient named Charles Thomas. If Fleming was makin' copies, the other records should have been right here in the room. Maybe that's what the perp was after. Someone tied into AKLC who suspected Fleming was copyin' the records for the police. He took the files but never realized there was one left in the copier.

On the drive back to headquarters to see the Chief, the tragedy begins to sink in. My worst fears have been realized, and it's totally my fault. I took advantage of this woman. Put her in danger. Scared the shit out of her and then used her fear to bludgeon her into helpin' me. God forgive me, I've become the kinda cop I never wanted to be. Maybe I should hang it up. Maybe the Chief will give me no choice. No matter, this'll be on my conscience forever. My mother, my wife, they told me to leave this *farshtunkener* job. Just feel like crawlin' into a hole and make this shitty world go away.

I got time to call Cassandra on the way to the station. She's the first person I can talk to who will understand my anguish. Besides, with another murder, I want to urge her to be more careful. If her cover gets blown, she could be the next victim. I begin to tell her, but she already knows. Guess I shouldn't be surprised. "I killed her, Cat. It's my fault. I never should've forced her to take such a chance."

"You can't do this to yourself, Martin. You had to make a judgement, and the balance between seeking justice and acting morally is not always clear. We use informants every day. If we didn't, half the criminals in jail would still be on the street. They would be out there hurting people. It's a dirty job. We deal in trade-offs with real people, and sometimes they get hurt. We have all been there and know how bad it feels, but it's not your fault."

"We'll see about that, Cat. On my way to meet with the Chief; prepared for a good shit-storm."

"Don't be so sure, Martin. This murder indicates you're on the right track and proves how serious this case has become. We'll find the bastards who did this. Keep your spirits up. I would give you a hug if I was there."

"Thanks Cat. Let you know how I make out."

Any self-confidence is absent by the time I walk into the Chief's office. Don't know what's comin' but expectin' the worst.

"Sit down, Martin. I'm sorry about what happened. You better explain what you were doing with Cynthia Fleming."

I tell the Chief that although Fleming knew about the illegal kidney sale, I don't think she was involved with the sellers. "My gut tells me she wasn't part of the trade. She was in love with Jensen and wanted to marry him. She wasn't goin' to turn him in or stop him from gettin' a new kidney. I used her involvement to pressure her to become an informant. It was a mistake. I feel responsible for her death."

"You didn't consult me, Martin. You probably thought I was better off not knowing, Plausible deniability. Maybe you were right, but did you think about the consequences? You just can't put the department at risk without good reason. If her family finds out she was an informant, the goddamn lawyers will be all over us. We'll all get fucked; especially you. I won't be able to give you any cover."

"I understand, Chief."

"Truth is, if you had asked me, I would have told you to go ahead. It looks like a mistake in hindsight, Martin. You may have underestimated what you were up against. But you must have been getting close, or else she wouldn't of got hit. It always sucks to lose an informant, but that's not my only concern. If the press discovers the link between these murders, they're going to find a love triangle, three murders, and an illegal trade in kidneys. It will make a hell of a story, and some asshole might eventually figure out she was an informant. I had to warn the commissioner that the story might become public. I'm sure he already told the mayor. You should have come to me first, but I don't blame you for what you did. It's a shitty business, and sometimes you have to play dirty to get what you need. If we didn't, they'd be all over us for not solving crimes. Just the same, if the shit hits the fan, we're both going to be covered. The press will be calling for our heads. The best thing we can do is find and arrest these assholes before anything else happens. If you need more support, just let me know."

"Thanks Chief. Sorry I got you into this. I'll work it as hard as I can." I walk outta his office knowin' what I love about bein' on the force. Despite all the shit you go through, you're part of a team. Other men and women on the force aren't simply work friends or colleagues. They're tightknit, loyal, dependable. They're brothers and sisters. Many of 'em would take a bullet to protect you. You fuck-up so bad, you could cost the Chief his job. Yet, you walk outta his office knowin' he's got your back.

Chapter 20

Cassandra

Yesterday, Keri had the most serious medical scare since she began dialysis. I don't know what caused the problem, but I know that fluid balance is critical for patients undergoing dialysis. Somehow, Keri had a severe imbalance that caused her heart to start fluttering. The nurse was able to get her under control, but the experience was terrifying. After putting her to bed, I was unable to sleep, imagining every kind of frightening scenario. At 5:00 a.m., I gave up, got out of bed, and brewed a hot cup of tea. It seemed like I'd been worrying about her forever and still had no indication she was anywhere near the top of the waiting list for a new kidney, I feared she couldn't wait much longer. I thought about this sting that has given me so much anxiety, and the possibility that it could somehow lead the way to a new kidney, even if it wasn't legal. I picked up the phone and dialed the number of Herman Poleskey.

I was still shaky this morning getting dressed. Trying on another new suit, strapping on heels that made my feet sore, putting on eye shadow and makeup I hadn't used since my twenties. By the time I left the house at 9:00 a.m., I was the stylish Sandra Ford, but I felt like the weary Cassandra Crawford.

I try to focus on my meeting with Herman Poleskey as I wait outside the front doors of Faneuil Hall. After fifteen minutes, there is still no sign of him, and, again, I have the eerie feeling of being watched. Perhaps this is part of their security plan, making sure I'm a legitimate mark and not part of a sting. A light rain starts to fall, but I have my Bloomingdales umbrella to protect my Armani suit. I feel so pretentious. If I wore these clothes to the office, everyone would figure I was on the take.

Herman finally arrives looking very Israeli with his sport jacket, no tie, and a pair of beige, linen slacks. He greets me warmly and leads me to the same café we visited before. They direct us to the same table, as if Herman had arranged this in advance. He is as charming as before, inquiring about Keri, her schoolwork, her health, her treatments. He is more like a generous uncle than a black-market kidney dealer. I have to remind myself that three people have been killed, and this is an investigation of criminals who sell human organs and commit murders. This is not just a nice man who is trying to save my daughter's life.

When we finally get down to business, Herman asks for confirmation of my decision. I have rehearsed my answer. I describe the episode Keri went through the day before. "I can't continue to watch her go through this," I tell him. "I want her to live a normal life. As I indicated on the phone, I have made the decision to go ahead."

"Did you bring the gift?"

From my Coach leather briefcase, I remove a small package with happy birthday giftwrapping. Inside the package is $10,000 in small bills. I was surprised to be able to fit so much money in such a small package. Herman accepts the package with a smile, like it's really his birthday, and this is his present.

"Thank you, you shouldn't have," he jokes. "The first thing you should do is sign a release for your daughter's medical records. A match is not likely to be a problem. It may surprise you, but we have many candidates who are willing to sell one of their kidneys. Nevertheless, we want to get you the best possible match, one that has the largest number of compatible antigens. Once we locate the right donor, we will give you all the information we can reasonably provide: the name and location of the hospital, the experience of the surgeon, and the basic information about the kidney match. When that happens, you will notify AKLC that you have found an altruistic donor. We will provide all the necessary paperwork. They will provide all the necessary pre-operative care. Our people will coordinate all the logistics except your airline reservations. You will make those reservations and notify us of the details. We will provide all other transportation and lodging."

"What if I am unhappy about the hospital or the doctor?" I ask. "I will not put my daughter's health at risk if I have doubts about her care."

"If you have any doubts, Ms. Ford, you can terminate the process, and there will be no repercussions. Of course, you will forfeit your $10,000 deposit. If you decide to go ahead, you must pay half the total bill before leaving the country."

I look Herman Poleskey straight in the eye. "You're asking me to risk $100,000 simply relying on your assurances?"

"I realize this involves a matter of trust," he replies. "You may think there will be no one at the other end, and we will keep your money. I can only give you my personal assurances. We have built a complex, international business to provide and transplant kidneys. Our profits are derived from the success of that process and not from stealing people's money and creating a group of angry victims who may go to the authorities. Believe me, there are much easier and less risky ways to steal."

"I suppose I have no choice, Mr. Poleskey. When do I have to pay the balance?"

"Once you get to your destination, the medical team will take over. If you do not like the people or the operation for any reason, you are free to change your mind. However, you will forfeit the money you have paid. Once the pre-op procedures have been completed, and the successful crossmatch with the donor confirmed, all that will be left is the surgical procedure. At that time, you will pay the balance. Do you have any questions?"

"I have a thousand questions, Mr. Poleskey. I'm afraid. I don't know if I'm doing the right thing. I have no idea what I'm getting myself into. Regardless, your instructions are clear, and I am prepared to go ahead."

"Ms. Ford, it has been a pleasure to meet you, and I sincerely wish you and your daughter the best. I will be informed of the outcome of the operation, but you will no longer be able to contact me, and you should not try. This cell phone is only for this one transaction between the two of us and will be destroyed. This meeting place will not be used again, and, as you know, my real name is not Herman Poleskey. Be that as it may, a live kidney is a gift of life, especially to a young child. I believe you have made the right choice. I only wish that it was legal. As we say in Yiddish, *zei gezunt*."

Chapter 21

Martin

"Dad, Dad, help me!" I hear Meredith's voice callin' over and over but can't find her. I run through the house. Somehow, it's a friend's house from thirty years ago. "Dad, help!" I go through the back door to an open field with woods at one end. There's a path through the trees. It's dark. I run through the forest and hear a gunshot. Meredith? Merideth? The kidney people. They've shot my daughter. Panicked, I thrash through the brush and trip over a tree root, fallin' face first on the ground. I wake up with my heart poundin' and the bed sheets damp with sweat.

Since Cynthia Fleming was killed, I've suffered from insomnia and nightmares. Weird dreams, violent scenes jumbled and makin' no sense, people outta time and place, some who I haven't seen in years. Tried sleepin' pills but felt like a zombie the next day. Work hasn't got to me like this for a long time. For years, Florence told me to give it up and go into private work. "You're too nice," she would say. "You're not callous like the others. You take it home and it eats at you." Thought all that was behind me. Finally, I was used to the violence. Now, after Fleming's death, I can't seem to quiet my mind; can't get the thoughts to stop racin' through my head. At least when Florence was here, I had someone to talk to. Maybe I drove her batty with my worries, but at least I had an outlet, a sympathetic ear. Maybe it's time to hang it up. But I can't. I'm responsible for Fleming's death and can't just walk away. I got an obligation to the Chief and the department to clear it up. And I got an appointment this morning with Colonel James Harris, a former AKLC patient whose medical record looks suspicious.

The guy was a hero in the Vietnam war. He flew B-52s outta Thailand and Guam. After the war, he was an airline pilot with a perfect record. He deserved a happy retirement, but at sixty-five he got kidney failure. He began dialysis at an AKLC on the north shore. Three years later, he stopped dialysis, but his records lack the usual detailed information. Today he is seventy-five and healthy.

Sun shines through the windshield, as I drive toward the Colonel's house. When I phoned him yesterday, he was resistant. Didn't want to talk about his kidney transplant. But when I told him it was an ongoin' murder investigation, he relented. The Colonel lives in Marblehead, a rich little elbow of land that juts out into Massachusetts Bay. His house is on a modest street named Drumlin Road. I park the Taurus in front and notice the house is in perfect condition. The yard is manicured, shrubbery trimmed, flowerbeds edged and surrounded by a thick coat of bark mulch. Unlike my yard, the place has the feel of military order.

The Colonel is a tall man with a thick shock of white hair combed neatly back from his forehead. Well-dressed, he looks younger than his age. Slacks are pressed, button-down shirt starched and wrinkle-free, shoes shined as if he was preparin' for inspection. His handshake's got the firmness of a man half his age. I follow him to a family room where his wife has already set a table with fresh baked scones and a pot of coffee. She was probably the perfect military wife, takin' her turn preparin' dinner parties for the senior officers and their wives. After a brief hello, the Colonel is all business: "Detective Goldberg, after I spoke with you on the phone, my wife and I had a long discussion about your visit. We have been married for fifty-three years, and we make our important decisions together. Initially, she was against my talking to you about the transplant, but after I explained how I felt, we both agreed that it was the responsible thing to do.

"Let me start by telling you a little bit about my life. I have been a most fortunate man. I was blessed with a successful military career in which I earned both high rank and numerous medals. As a civilian, I became a commercial airline pilot when that was one of the highest paid occupations in the country. I have a loving wife and family including two children, five grandchildren, and seven great grandchildren. Aside from my kidney transplant, my health has been excellent. This wonderful country has been good to me, and the Lord has been even better. An observer might say, I have lived a near perfect life."

"You have served your country well, Colonel."

"Thank you, Detective. But despite all those things, I have some regrets. You see, I was a bomber pilot in the Vietnam war. I flew those huge B-52s they called Stratofortresses. They flew at over 30,000 feet, where the chance of getting shot down was remote, and they carried 70,000 pounds of bombs. Those planes were not used in the beginning of the war. They used to fly for the Strategic Air Command and held nuclear weapons. But as you know, the war in Vietnam did not go well for the U.S. We thought we could win with a little counterinsurgency. Then, we thought we could turn the tide by bombing only military targets. When those efforts failed to stop the men and weapons coming from North Vietnam, we turned to punishing the North Vietnamese to break their will and draw them to the conference table. So, the B-52s were converted for one of the most intense bombing campaigns in history. We took off from Guam or Thailand, high in the sky, far above the death and destruction, and we carpet-bombed that tiny little country, often with napalm. God knows how many thousands of innocent people—women and children—that we killed. Of course, it didn't do any good. Rather than break their spirit, we toughened their resolve. I hated what I was doing, but I didn't have the guts to stand down, to ruin my career, or worse, to face a court martial and disgrace. Every day, I climbed into the cockpit and dropped tens of thousands of pounds of bombs, killing everything and everyone below me. At night, I prayed to God to forgive me. Even now, I have nightmares of people burning and screaming.

"When my tour of duty was up, I left the military, a decorated hero. Almost immediately, I was hired by one of the major airlines. The salary was more than I ever dreamed of making. Many of the people who ran the company and flew the planes were ex-military. The anti-war movement was growing, and I wanted to speak out, but I didn't have the guts. I thought I would lose my job. I told myself I had a responsibility to support my family. I kept my mouth shut and had a long, lucrative, and successful career.

"Now, you come to talk to me, Detective. You said that if I tell you about my transplant, I can prevent some evil, put dangerous criminals behind bars, and perhaps save the lives of people who might otherwise be harmed. Of course, I wish you had never called. I don't want to revisit a decision I made that I know was illegal. I don't want to besmirch my stellar reputation. Wouldn't it be better for me to continue my happy, peaceful life and not get involved with your ugly investigation? Don't I owe it to my family to maintain the respect of the Harris name? Shouldn't I just keep quiet and not drag my family into this mess, which, if it goes to court, will undoubtedly be headlines in the local newspapers?

"I'm sure by now you see where I am going. I cannot remain silent again. I cannot, again, opt for the easy way out. My conscience still aches from my guilt about the war. I do not want to lie on my deathbed regretting the decisions I should have made.

"So, after you called, I shared my thoughts with my wife. Of course, she already knows about my past regrets. Just the same, after all these years, she still thinks I'm the proud military hero—the handsome, brave, all-American fly-boy she fell in love with and married. She has always believed in me; believed that deep in my heart, I was the person who always tried to do the right thing. I am not going to disappoint her, Detective. Not this time."

I gotta stop my eyes from tearin' up in front of this military man who probably wonders if I ever served. Course not. I had an exemption for bein' in law enforcement. "Colonel," I manage to speak over the lump in my throat, "I appreciate your honesty."

"Thank you, Detective. I am prepared to tell you about my kidney transplant. I have made some notes, so I don't leave anything out."

I'm dyin' to hear his story after so many other interviews and false leads, but I gotta pee somethin' awful. It's probably from the coffee, but when it comes on, I need to go right away. I imagine the look on this Colonel's face if I pissed in my pants. "Excuse me, sir, but can I use your bathroom before we begin?"

"Certainly, down the hall, first door on the left."

Bathroom looks spit-shined, and with my weak stream I'm careful not to dribble on the rim of the toilet. I wash my hands and re-fold the perfectly folded towel back on the rack. Returnin' to the alcove, I ask the Colonel to begin. But he discreetly lowers his eyes, and I realize my fly is unzipped. I give the Colonel a manly nod and quickly close the zipper.

The Colonel relates his story in detail, frequently checkin' his notes. He describes how he was approached by an AKLC technician, and how he later met with an Israeli broker. He tells about his preparation and his trip to India for the operation. I ask him about the payments, and he describes how he paid $150,000.

"Colonel Harris," I ask. "Are you willin' to give a formal deposition and testify in court if the need arises? I can promise you complete immunity from prosecution."

"Yes, detective. I believe it is my duty to do so. But, if I am judged to be wrong in a court of law, I will accept the consequences."

Chapter 22

Cassandra

Kids love macaroni and cheese. I place the plate on the table noticing my daughter's eager smile. I probably should give her a healthier meal, but it's hard to say no. Keri just finished four hours of dialysis, sitting patiently like a little angel, while her friends were out playing and visiting each other's houses. Poor girl feels different, left out, that girl with the kidney disease. "Can I have more mac and cheese, Mom? Please?" I don't have the heart to refuse. Plus, I feel guilty that I'm going out and leaving her at home with a babysitter; my last meeting with Martin before I leave the country.

What a relief to get out of these clothes. I am so Sandra Ford at the dialysis center with designer suits and high heels. My feet feel like they have undergone Chinese foot binding. In the hot shower, I scrub off the makeup and eye shadow, stare at my French nails. It is so not me. I squeeze into skinny gray jeans, a black blouse with balloon sleeves, and a pair of low-heeled black pumps and feel more like myself. I give instructions to the sitter and kiss Keri goodbye. Out the door, I surveil the area around the house. No one who knows Sandra Ford has this address, but I need to be careful just the same. All clear, I climb into the Lexus and drive to Spadaro's.

Having committed to the sting, I know Martin is going to be upset. There was little choice. After Herman set it up, I was too involved to say no. Donaldson sucked me in all along. Martin is sitting in his usual booth when I walk in. He greets me with his usual hug. He can't wait to tell me about Colonel Harris. We have barely sat down when he begins to blurt out the news. "You don't need to worry about followin' up with your kidney dealer," he says. "I will have enough evidence—

but I interrupt. I need to tell him straight out. "It's too late, Martin. I know you're going to be upset, but the sting is all set. Keri and I are going to India." Immediately, I see the disappointment in his face. His eyes droop and his cheeks and chin scrunch together in pain. "I know you are worried, but this is the best way. The FBI has conducted sting operations like this forever. They know what they are doing."

"I had a feeling you were goin' to tell me this, Cat, but the case has got a new turn. With this witness, I can solve it from here. Nobody's got to go to India. Let me tell…"

"Martin, forget it. The strike team is set. There is no going back."

"Listen, please. Let me tell you about my meeting with the Colonel." Martin relates the details of the meeting while I try to listen patiently, knowing that whatever he says is not going to change anything. "AKLC is up to their necks in this," he tells me. "We got enough on Bradley Stone to scare the shit outta him. Think of what he has to protect in his little empire. We can break him and pick up the whole ring. You don't gotta go to India. No matter how careful, you and Keri will be in danger. I can bust them from here, Cat, without the risk."

"Don't be naïve, Martin. You have to focus on your own local area, but the FBI is itching for an international breakthrough. They cooperate with other countries, and they think this could help them identify organ traders all over the world. The local picture is small potatoes to them. Besides, you know the Bureau. This is their case now, and they are not about to give it away to some Boston Detective. I'm sorry, Martin. I know it was your case, and you're worried about me, but this decision is already over my head."

"These people are killers, Cat. Howd'ya know you'll be safe?"

I take a quick glance around the restaurant. Even though we're in a quiet booth, I can't take the chance of being overheard. Not sensing any danger, I outline the plan to Martin. "The back-up team is already in the country. Keri and I can go in unaccompanied because they're already set up. The Bureau has confirmed that these people really do provide kidneys and arrange transplants. They have a profitable business. The only reason they would resort to violence is the fear of being caught. Besides, there is still a $95,000 hold-back that I don't deliver until all the clinical tests are complete."

"Will they actually conduct the tests on Keri?"

"Martin, the whole schedule is worked out." I access a hidden file in my cell phone and read off the timeline of Keri's preparations. "Barring any unexpected development, the team will stay hidden while we go through all the required procedures. Then, on the morning the final pre-op is scheduled, Keri and I will be on a chartered FBI transport making our way back home. Instead of us, the strike team will show up at the hospital and conduct the sting."

"Sounds simple, Cat, but if they find out what you're doin', your backup won't mean shit."

Could things go wrong? Undoubtedly, but I've taken these risks all my life. What kind of career would I have had otherwise? Of course, I never had to involve Keri, and I feel guilty, wondering if I'm a terrible mother, afraid I'm doing the wrong thing. It's a screwed-up situation, but I have to take the risk if I'm ever going to get a promotion and make enough money to send Keri to college.

"You don't have to make that choice. I could bust them without the risk."

"Forget it, Martin. This plan is going to require your cooperation. We can't let these people know we're hot on their trail before the sting takes place. There can be no arrests. The Bureau has already cleared this with your boss. I know how you must feel. It was your case and the Feds have pretty much taken over. But the send button has already been pressed, and I know you don't want to do anything that could blow my cover."

"Great! You're tellin' me I'm done. I'm outta the loop."

"I'm sorry, Martin. It is what it is, and don't think I'm happy about it. I could hardly be more conflicted. I know three people have been killed. I'm sure these organ traders are tied to AKLC, and I know they prey on poor, desperate people. They are reverse Robin Hoods, taking kidneys from the poor and selling them to the rich. Yet, against all my better instincts, I keep trusting them. I was totally on my guard against Herman Poleskey, but as much as I wanted to doubt him, he came across as caring and concerned. Maybe he was a great actor, but I couldn't help feeling he was genuine. A little voice kept telling me, 'Beware, this man is a criminal; a person who exploits poor people for their organs and looks the other way when his gang members murder anyone who gets in their way.' But it didn't ring true. He was polite and considerate at every point. He looked me in the eye, and I felt he was telling me the truth."

"And he took your money."

"Yes, $105,000. But his operators have been impressive. They have taken care of every detail I can imagine. I wish I could find travel agents who are so thorough. And they have been surprisingly transparent; giving me all the clinical details about the donor kidney and a thorough description of the transplant process. I don't get treated half as well from doctors in the states.

"Most unsettling is the knowledge that they actually do some good. They save people's lives. I have this nagging uncertainty that I may be arresting the wrong people. These are people who could save my daughter and give her a normal life. Maybe they are doing the right thing, and the rest of us are wrong. Maybe we are the ones who are guilty of letting people die while we sit on our high horse calling the condemned immoral. Look at your upstanding Colonel, healthy and well for years after buying an illegal kidney. What if we are wrong,

Martin? What if the biggest risk for my daughter is not the sting? What if it's my fear of cooperating with them?"

"You can't think that way, Cat. These are murderers who are breakin' the law. Even if you're convinced the law is wrong, you can't just break it. That's what you and I spend our lives fightin'. We can't be on the other side a the fence."

"Sounds great, Martin, but somewhere, inside of whatever maternal instincts I have, is the horrible fear of letting my daughter die a preventable death."

There is no way for the two of us to salvage a happy night out. We will not see each other before the flight to India, and if something goes wrong, we may never see each other again. Both of us know the stakes, and we linger over cold cups of coffee, not wanting this woeful mood to define our final meeting. I know Martin is uncomfortable with sentimentality, but I put my hands over his and stares into his eyes.

"Martin, whatever happens, I want you to know you have a special place in my heart. I want you to know how much I care about you."

Poor guy, his eyes begin to fill up with tears and his face turns red. He can barely get out the words, and, while they may not sound like much, they are the most the big guy can muster.

"Thank you, Cat. I feel the same way."

Chapter 23

Cassandra

I am bleary-eyed when the plane touches down in New Delhi. Keri has been sleeping on my shoulder for the past hour, and I'm so stiff I can hardly get out of my seat. We exit the plane and walk through a maze of corridors. Following signs for passport control, we emerge in a cavernous room with hordes of people and interminable lines. Keri is tired and cranky as we inch along toward customs. After nearly an hour, we are able to retrieve our luggage, pass through the final check, and walk through the doors into the main terminal. A sea of people waits on the other side, some hugging long-lost relatives, kissing returning partners, searching for missing friends. The crowded scene is overwhelming, and I wonder how anybody can find us in this mass of humanity. Yet, just a few steps in front of us, a man is holding a bold, red, handwritten sign with the name Sandra Ford.

He introduces himself as Anish, a well-dressed, well-groomed, good-looking young man. I detect a British undertone to his Indian accent, probably learned in private schools or overseas in England. He helps with our bags as we follow him outside the terminal to his car. By the time we settle in to his air-conditioned Mercedes, it is clear he is not simply a taxi driver.

"Welcome to New Delhi," he says to Keri. "It is a very big city, much larger than you're used to in Boston. But the people are very nice. We will take good care of you. You must be tired after your long flight."

"Yes," Keri murmurs a one-word answer, overwhelmed by the gigantic size of the airport, the crowds of people, the noise, the heat.

"Mrs. Ford, I work for the Apollo Hospital, and I will be your guide and your liaison to the medical team for your entire stay. I will give you my cell phone number and you should feel free to call me at any time of day for anything you need. We have prepared a booklet to provide you with the details of this entire process, but while we are in the car, I will give you some basic information."

"Thank you, Anish. I should give you my cell and my e-mail also."

"Not necessary, I already have that. I know you must be anxious because you are in a strange country. I am happy to put your mind at ease. You are most fortunate that this procedure will be performed at the Apollo Hospital in New Delhi. The Apollo Transplant Institutes are among the most technically advanced and experienced in the world. They perform kidney, heart, liver, corneal, intestinal and bone marrow transplants. The Institutes perform more than 1,000 kidney transplants a year making us the largest outside the United States. About three-quarters of them are done here in New Delhi. Our success rate is over 90 percent, and that includes many elderly people with multiple medical problems. Among young people, the success rate is much higher. We have an excellent pediatric transplant department. With the possible exception of a few places in your own country, you could not have come to a better place."

"Thanks, Anish. As you can imagine, I have read quite a bit about the Apollo hospitals. They do have an impressive reputation."

"Have you ever been to New Delhi before, Mrs. Ford?"

"No. I have never been to any part of India."

"The city has become quite cosmopolitan. You will be staying in a modern, high-rise apartment with all the conveniences you are accustomed to at home. It will be a short distance from the hospital. The unit has a full kitchen, but there are many restaurants in the immediate area. I can tell you some of my favorites. As you can see, traffic around the city is horrific. I would strongly advise you not to drive or rent a car. Taxis are inexpensive, and I will also be at your service. This is your building coming up on the right. I will pull into the underground garage and we can take the elevator up to your suite."

Anish helps carry our luggage up to the apartment and checks to make sure everything is satisfactory before taking his leave. The two-bedroom apartment is small, but certainly adequate and spotlessly clean. I check the kitchen and am pleased to see it has been stocked with simple basics like salt, pepper, sugar, milk, cereal, and a few soft drinks. I'm relieved to see numerous "pods" of coffee placed next to a Keurig coffee maker, so I will not have to wait hours for Keri to wake up before having my morning fix.

"How do you like our new place, honeybun?"

Keri has been watching me scuttle around, checking for little details like toilet paper and soap, and she is whiney and cranky. "I'm tired, Mommy," says the little girl who always resists bedtime. I help getting her ready for bed, pull back the crisp white sheets, and kiss her goodnight. She is asleep in minutes. Feeling alone, and somewhat disoriented in this strange and unfamiliar place, I pace the room and ponder my situation.

Here I am at one of the world's most respected hospitals. Is there an obvious contradiction? How can a ring of international organ traders cooperate with a renowned medical center? I consider the whole process. Everything that was illegal must have been completed on the front end. The discreet offer to the recipient, the search for the donor, the clinical lab work, the money that changed hands. Once those were accomplished, it would simply be a matter of producing believable paperwork—an altruistic donor giving a kidney to an ailing person, possibly identified as a close friend or distant relative. A charitable organization assisting a sick patient in finding a compatible donor. A life saved by a human being with heroic compassion. Why would anyone object? The paperwork would show it all. Signed and notarized by all parties. Stating the transaction was voluntary with no remuneration. Why would someone, without evidence, object to the operation and condemn the diseased recipient to an early death? What motivation would the hospital have to investigate the carefully prepared legal documents? Why would the surgeon refuse to conduct the life-saving transplant? Add to that, the fact that the hospital and doctors gain valuable experience and receive handsome payments. The transaction between the kidney-procuring organization and the hospital is a mutually beneficial and highly profitable joint venture. You could hardly devise a better plan at the Harvard Business School.

So far, everything has gone like clockwork, and that is what is eating away at my conscience. Had this ring of people been ugly and nefarious; had the site of this operation been some filthy, third world clinic; had the accommodations not been so perfect; had the planning not been so meticulous, it would be easy to betray them and plan their demise. Instead, everything has been totally professional. Every person has been considerate. Every detail has been managed. There has never been a hint of subterfuge or violence. The whole God-dammed setup that I am here to destroy seems almost too good to be true.

It is certainly not the first time the thought has occurred to me. What would happen? What would happen if I did nothing? What would happen if I deceived the FBI and let the operation take place? Chances are 95 percent or better that it would save Keri's life. A kidney from a live donor would last twice as long as one I might get in the future from someone who died. Besides, Keri might never even get a deceased donor from the waiting list. What would the FBI do if I deceived them? It would certainly be the end of my career. It would quite likely land me in jail. How much compassion would a judge have for an FBI investigator who effectively turned double agent and paid off a ring of people suspected of multiple murders? Even a single mother with a dying child would not get enough sympathy to keep her out of the slammer.

Chapter 24

Martin

After my dinner with Cassandra, I return home dejected. I got no one to blame but myself for what happened. I pace around the house havin' an ugly conversation with myself. The stupidest thing was handin' my case to the FBI. After all these years in the force, how could I not know better? They have this grand image of themselves as the saviors of law enforcement and they piss on everyone else, especially city police departments. Still think they're like Elliot Ness, chasin' down Al Capone and the Chicago mob, makin' the country safe for democracy. Same fuckin' agency that was a laughin' stock for years as a tool of J. Edgar Hoover. Same people who supported Joe McCarthy and tried to screw Martin Luther King. They never consider cooperating with local police. If it wasn't for Cassandra, they wouldn't have given me shit. Chief told me to talk to her, not to make her my partner. Losin' control and lettin' them take over was completely my fault. I coulda broken the case with the colonel's testimony. She never woulda gone to India with that little girl so the FBI could chase their big score.

At 10 o'clock, I'm getting' ready for bed when the phone rings. "Martin, I got news," Tony D'Angelo says. "We picked up some good shit from the wiretap on Cohnheim's phone."

One thing I managed to get for this investigation was a court order allowin' a wiretap on Roni Cohnheim's phone. Judge had been reluctant, but considerin' her history in Israel and her association with Bradley Stone and AKLC, we were able to convince him that a wiretap was justified.

D'Angelo queues the recording. "Listen to this, Martin. It's a call from Cohnheim to Stone. It came in around nine o'clock."

"Hello, darling. I figured it was okay to call on this line while she's away."

"Yes, it's fine. Is anything wrong?"

"I'm worried about the police. They have been nosing around. A couple of old patients called my techs saying the police had contacted them and were asking all kinds of questions about us. I'm worried about that guy Goldberg, the Jewish detective. The same one who spoke to you. I don't know if he has any evidence or suspects we are doing something illegal. Do you think we have anything to worry about?"

"Honey, you're too anxious. We don't have anything to fear from that guy. He's just some local cop. He's got three murders to solve and his boss must be putting enormous pressure on him. You know how it works. The mayor doesn't want the bad publicity from a rash of unsolved murders. He gets on the back of the police commissioner who lights a fire under his precinct chiefs. We run a tight ship. We've covered our asses. He's got nothing on us. You don't need to worry."

"I'm sorry. It just gets to me after everything I went through in Israel. I haven't been sleeping well."

"Hey, it's only a little past nine. My wife is doing a three-day yoga retreat with some Indian guru out in Western Massachusetts. Why don't you take a cab over? Have the driver come around the rear of the building and call me on my cell when you're outside. I can let you in the back entrance, and we can take the service elevator directly up to the penthouse without anyone seeing us."

"Are you sure? You're always so careful about no one seeing us together, especially around your place."

"Don't worry. I'll put a nice sauvignon blanc in the refrigerator and fire up the Jacuzzi. Wear something that comes off easy."

"Absolutely. See you around ten o'clock."

"Good stuff, Tony," I tell him. "If we ever doubted they're in this together, we can put those thoughts to rest. They're both in it up to their necks. '*We run a tight ship. We've covered our asses. He's got nothing on us. You don't need to worry.*' We'll see about that Mr. Bradley Stone. We got plenty for you to worry about and the Colonel as a witness."

The recordin' helps lift my spirits and gives me more confidence to push on. It's another piece that might help break open the case. I can't let Cassandra walk into a trap with these people. If she or her daughter were ever harmed, I could never forgive myself. Can't take any chances that could blow her cover, but if there's information that might protect her, I need to find it out. I can dig a little deeper without endangerin' her operation, and the first place I wanna dig is the Nattai Institute.

First thing next mornin', I make an appointment with Roni Cohnheim. Then, I meet with D'Angelo. "Glad you want to push ahead," he tells me. "I was afraid we'd have to chill with Cassandra in New Delhi, but as long as we're careful, there's still a bunch of leads we need to follow."

"Agreed. After that phone tap last night, I made an appointment to see Cohnheim at the Nattai Institute. We gotta leave in a few minutes."

"Great. After that, we oughta have a talk with Clayton Thurmond."

The Nattai Institute is located in a modern, steel and glass building in Cambridge, the home of Harvard and MIT. The schools have been a force, turnin' the empty lots and old mill buildings in East Cambridge into the headquarters of high-tech start-ups.

Enterin' the building, we're surrounded by a swarm of activity. Young people with backpacks rush around in all directions. Average age must be no more than thirty, and I can't help but notice some very attractive young women who find me totally invisible. To be honest, I never felt very visible to them even when I was young.

We take the elevator to the fourth floor. Light maple double doors bear a sign "Office of the President," but when we enter, the rooms are nothin' like the corporate offices at AKLC. The furnishin's are more like IKEA than Roche Bubois. Atmosphere is casual, and no one is dressed up. Jeans seem to be the uniform of the day. Receptionist looks like a student who's probably workin' for tuition. I tell her we got an appointment with President Cohnheim.

We don't have to undergo the usual "please have a seat and the President will be with you shortly." Receptionist simply points to the hallway and tells us it's the last door on the left. No one accompanies us to the executive office. Door is open, and before we can knock, Roni Cohnheim tells us to come in. She's an attractive woman, probably in her early forties. Has the features of an Israeli sabra: olive skin, curly black hair, large brown eyes. She's about five foot six, slim, and obviously in good shape. I make the introductions, and we both show her our badges.

"Good morning, detectives. No need for your badge. As you undoubtedly know, I'm used to speaking with Israeli detectives, but this is my first opportunity in the U.S. To what do I owe this visit?"

"We're hopin' you can help us, Ms. Cohnheim," I respond. "But first let me thank you for takin' the time to meet with us. I'm sure you're busy, so I'll explain why we're here. A few weeks ago, a dialysis patient at one of the American Kidney Life Centers was murdered. His autopsy and other evidence indicated that he might have undergone an illegal kidney transplant. Around the same time, a young man who was a close friend of a dialysis tech at a different AKLC was found murdered in Mexico. All his valuable organs had been removed from his body. A short time after that, another AKLC dialysis tech was murdered in her home. We believe these murders may be connected and are likely related to the trade in illegal organs."

"That is horrible, but what does that have to do with me?"

"We're in the beginning of our investigation. As of this time, we have no suspects but are gathering information. A logical place to start is to learn everything we can about AKLC and the people who work there. Since your institute supplies many of their technicians, I am hopin' you can help."

"I am happy to cooperate, but not sure I can be of any help. It is true that we place many of our graduating students at AKLC. The great majority are very young; many in their teens and twenties. Some attend college and work part-time as dialysis techs to help pay their tuition. These kids are not long out of high school, just starting out in their careers. They are hardly the type to know anything about the international trade in illegal organs."

"Right, I understand. What about your client, AKLC?"

"As you can imagine, we place our students in medical centers all over the country, but AKLC is our largest client. We have a very good relationship with them, and they have an excellent reputation. They are highly regarded in the industry, and our graduates give us positive feedback about their operation. They are also highly profitable, so I can't imagine they would be involved in anything that could threaten their business. But my knowledge is almost entirely limited to recruiting. I don't know much about the details of their operation."

D'Angelo gives Cohnheim a disbelievin' look. "What about their CEO, Bradley Stone?" he asks.

"What about him, Detective?"

"I understand you know him quite well."

"Let's be frank. Bradley told me that you interviewed him and asked about me. I was not surprised when you called."

"So, I assume as his major source for personnel and his romantic partner, you might have quite a bit of knowledge about Mr. Stone and his business."

"I don't appreciate you associating my personal life with your investigation. I have a complex business to run, and I don't have the time or inclination to learn about the inner workings of AKLC."

Tony D'Angelo is like a dog with a bone. "Ms. Cohnheim, three people connected to AKLC have been murdered. It ain't coincidence. Somebody who is somehow connected with AKLC is probably the killer. Stone runs the show, you supply the help, and you two are like this." (D'Angelo makes a somewhat obscene gesture sticking his finger through a hole in his balled-up fist). "Both of you are what we call persons of interest."

"I understand, but what is it that I can tell you?"

I pick up the questionin', afraid that Tony is getting' too offensive. "Let's start with Mr. Stone. He appears to be a meticulous man who likes to be in control. Is it likely that someone on the staff could be referrin' people to organ traders without his knowledge?"

"I doubt it. Bradley is both cautious and thorough. His staff vets all our referrals very carefully. Even people who we highly recommend go through a lengthy hiring process. He does not delegate well. You are correct in assuming he is very much in control."

"I asked him whether patients talk to the technicians about findin' organs. I would've expected him to say no; to tell me his staff would never be permitted to do so or they'd be fired. Instead, he told me quite the opposite. It was almost as if he encouraged his staff to let patients know about purchasin' organs on the black-market."

"You were suspicious because he was being honest? I assume you know about his son."

"Yes, he told me."

"Then I think you would understand what motivates him. His son might be alive if Bradley had bought him a kidney. What if it was your son, Detective Goldberg?"

"I don't believe in breakin' the law. In the long run, when people don't respect the law, society breaks down. What if it was your son, Ms. Cohnheim?"

"I would not watch him die a needless death. I think the law is anachronistic. The capabilities of medicine have advanced faster than the attitudes of politicians and judges. Sometimes it is immoral not to act."

"Is that why you were involved in the organ trade in Haifa?" D'Angelo asks.

"Don't try to bully me, Detective. I had enough of that in Israel. I'm sure you already know I was not involved in that situation. I was never charged with any offense. That situation was the reason I left."

"You bolted."

"I did not bolt. Those people were out for themselves and I did not want to be associated with them. I came to your country and started an honest, reputable business."

"How long have you known Bradley Stone?" D'Angelo asks.

"I met him around the time I opened the first location, about two years after I arrived here."

"And when did you hook-up?"

"I don't think that is any of your business."

D'Angelo ignores her answer. "Was it before your students were getting in or after?"

"I don't appreciate your insinuations. AKLC and the Institute have a mutually beneficial business relationship that has worked well for both companies irrespective of my relationship with Bradley Stone. You cops are all alike. You're just like the ones in Israel. You see too much filth. You get to think every business is dishonest and every relationship is dirty. You bludgeon innocent people with your prejudices. If you had any sense, any *sachel*, you would realize that it would be crazy for me to get involved in anything suspicious after what

I went through in Israel. Now, are we done? I have a busy day, Detectives. I doubt if I have any information that will help your investigation."

"Not quite true," I answer. "It would help if you could give us access to your personnel files—to your graduates who are employed in two AKLC locations."

"Why would I do that? Those files have confidential, personal information, and you are on nothing more than a fishing expedition. Imagine the reaction of my students and alums if I gave all their personal information to the police. I absolutely refuse. You have no reason to suspect that I, or anyone from my institute, is involved in your case."

"No reason Ms. Cohnheim? Let me see: a woman works in a small hospital department that is sellin' illegal kidneys. Members of the department are arrested and convicted. She flees to the United States and within two years somehow has the money to open a new trainin' institute for kidney dialysis. She enters into an affair with the CEO of one of the largest dialysis companies in the country. Soon, she stacks the staff of the dialysis centers with her own graduates. It so happens that if you're lookin' for potential buyers of illegal kidneys, there's no better place to look than a dialysis center. In another coincidence, three murders are connected with the centers and at least two of 'em involve illegal organs. What do you think are the odds that those murders are random and have nothin' to do with the dialysis company or someone on its staff?"

"I think you are trying to piece together unrelated facts. The crimes you refer to may be connected, but you have no reason to connect me with those occurrences."

"As my partner said, you are a person of interest in this investigation. Those personnel records for a few employees currently employed in two centers could help our investigation. I would advise you to reconsider."

"I am not intimidated by your threats, Detective. I run an honest, respectable institute and have a responsibility to protect the privacy of our graduates. If you choose to pursue the matter, you will have to deal with our attorneys. I suspect we have nothing more to discuss."

Back in the Taurus, we share our impressions. "Tough lady," D'Angelo says. "Think she and Mr. Kidney Stone are tellin' the truth?"

"She may be as tough as Stone, but she doesn't strike me as a person who would conspire with murderers."

"Wasn't scared of us, though. Said she would break the law to get her son a kidney."

I think back to my arguments with Cassandra. Not that different from what I heard from Cohnheim.

Chapter 25

Cassandra

I am thankful for the Keurig machine and my morning cup of coffee. The long trip yesterday was exhausting. I should have slept like a baby. Instead, I was anxious being in this strange place. I worried about Keri. I tossed and turned for hours and had bizarre dreams. Altogether, I slept for only three or four hours. Fortunately, Keri has been down for more than ten, but now I must wake her to go to the medical center. She needs to get her regular dialysis. Meanwhile, they have scheduled me to get a tour of the facilities and an opportunity to meet the medical team. The doctors probably know nothing about the source of the kidney, but I will collect their names for the strike team. After the sting, they will be rounded up and interrogated, but they are unlikely to provide any actionable intelligence.

At 10:00, I call Anish. He will help us register at the hospital and guide us to wherever we need to go. He answers the phone on the first ring as if he was waiting for the call. A perfect gentleman, he asks if the accommodations are satisfactory, whether we slept well, if there is anything we need before leaving for the hospital.

After hanging up the phone, I go to Keri's room to wake her up. There is nothing more beautiful but heart-rending than watching my baby sleep. Beautiful, because she looks like an angel, so peaceful and serene—a magical, perfect little package, so innocent and pure. Heart-rending because of the seriousness of her illness, and how unfair for her childhood to be hijacked by this shitty condition. I stand in the doorway not wanting to wake her. I just want to watch her sleep; to capture this moment and freeze it in time; to make the world go away so there is just the two of us—no kidney disease, no dialysis, no transplants, no FBI, not even any growing up. Just the swelling of my heart as I watch my precious girl sleep.

But it is not to be. My poor baby needs dialysis three times a week to keep her alive. I wake her ever so gently, sitting on the edge of the bed and stroking her head. "It's time to get up, honeybun. I put your Corn Flakes on the table."

One hour later, the intercom buzzes, and Anish says he is waiting in the lobby. Keri is dressed and ready with a little backpack filled with her teddy bear, crayons, coloring books, and iPad—diversions that will help her sit through another four hours of dialysis. We take the elevator down to the lobby, and Anish greets Keri with a big smile. "I have a surprise for you, little one," he says, and produces a beautiful doll with a white sari and movable arms and legs. He looks at me for approval, and, of course, I am thankful for his thoughtfulness.

Anish walks us to the hospital and helps with the registration. The number of forms is overwhelming, almost as bureaucratic as in the States. Hasn't anyone in the world figured out how to do this better? After registration, Anish directs us to the dialysis center. Except for the accents and the number of dark-skinned people, you might think you were back at AKLC. The room and the machines look nearly identical. I am relieved to see the modern equipment, knowing the familiar look of the machines will make Keri more comfortable. I stay with her for the first hour, until my appointments with the hospital staff.

I am scheduled to tour the facility and then meet with Keri's medical team. Anish arrives promptly at the dialysis center to direct me to the first appointment. With so many international patients, the Apollo Hospital has learned how to accommodate people who are anxious about traveling out of their own country for surgery. One of the ways they ease peoples' concerns is by providing a tour of their impressive facilities. Anish introduces me to the woman who will conduct the tour.

"I am pleased to meet you, Ms. Ford. My name is Anniya, and I will be your guide."

"My pleasure. Please call me Sandra," I reply, noticing the young woman's appearance. She is dressed in a conservative, Western-style business suit with matching pumps. She wears earrings and a thin necklace with a green stone, possibly jade. She speaks English with just a modest Indian accent.

"I know you are probably anxious, Sandra, being out of your own country, but you have come to a very wonderful place. I am going to take you to the transplant institute right away, because one of the operating rooms is empty, and we can peek inside. As you probably know, our transplant institute is the busiest in the world, and many of our doctors are board certified in the United States."

"I *do* know, Anniya. I have read much about the Apollo Institute."

I follow behind the guide, whose heels click on the tile as she walks hurriedly down the gleaming corridors. We follow signs for the Institute and take the elevator to the third floor. Even though the O.R. is empty, Anniya opens a closet and takes out gowns and masks to wear inside. "This is one of our dedicated operating theatres designed only for transplants," she explains. "Everything the surgical team might need is stored within the theatre for quick retrieval."

Anniya turns on some switches and incredibly bright lights illuminate the operating table. The room is spotless, and the equipment looks brand new. "I haven't been in an operating room since I gave birth," I tell her. "But I'm very impressed. The birthing room looked nothing like this."

For the next half hour, Anniya guides me through the Institute, explaining all its attributes. A specialized blood bank and an intensive care unit exist specifically for transplant patients. She is particularly proud of the Institute's radiological capabilities. "We have the latest high-tech imaging equipment," she explains, "including color doppler ultrasonography, computed tomography, magnetic resonance imaging, and nuclear medicine for molecular imaging."

"Does the government pay for this equipment?" I ask.

"No, Apollo is a private, for-profit corporation," she replies, as she guides me through separate wards and private rooms designed specifically for patients undergoing transplants. We finish the tour barely in time to meet the transplant team.

Anniya leads us to a boardroom with a long rosewood table and swivel chairs. A nurse is already in the room, and shortly after we sit down, the surgeon and anesthetist join us. The surgeon is a young, Indian national who attended medical school at Johns Hopkins and is board certified in the U.S. I ask him how long he has been doing kidney transplants.

"I conduct these kidney transplants every day," he answers. "I have done well over a thousand, often with patients who are elderly and much sicker than your daughter."

"What about pediatric transplants?" I ask.

"I specialize in those, although they are a minority of cases. Your daughter should do fine. Except for her kidneys, she is in excellent health, and there is every reason to believe the operation will be routine. I also have some good news for you. We had a cancellation, so we can perform the transplant earlier than scheduled. We can do your daughter's pre-op procedures tomorrow afternoon, and, assuming all is well, we can perform the transplant on Wednesday morning. I think the less time you wait and worry, the better it will be. Don't you agree?"

I hesitate, not knowing how to answer. Keri was not supposed to actually undergo the final pre-op procedures. The plan was to conduct the sting at the time of the scheduled pre-op. The strike team was not planning on that occurring tomorrow. I do not know if everything is in place. "Umm, I'm not sure, doctor. I wasn't expecting it to be so soon.

All of this has been strange and disorienting to Keri. I'm not sure if she's ready. Can I think it over?"

"Certainly, I understand. At this point, no one else is going to fill that slot. If you talk to your liaison first thing tomorrow morning, we can finalize the schedule. Now, let me give you a brief overview of the process. During the pre-operative procedure, we will review your daughter's health history and give her a routine physical exam. That will include an EKG and a chest x-ray. We will perform an extensive amount of bloodwork because, as you probably know, kidney disease can bring about a number of chemical imbalances. Hence, we check for such things as metabolic acidosis, pre-operative electrolytes, uremia, hypervolemia, levels of potassium, calcium, phosphates, sodium, chloride, creatinine, and other potential imbalances. Lastly, we will conduct a final crossmatch test for donor compatibility."

"Hasn't the donor match already been determined?"

"Yes, it has, and the organ looks to be very compatible. However, before we remove your daughter's kidney, we do a final re-check, just to be completely safe. Assuming all of the pre-op tests are satisfactory, we will do a final dialysis. She will have to fast for eight hours prior to the surgery. In the operating room, she will be connected to an IV and will have several cuffs to monitor her heart rate and blood pressure. The anesthesiologist will administer a general anesthetic. She will have a catheter for her bladder and a ventilating tube to breathe for her while she is under anesthesia. The anesthetist will continually monitor her heart rate, blood pressure, breathing, and blood oxygen levels.

"I will begin by making an incision in her lower abdomen. The best space to fit the new kidney is in the iliac fossa. There are three fused bones, and the interior space between those bones is where we place the new organ. Here, I have a plastic replica of a kidney. It is basically a little blood cleaning machine with three connecting tubes."

I examine the plastic kidney and the three colored tubes that protrude from it. "What are each of these tubes for?" I ask.

"The blood flows into the kidney through the red tube, which is the renal artery. The kidney cleans the blood, and it then flows out of the blue tube, which is the renal vein. The residue, or urine, from the cleansing of the blood, flows out this last tube. It is called the ureter, and it drains the urine from the kidney into the bladder."

"Thank you, doctor. You make it sound simple. But how do you connect the tubes to the new kidney?"

"I have to hook up these three connections to your daughter's blood system and bladder. The renal artery will be sutured to your daughter's iliac artery and the renal vein to her iliac vein. Once the sutures are complete, clamps will be removed from the existing vessels and the blood will flow in and out of the new kidney. At that time, we will ensure that there is no bleeding around the sutured vessels. The ureter will then be connected to the bladder so that urine will flow out of the kidney and eventually be excreted. A stent will be placed in the ureter for several weeks to promote healing and will be removed in an outpatient procedure. Finally, I will stitch up the incision, probably inserting a drain to reduce inflammation. The entire procedure should take about three hours."

"I didn't expect it to take so long," I say. "It seems like a long time to be under anesthesia. What will her post-operative recovery be like?"

"Immediately after the operation, your daughter will be closely monitored in the surgical recovery room. From there, she will be moved to the ICU or possibly her own hospital room. Her new kidney should start making urine immediately, but it usually takes three to five days to attain normal function. If function is delayed, dialysis may be required. Your daughter will have a urinary catheter, and nurses will carefully measure her output to assess how the new kidney is working. During her recovery, the nurses will take frequent blood samples to monitor the function of the new kidney as well as the status of other systems such as the liver and lungs. She will be able to get out of bed the day after the surgery and gradually progress from a liquid diet to ordinary food. The total length of her hospital stay will likely be four to seven days."

"Will she then be on medication?"

"Yes, right away. As you probably know, the body naturally rejects a foreign organ, so your daughter will be on a regimen of immunosuppressant drugs. She will have to take those drugs for the rest of her life."

I summon the courage to ask what worries me the most. "If the operation is successful, will Keri have a normal life expectancy?" I ask, fearing the answer I don't want to hear.

The doctor hesitates, responding carefully. "Once the new kidney is functioning, your daughter will have an excellent prognosis. However, her life expectancy will still be less than average. The longest anyone has lived with a new kidney is a little over fifty-four years. However, our methods and science are continually improving, and it may well be that fifty years from now we will have the capabilities of extending her life much further. Of course, she can also have a second transplant. It would not be unreasonable to hope for a normal life span."

His answer makes me cringe. It is, of course, the "less than average" that reverberates in my mind.

"I know all of this sounds complicated," the doctor says, "but we live in a remarkable world in which our state of knowledge makes operations like this little more than routine. In a few months, your daughter will be living a healthy life, practically indistinguishable from her friends. Is there anything else you want to ask?"

"No, I appreciate the time you have given me. I'm sure you're very busy. Thank you, doctor, for being so considerate."

"My pleasure, Ms. Ford. I have to leave for my next surgery but let me introduce you to Dr. Singh. He will be your anesthesiologist. He will ask you a few routine questions about your daughter's medications, allergies, and such. Please feel free to contact my office if you have any further questions."

After speaking to the anesthesiologist, I seek out the nearest lady's room. Thank God it is a single room with a locked door. I am barely able to enter and lock the door before bursting into tears. How can I reconcile what I am doing with everything I've observed. The hospital is impressive. The transplant institute is one of the best in the world. The doctors and the staff are competent and dedicated. They can give Keri a new life. Sure, they must know that some of these kidneys come from the black-market, but why should they care? They're saving lives. That's their business—to help people like Keri live a normal, healthy life. And I am here to have them interrogated? Arrested? Instead of getting Keri a transplant, a new lease on life, we will fly back home and she will still have kidney failure. She will still need dialysis four hours a day, three days a week, and she may never get a new kidney. How can I let that happen? What the fuck am I going to do?

Chapter 26

Martin

After the interview with Roni Cohnheim, D'Angelo and I drive outta East Cambridge and turn on to Memorial Drive. The road runs along the Charles River and passes the boat houses of Harvard and M.I.T. I can see the crews practicin' on the water. Hear the coxswain callin' out to the crew as one a the "eights" glides through the water. But I gotta shift my attention to Clayton Thurmond, Cynthia Fleming's widower.

Thurmond lives in an apartment buildin' in Brighton, not far from Boston College. Although much of Brighton is home to run-down student housin', the area near Boston College and the city of Newton is more upscale. Thurmond's buildin' is attractive and well-maintained. Grounds are clean and carefully tended. We called earlier in the mornin' and got no answer, so we decided to take a shot.

The vestibule has a buzzer and intercom, but the door is ajar. We decide not to ring and give Thurmond the opportunity to make excuses, like pretendin' it's not him who is answerin', so we go right up and knock on his door.

It takes a second try before someone answers. "Who is it?" comes the reply.

"Detective Martin Goldberg, Boston Police."

"I just stepped out of the shower, officer. Give me a minute to get dressed and I'll be right with you."

It's not the first time I've heard that. Puttin' my ear against the door, I listen for sounds from inside. I hear the toilet flush. They don't make walls and doors like they used to. After another minute Thurmond opens the door. We hold up our badges and Thurmond greets us politely and invites us in. “Can I get you guys a cold drink or a glass of water?” he asks. I take note of Thurmond’s good looks and easy manner. He wears a clean pair of jeans cut wide at the bottom for boots, and a black belt with a large silver buckle. Has on a Western-style shirt with two pockets. Hair is thick, wavy, and neatly combed back. I recall Fleming’s description and can picture him as a car salesman, tellin’ the customer that at the price he’s offerin’, the dealership don’t make any profit. We enter the apartment which appears clean and nicely furnished.

“Mr. Thurmond,” I begin as I have so many times, “I’m so sorry about your wife. I apologize for havin’ to bother you at this difficult time. The worst part of my job is havin’ to visit bereaved family members. However, I’m in charge of this investigation, and I need to pursue it as quickly as possible. We’d like to ask you a few questions.”

“I’d be happy to help you any way I can. Cynthia was a great gal, and I lost her. I still can’t believe what happened.”

Thurmond leads us into the living room and sits down on a chair, leavin’ the two of us to share the couch. “Let me begin by askin’ you a few routine questions, Mr. Thurmond. When was the last time you saw Ms. Fleming?”

“Not since she got a restraining order. I’m sure you know about that.”

“What about calls?”

“I tried to call her a few times. I know I wasn’t supposed to, but I wanted her back. I was stupid and wanted another chance, but she wouldn’t talk to me.”

“You never tried to see her?” D’Angelo asks. “Kinda accidentally on purpose; run into her after work or on the way home?”

“No never. Wouldn’t have done any good. She made it clear that she didn’t want to see me.”

“What about Neal Jensen?” I ask. “You ever meet him?”

"No. That all happened after we split. Never met the guy."

"But you knew his son, Blake?"

"Blake tell you that? Yeah, weird dude. His saddle ain't cinched to his horse."

"How did you meet Blake?"

"At his store. I read about the bust in the papers. Y'know, noticed the last name right away. I was feeling lonely; wanted Cynthia back. I thought he might know how serious they were—whether I had a chance."

"What'd he say?"

"He thought they were tight. Probably gonna get hitched."

"Blake had a side business," D'Angelo says. "You a customer?"

"You mean drugs? I don't do that shit. I drink beer, Coors mostly or sometimes Modelo. That's what got me in trouble with Cynthia. I had a few too many and we got into a fight. I been trying to lay off."

"You got into a fight in Dallas too, didn't you Clayton?"

"That was a bum rap. It wasn't my fault. But I admit I had a drinking problem. I'm trying hard to straighten out."

"You tellin' us, you hung out at Blake's store but never bought any drugs," D'Angelo stares hard at Clayton.

"Nope. Not my thing. You can search my place if you want."

"Maybe too late. Is that why you flushed the toilet?"

"Aw, c'mon. I told you. I was in the bathroom when you knocked."

"Blake ever mention his father's will?" D'Angelo asks.

"Don't think so. He didn't talk much. Didn't really want to talk to me."

"You never asked Blake about his father's will?"

"No, why would I care?'

"Inheritance, Clayton. You're still married to Cynthia."

"Cynthia didn't have no money. Her dads a preacher-man. I sure as hell didn't want her back for her money."

"C'mon Clayton," D'Angelo says. "If Jensen left his dough to Cynthia, you get the whole gravy train."

"What? I never even thought… You're saying that if my almost ex-wife started going with a rich guy and he changed his will and then he got murdered and then she got murdered that I was planning it all along? You think I planned all that and killed them both? You guys must be smokin' Blake Jensen's shit."

D'Angelo points his finger right at Clayton Thurmond's chest. "You and Blake had something in common. You were both interested in the old man's will. Why else do you keep visiting a low life like Blake? Unless you were also scorin' some dugs."

"Hey, you guys got a great imagination. I loved Cynthia. I wanted her back. I hope you find the bastard who killed her. If I can do anything to help your case, I'd be more than happy to cooperate. Here's my card with my personal cell. Call me anytime."

"Car salesman! Guy's as smooth as a ride on a new Mercedes," I say, after we get back in the Taurus.

"And the kind who can sell you the five-year maintenance package," D'Angelo replies. "Couldn't get him ruffled."

"Guess not, but I'm always suspicious about a suspect who lies. We know from Blake that they talked about the will. We know from the Dallas police that his assault was not anything like a bum rap. We know from Cynthia that he smoked dope; and he wasn't flushin' Coors beer down the toilet when we knocked on his door."

Chapter 27

Martin

Back at my desk, I'm in a funk. Feel like I'm lettin' everybody down. The department has three unsolved murders and I'm the guy in charge. Got a buncha suspects, but no hard evidence. No fingerprints, no murder weapon, no witnesses. I pressured an innocent woman to become an informant, and she paid for it with her life. Got the Chief in a pickle, afraid that the deal with Cynthia Fleming will leak out to the press. Let the FBI take over my investigation. Now they got Cassandra and her little girl in India, and if their cover gets blown, they both could get killed.

Bein' so upset, I get little done durin' the rest of the day. I head home in the late afternoon, and it's unusually hot and humid. The air conditioner in the old Taurus produces more noise than cool air, and rush hour traffic in Boston moves slower than the U.S. mail. Nobody here ever considered layin' out the roads in grids instead of crisscrossin' randomly. It's like city planners thought automobiles were just a passin' fad. When I finally arrive home, rings of perspiration bleed through my shirt. I take a cool shower and open my bureau drawer for some fresh underwear, but I'm all out. I consider takin' a worn pair from the hamper, but the aroma of sweaty clothes overflowin' the lid convinces me otherwise. Puttin' on an old bathin' suit and a tee shirt, I gather a huge pile of clothes and carry them down to the basement washin' machine. Florence always yelled at me for mixin' colors and whites, but I'm hungry and tired and not in the mood to sort everything out. I stuff the clothes up to the top of the washer, throw in a cup of detergent, and turn on the machine. By the time I finish dinner, the clothes'll be ready for the dryer.

Back upstairs, I take a three-cheese frozen pizza from the freezer and stick it in the oven. The Sox are on TV, so I can watch a coupla innings during dinner. When the pizza comes outta the oven, I set it on the coffee table in front of the TV and take out a can of beer. No sooner do I take my first sip than the phone rings. I'd like to ignore it, but if you're a cop, you always gotta answer.

"Goldberg here."

"Martin," D'Angelo says. "We just picked up another conversation between Rony Cohnheim and Bradley Stone. They know about Cassandra. Her cover is blown. You'd better get down here right away."

"Aw shit! I'll be right down." I look longingly at the pizza, gulp down two slices as fast as I can, and head outta the house. I gotta sick feelin' in my stomach, and it's not from the food. Again, I'm ready to blame myself. This was my case, and if I hadn't given it to the FBI, none of this woulda happened. Cynthia Fleming's copies led to Colonel Harris. I didn't need the FBI. If somethin' happens to Cassandra, I have no one to blame but myself.

When I arrive at the station, O'Donnell is waitin' with other team members. Chief does not look happy. Probably thinkin' we should have washed our hands of this case and given it to the Feds right away. That way, there was no chance of blowback and embarrassment. Well, they're stuck with it now, and we just gotta make the best of it. A recorder is set up on the table, waitin' for me to listen through a pair of headphones. The connection is good and the voices clear.

"Sally, it's so good to talk to you," comes the voice with a slight Israeli accent that I recognize is Roni Cohnheim.

"We haven't seen each other in so long, Roni. I thought we could make some plans. Maybe meet for lunch."

"Great idea. It's been much too long, Sally. We used to see each other often, before our busy lives got in the way."

"Our busy lives! It's you who have become the big entrepreneur. I keep hearing about your new schools and all your graduates. What a fabulous idea you had, and what an accomplishment to carry it off."

"Luck played a big role. I happened to be in the right place at the right time."

"Don't belittle what you've done, Roni. Here I am, doing HR for our little company while you created an institute that trains and places techs all over the country. I heard AKLC gets most of their techs from your program."

"It's true. We've managed to develop a great relationship with them. They have become our biggest source for job placements."

"Yeah, and they keep opening new centers and stealing our patients. One of my favorite patients was this black woman who had the most adorable daughter. The center that houses my office is always crowded with old people, and they just brightened up when they saw this cute little girl. We had them for over two years, and then they up and left to switch to AKLC."

"Really? I may know them. Do you recall their names?"

"I remember them well. The woman's name was Cassandra Crawford and her daughter's name was Keri."

"Hmm, I don't recall the name Cassandra Crawford. What was she like?"

"She was an attractive black woman. Very professional. I got to know her quite well. She was actually an FBI agent. I remember when she told me what she did. I never would have suspected."

"An FBI Agent? No kidding. I thought I knew who you were talking about, but I must have confused her with someone else. So many people needing dialysis—even children. Over 75,000 people on the waiting list for a kidney. It's a tragedy. The kidney shortage is getting worse than ever."

The rest of the conversation is small talk, and when the call ends, I reach up to take off my headphones.

"Keep 'em on," D'Angelo tells me. "There's a second call."

I look at Tony and roll my eyes, like oh-my-God what's comin' next? Is Cohnheim going to call Herman Poleskey or one of his gang? I imagine what could happen next. These people have to protect their business. In some God forsaken place in India, their thugs are goin' to break into Cassandra's room and assassinate her. I also realize I'm about to hear the person she calls. It could give us our first big break; ID someone in the criminal organization. Would hardly be a trade-off for Cassandra's life but could enable the FBI to move fast. The second call comes through my headset.

"Hello."

"Brad, this is Roni. This is an em...."

"Roni, what are you doing calling me on this phone. Thank God, my wife didn't pick up. She's in the other room. What could possibly be so imp...?"

"Brad, calm down. We have a major problem. The woman with the little girl? The one that just flew to New Delhi to get a kidney? She's an undercover FBI agent."

"What! How do you know?"

"I was talking with an old friend who works at another dialysis center. Sandra Ford's little daughter used to be one of their patients before they transferred to us. Only her real name is not Sandra Ford. It's Cassandra Crawford, and she works for the FBI."

"Holy shit! I always feared something like this would happen. We need to alert the people on the other end. How well do you know them?"

"I don't. I only deal with Herman Poleskey. They are careful and keep everything encapsulated. Herman has never let me know about

anyone else in the organization. In fact, his name isn't even Herman Poleskey. I don't know his real name."

"All the better for us. Can you get in touch with Herman? Is he reliable?"

"Absolutely. I have his cell that he always carries in case of emergencies. Herman has always been responsible. He will respond quickly and do what has to be done. The problem is, I don't know anything about the people on the other end—the ones that procure the kidneys. I don't know where they get them or, more importantly, how they get them. Herman says there are plenty of people in the third world who are happy to sell their kidneys for money. He says everything is voluntary, and they line up to donate. But even if it's voluntary, it's still illegal, and they could go to prison. We don't know what they might do to protect their network. Sandra Ford, or rather Cassandra Crawford and her little girl could be in danger."

"How long ago did she arrive in India?"

"She's been there two days. They're ten and a half hours ahead of us. I don't know much about their protocols, but I know the girl must go through tests and a final dialysis before they can operate. We may still have time to abort the whole thing."

"What about the hospital and the doctors? Are they part of the organization?"

"I doubt it, but I don't know for sure. Everything is compartmentalized. I know from my experience in Israel that the hospitals and doctors don't usually know. By the time the transplant is requested, all the paperwork is in order, signed and notarized. It looks official, even though it is fabricated. The hospital and the doctors must suspect that many of the transplants involve kidneys that were purchased illegally, but they have neither the reason nor the resources to examine the paperwork. Besides, it's in their interest to gain the

experience and the revenue from the operation; not to mention the fact that they are saving peoples' lives."

"Doesn't matter what they know. The FBI will arrest everyone. We have to call it off and get everyone in the organization out of there before they are ready to conduct the sting."

"Okay, I'll call Herman right away."

"Not so fast, Roni. Be careful. If the FBI is involved, I wouldn't be surprised if our phones are tapped. See if you can find a public phone somewhere."

"I'll try. There aren't many left."

"One more thing, Roni. They will come after us at the same time they execute the sting. We always knew it might happen and we have taken precautions. Just the same, you should check your files and destroy any incriminating evidence."

"What about the Jensen case? That nosy detective suspects us."

"Stay calm. We have good lawyers. They will bail us out if the police try to hold us. I'm not that worried. The only thing we have ever done is dropped some names. We never took money or benefited in any way. The state can't convict us for that. We should be careful about talking to each other and avoid being seen together. We'll get through this. Don't worry. Go call Herman right away."

I take off the headphones, and my heart is thumpin'. I'm shaken by the frank conversation and worried for Cassandra's safety. But I need to control my emotions, because I know that everyone is watchin' me and waitin' for my response. I gotta act like a cop, not Cassandra's close friend. I turn to the Chief.

"Obviously, we need to notify the FBI right away and share the contents of the recordin'. Not much else we can do. I know from meetin' with Crawford that the FBI backup team was in place before she got there. Their assets should already be in place to deal with this. Their top priority will be gettin' Cassandra and her daughter outta there.

The FBI will protect its own, even at the expense of blowin' the operation. As for Cohnheim and Stone, they committed federal crimes and deserve to pay the price. I assume the FBI will want to arrest them, and they don't want us in the way. Just the same, I'd be more than happy to do the deed. We still have three unsolved murders and puttin' some pressure on them might break the case. Cohnheim doesn't want to be sent back to Israel, and Stone doesn't want to lose his little empire."

"I've already notified the FBI," O'Donnell says disdainfully.

Of course, he has. I must have sounded like an idiot. The Chief wasn't goin' to wait for me to drive over before takin' action. In fact, the Chief looks pissed and probably blames me for gettin' the department into this mess in the first place. No point remindin' him that he was the one who suggested the contact with Cassandra and the FBI.

The Chief disbands the meeting and says, "Goldberg, I want to see you in my office." I steel myself to accept the blame. I follow him upstairs and sit in the chair facin' his desk. Pictures of O'Donnell with the mayor, a couple of senators, and the last two governors stare down from the walls. He looks disgruntled, but he is not an unreasonable man.

"Moishe, the other day the Globe ran an article about the number of unsolved murders in the city. You must have seen it. No secret the mayor would like to run for statewide office, and he's telling the commissioner he wants to see some action. Nobody pays much attention to the drug murders in the projects, but the Jensen and Fleming murders got a lot of press. Sounds racist, but that's the way it is. Assuming your friend Crawford gets flown out safely, this will still be her case. She should be back in time to interrogate Cohnheim and Stone after the FBI picks them up, but before they get out on bail. I assume you have been sharing information with her. I'm not sure what else you two are sharing. Whatever it is, I want you to stay involved in this case. If either of those two cracks, we can solve the murders. The Bureau will try to take all the credit, but we need to be part of the story. I have good press connections. We can probably spin it so the powers that be are happy. Understand?"

"I'm on it. And by the way, we're just friends."

I walk back to my office thinkin' about the Chief. Guy is a decent police chief, but his real concern is politics. If the mayor runs statewide and the commissioner runs for mayor, he's in line to be commissioner. And that's just his first step. What a fuckin world. We have three unsolved murders. Cassandra and her daughter are in mortal danger. The international kidney trade is operatin' in Boston. People are gettin' murdered for their organs. And what's the police chief most worried about? Becomin' commissioner!

Chapter 28

Cassandra

It hits me like a rogue wave. The strike team expects Keri to undergo pre-op on Wednesday afternoon. If I don't tell them about the schedule change, Keri can do the pre-op tomorrow and get the transplant Wednesday morning. By the time the strike team is ready to act, she'll have a new kidney. I break out in a cold sweat.

"What's the matter, Mommy?" Keri asks, as I tuck her into bed.

"Oh, nothing darling. I was just daydreaming. You pull up the covers and get yourself a good night's sleep. I love you honey-bun."

I bend over, give my daughter a goodnight kiss, and shut off the light. It's going to be a long night. I put up a pot of coffee, knowing sleep is not coming anytime soon. Could I really consider this? Break the law? Deceive the FBI? Sabotage the sting? Back home, I thought the sting might teach me how to buy an illegal kidney, but I never thought the opportunity would arise on this trip. It never seemed like a realistic possibility. I feared we were dealing with a group of dangerous criminals, international organ traders, murderers, gangsters selling kidneys from God knows where, conducting secretive medical operations in places that might be dirty and unsterile, and using criminal surgeons who lacked proper training. But it's not like that at all. The hospital is top-notch. The medical team is as good as it gets. The donor kidney is an excellent match. I can give my daughter a new life. I only have to deal with the consequences. What would happen to me? Should I care? This is my precious little girl. Suppose, in another context, someone offered me a deal: you spend time in prison and we will save your daughter's life with a new kidney. I wouldn't hesitate.

Is it that simple? It could be the most important decision of my life. I can't simply rely on my gut. I need to consider all the possibilities, all the implications. How do I even begin to think about it? To organize my thoughts? What are my obligations and responsibilities as a mother? As a citizen? As an FBI agent?

I think about being a mother. Would any mother say no? Wouldn't a loving mother do almost anything to save her daughter's life? I know my mother would. What if Keri never gets another kidney? Or, by the time a kidney becomes available, she has been on dialysis so long that she can't tolerate the transplant? Even if she gets a cadaver kidney from the official list, it will last only half as long as one from a live donor. Would any mother watch her daughter suffer and die when she could have saved her? When she could have prolonged her life?

What moral compromises would I make to save my daughter? Would I obstruct justice? Would I purposely foil an investigation that would put international organ traders behind bars? Would I let murderers go free? Murderers who would no doubt kill other people? After all, that is probably what I am considering; Foiling the sting and letting murderers go free.

I pace around the living room trying to relieve my tension. I pause to look out the window at the city below. The streets and sidewalks are empty. Everything is still. The city that is so tumultuous during the daylight is eerily quiet, like an empty function hall after the wedding. But the inside of my head is noisy, crowded, with thoughts streaking through like tracer bullets in the night.

What would the world be like if people were free to buy organs. It would be a one-way street. The rich would not sell their body parts to help the poor or anyone else. The poor and the desperate would sell their body parts to the rich in order to survive. The other day, I read a true story about the women of Banda Ache,[1] the city in Indonesia that experienced a massive earthquake in 2004. Over 200,000 people died and many more were left homeless. About 2,500 were resettled in a refugee camp called Tsunami Nagar. Kidney brokers saw the desperately poor population as an opportunity to make money. The people in the camps were so destitute that the money they could get for selling a kidney became a life-saving gift for their families. They could get $800 for a kidney. For many, that represented two years of income. The many did not include males. Almost all the donors from Tsunami Nagar were women—mothers. And almost all the women of Tsunami Nagar have a foot-long scar from where their kidney was removed; so many that the camp is nicknamed "Kidneyvakkam" or "Kidneyville." If a free market existed for kidneys, Bande Ache would be the reality for thousands of the world's most desperate people. Who would want to live in that kind of world?

I know that question is essential, because any person who buys an illegal kidney enables that black-market to exist. That person cannot deny their responsibility. If no one bought illegal kidneys, there would be no black-market, and no pressure on the desperately poor to sell their organs.

I also have to consider that anyone who buys an illegal kidney has a responsibility to the donor? The donor might be an innocent person from the third world who is desperate, but willing to sell her kidney to pay for her family's needs. But she also might have been coerced or kidnapped for her organs. She might have been forced to sell her kidney to pay off the family's debts. She might have been an innocent seller who was grievously harmed from the operation. Who would compensate her? Who would care for her? The black market would leave her to suffer.

---

[1] This is an account taken from the book "The Red Market" by Scott Carney, HarperCollins Publishers, Inc. 2011.

And what about enabling the procurers. The members of criminal organizations who take advantage of the desperately poor; who kidnap people for organs; who pay unscrupulous doctors to remove organs from unsuspecting people undergoing surgery; who kill people for their organs and murder those that might expose their organization. How can one rationalize letting those people go free?

On the other hand, what if the laws against buying kidneys are outdated and unjust? Does that confer the moral right to ignore them? Clearly, thousands of people die of kidney disease every year, while thousands of other people are perfectly willing to sell their kidneys and save those peoples' lives. We already let people sell body parts and services. We let people sell their blood and blood platelets. There is a legal market for hair. We let men sell their sperm, and we sometimes pay huge amounts to women who sell their eggs. A good-looking woman with a high IQ can get $50,000 for her eggs. We pay surrogates to carry someone else's baby for nine months and undergo the painful process of childbirth. If those markets are legal, why should we deny a willing person the right to sell their life-saving kidney to a willing buyer? What right do we have to tell the seller that they do not have autonomous control of their own body? Is the state in a better position to make that decision than the individual?

Too many questions. Not enough answers. I feel like a rat caught in a maze. I keep trying new avenues of thought, but every one of them just makes the issue more complex. What is right and wrong? None of these thoughts provide a definitive answer. I get up from the couch and take a pint of ice cream from the refrigerator. Food provides comfort when I'm feeling empty and confused. I understand why people eat to feel better. I take a tablespoon from the drawer and try to dig out a scoop. Either the ice cream is too frozen or the Indian silverware is too cheap, but the spoon bends before it even makes a dent. I wait for the ice cream to thaw, standing there watching, like a dog sitting at the foot of the table hoping for scraps.

For a few moments, I'm focused on eating the ice cream. I take small spoonfuls, trying to make it last longer. After finishing, I tip the plate and scrape my spoon along the sides to get the last bit of the melted snack. The respite only lasts a few moments before my mind is back racing, thinking about being an FBI agent.

I do solemnly swear that I will support and defend the Constitution of the United States against all enemies, foreign and domestic; that I will bear true faith and allegiance to the same; that I take this obligation freely, without any mental reservation or purpose of evasion; and that I will well and faithfully discharge the duties of the office on which I am about to enter. So help me God.

I raised my right hand and took that oath the day I became an agent for the Federal Bureau of Investigation. I remained faithful to that oath for close to two decades and built a good life and a successful career. It has given me a sense of purpose and self-worth. Now, I'm considering breaking that oath, betraying the Bureau, deceiving my boss, double-crossing my colleagues, breaking the law, and probably letting murderers go free. Is my oath more important than my daughter's life? Is my integrity worth condemning my daughter to a restricted life and an early death? Would I go ahead and get Keri an illegal kidney if I was just an average mother and not a law enforcement officer? If that is the case, should my choice of occupation determine my daughter's life and death?

I think about the consequences of breaking the law. I will certainly be fired. I most definitely will be prosecuted. The FBI cannot allow one of its own to become a kind of double agent without facing the harshest reprisals, without making an example, so that agents in the future will fear to do likewise. They will charge me with numerous crimes: obstruction of justice, conspiracy to trade in illegal organs, racketeering under the RICO Act, accessory to murder, and any other charge they can imagine. A judge may be sympathetic, but he or she will not be lenient. No judge can forgive an FBI officer for turning double agent. I will go to jail. My mother is too old to care for Keri, and my deadbeat former husband may not even be in the country, so they will not be considered for custody. My eight-year-old daughter will be placed in a foster home. She will be an orphan. She will gain a kidney but lose a mother and grow up without either parent.

How important are these consequences relative to Keri's life? How can I weigh them and fit them into the equation? Am I foremost a mother? A responsible citizen and member of a law-abiding society? A law enforcement officer? When all is said and done, how will I feel when I look in the mirror? How will I live with my decision? I think about Bradley Stone and his lost son. When my life is coming to an end, will my last thoughts be ones of regret for what I did or did not do?

The more I consider all the conflicting issues, the muddier things get. I go back and forth, changing my mind after every argument. It seems to come down to this: what is morality in the face of death? Strictly speaking, my decision to buy this kidney and deceive the FBI would be immoral. Yet, as a law enforcement officer, I would kill a person if I thought it would save an innocent life.

Should I just stop ruminating? Should I stop intellectualizing and go with my gut? I wish I had someone to talk to. I wish Martin was here. He is the only person I could confide in, knowing he would listen—knowing he would be compassionate. Martin the *mensch*. But I can't talk to Martin. I am all alone, and the first glint of sunlight is beginning to shine through the east-facing window. Delay is not possible. I have to make my decision.

According to the plan, the sting would be executed at the time the final pre-op exam is scheduled. Just before Anish would arrive to accompany us to the hospital, we would be put on a chartered FBI flight back to the states. Agents would arrest Anish, the hospital administrator, and all the people that were part of the medical team. At the same time, they would arrest Bradley Stone, Roni Cohnheim, Susan Landis, and Herman Poleskey, if they could find him.

Presently, the strike team is staying out of sight to minimize the chance of discovery. They expect the pre-op to be conducted on Wednesday afternoon, and they have made their plans accordingly. But these things often change, so they are hiding, waiting for me to give them the final confirmation.

I have promised to call Anish at 7:00 a.m. to tell him if I want to re-schedule the pre-op. If I say yes, Keri will have a new kidney before the team is ready to strike. If I say no, the strike team will arrest everyone on Wednesday afternoon. Keri and I will fly back to the states without getting a kidney. My decision will seal all of their fates.

At 7:01, Anish answers his phone, and I tell him my decision. "I will inform the hospital," he says, "and call you back in 15 minutes to confirm the final schedule." I distract myself with another cup of coffee. I sit at the counter of the modern kitchenette; in this place that is so foreign to me. I can see out the window as the city begins to wake up. Traffic noises below are a distant but constant hum, like busy bees hovering around their hive. Soon the streets will be overflowing with people, commotion, and congestion of the kind you see only in the world's busiest cities. The entire scene feels surreal, like I'm watching a movie—like this is not really happening to me. I am merely a spectator at the amusement park of life, watching the carousel go round and round, not realizing it's me riding one of the horses.

At 7:30, Anish has not called back. Should I worry something has gone wrong? The hospital is busy. He's probably just waiting for a call back. After another fifteen minutes, my anxiety level is becoming unbearable. I decide to call and ask him if anything is wrong. My heart feels like the Eveready bunny as the phone rings four, five, six times. After eight rings, I realize no one is going to answer. Maybe he is still waiting to hear from the medical team. Perhaps he is in the shower and can't hear the phone. Regardless, he should have called back. I wait ten more minutes and call again, even more nervous than the first time. The phone rings four, five times. This time I am more patient. Who knows about the Indian telephone system? On the tenth ring, I get a recording. "The number you are calling is no longer in service. No further information is available."

I stand in the little kitchen, shocked, holding my cell phone, my mind racing. This should not have happened. Something has gone wrong. In my profession, I have been trained to react quickly. The first thing I do is check the locks on all the doors. However, I know they could have keys. There is no chain that would stop or delay them. I hurry into the bedroom and get my service revolver. I check to make sure it's armed. Keri is still asleep, and I quietly shut her bedroom door.

It could be an innocent mistake. A foul-up with the cell phone company. Maybe Anish had to change phones. After all, he's in a dangerous occupation. He must change cell phones frequently. But what if something went wrong? What are the chances they discovered the sting? I try to remember any lapses or mistakes; information that might have leaked out. Did I say anything that could have blown my cover? Did my hesitation to re-schedule the operation set off an alarm?

My senses are on high alert. I hear the elevator stop down the hall. Footsteps approach my doorway. I assume a defensive position kneeling behind the leather couch. Can a bullet go through it, finding me on the other side? I remove the trigger safety on my service revolver. Then, I kneel on my left knee. My right leg is bent 90 degrees with my foot firmly braced against the floor. The barrel of my gun sits cradled in my left palm, which rests on the top of the couch for support.

My right index finger curls against the trigger. With my eyes just over the back of the couch, I aim my pistol at the front door.

Chapter 29

Martin

Waitin' is harder than doin'. The FBI's in charge and will make all the arrests. For now, I'm shut out. I got no active role. I sit behind my desk with a cup of coffee and stare at the telephone and the police radio. The team in New Delhi has been sent to rescue Crawford and get her and Keri outta the country. At the same time, they'll sweep the hospital, arrestin' the administrators and doctors involved in the case. Back here, they'll take Stone, Cohnheim, and Landis into custody and get whatever they can before the lawyers bail 'em out. I feel helpless, unneeded, worried. All I can do is sit and wait for the news like a parent waitin' for a child to come outta surgery. Crawford is in mortal danger. We know nothin' about the people who are operatin' in India.

Fidgetin' at my desk, waitin' for the phone to ring, I'm like a forsaken lover, hopin' my mate will call. Gradually, the news filters in. Stone was arrested at his penthouse condominium. It musta been quite a shock for the wealthy condo owners who are usually shielded from unpleasantness by a wall of security guards. Apparently, Stone was furious, bein' treated like a common criminal by the arrestin' officers. His complaints only drew more attention as he was led out with hands cuffed behind his back. It's unfair, but police usually show more deference when arrestin' someone from the upper class.

At nearly the same time, they arrested Roni Cohnheim. She wasn't surprised and went quietly. She'd been there before and was smart enough to keep quiet until she had lawyers. Cohnheim doesn't have the same presence as Bradley Stone, but she's got better control of her emotions.

It's good the Bureau was able to make the arrests without incident, but those aren't the focus of my worries. I imagine Cassandra, holed up in some apartment or hotel room in New Delhi, crouchin' in some corner of the room, her gun at the ready, scared for her daughter as well as herself; probably cursin' herself for puttin' her daughter at risk. No one knows how well these criminals are connected. Whether the police in New Delhi are honest or complicit. Possibilities are wide open. Anythin' can happen. Chief promised he would call as soon as he hears. All I can do is sit and wait.

Time passes so slowly that I check the clock on my desk to make sure it's still runnin'. The old timepiece was a genuine Yunghans clock that my mother's family brought from Germany. My father kept it on a shelf behind the counter in the Blue Hill Avenue store. Although the store was robbed twice, the thieves only wanted cash. They couldn't be bothered tryin' to fence an old clock. When my mother finally retired, she brought the clock home and put it on the mantle above the livin' room fireplace. It was one of the few things I kept when I cleared out the apartment after she passed. I was lucky to find a watchmaker who specialized in antique timepieces. Since then, the old clock has kept runnin', and it still sits in the center of my desk.

Strangely, the clock reminds me of a joke. One a my college professors used to say that he didn't mind students checkin' their watches while he was lecturin'. It was when they took them off and started shakin' them that he got upset.

Finally, the telephone rings. The digital readout says "Chief." My pulse beats in my temples as I pick up the receiver. "Moishe," he says. "We got more trouble."

I grimace and shut my eyes, imaginin' the worst. The organization has retaliated. They had to in order to protect themselves. Cassandra is dead. They stormed the apartment with automatic weapons, killing her and her daughter. It's my fault. How can I ever forgive myself?

“Martin? Martin, are you still there?”

“Yes,” I manage to squeak out. Feels like one of those blood pressure cuffs are around my throat squeezin’ tighter and tighter. I know what the Chief is goin’ to say and don’t want to hear it.

“Oh, it’s not that, Martin,” the Chief says, somehow knowin’ that the only thought on my mind is Cassandra. “I haven’t heard anything from New Delhi about Crawford. It’s about Neil Jensen’s son, Blake; the one that was dealing drugs out of his convenience store.”

“Yeah,” I answer, feelin’ annoyed. Why the fuck is he callin’ about a drug dealer when all this is goin’ on?

“I was just on the phone with the Chief in Quincy. One of their patrolmen answered a call and found Blake Jensen dead in his house in Wollaston. Died of multiple stab wounds. Looks like a homicide. Likely has nothing to do with our case. The guy was a drug dealer who probably cut in on somebody else’s territory. Just the same, you better check it out. I told the Quincy police I was sending you over.”

“I’m on it, Chief. Leavin’ right away. Gimme me a call if you hear anythin’ from New Delhi.”

Chapter 30

Cassandra

The footsteps echo down the hallway, getting louder, drawing closer. As they approach the door, my body tenses. My left hand steadies the revolver. My right index finger presses against the trigger. How many of them are there? Will they knock on the door, break it down, or just enter with their key? The footsteps get louder until they are directly behind my door, and then, they proceed down the hallway. I remain on alert. They could be making sure I have no backup. They could be checking out the stairway at the end of the hall. Suddenly, the silence is broken, a key turning in the lock next door followed by voices and laughter. Just some hotel guests. I exhale, unaware I had been holding my breath.

Just as my heartbeat returns to normal, my cell phone rings, startling me again. Who would call here? At this hour? It must be Anish. Only a few minutes have passed since my last call. Something must have held him up. I had panicked for nothing. Things are okay after all. I breathe a sigh of relief and answer my cell. But it is not Anish. The voice over the cell phone is crackly. It sounds far away. "Hello, hello? Is this Cassandra? Sandra? Hello?" Far away, yes, but I recognize the familiar voice of the Director of Operations.

"Crawford, they discovered the sting. Your cover is blown, and you could be in danger. Agents are on the way over to your place. They will knock on your door and give you the password. I will spell it out: Y-a-s-t-r-z-e-m-s-k-i. Without the password, don't let anyone in. Are you armed?"

"Yes, of course."

"Hold tight. All of them probably have fled but be careful just the same. We'll get you out of there in no time. Meanwhile, make sure your little one is safe and assume a defensive position. Our agents should be there within ten minutes. I'm getting off so you can get set up. Be careful and good luck."

I resume my position behind the couch. For a few seconds, after the false alarm with the footsteps, my fear seemed foolish, panicking because Anish hadn't answered my call. Get a hold of yourself, I thought. You've been in these situations before. But, as it turns out, my fear was justified. My initial instincts were correct. Somehow, the operation was compromised. Now, there will have to be an internal investigation to find out what happened; to find out if someone leaked information by mistake, or worse, to make sure there isn't a mole or someone with access to our communications. That may be the reason for spelling that password, a name only a local person would pronounce correctly. No time to think about that now. I need to get through the next few minutes until the backup team arrives.

The sounds of the morning rush hour penetrate the room from the street below. Thousands of people pursuing their daily routines: getting their morning cup of coffee, walking to the train, driving to the office, passing the day performing their usual tasks before returning home to their families and an evening meal. How many times have I yearned for a more normal life? Questioned whether my career as an FBI agent has robbed me of the simple everyday rhythms that other people enjoy; longed for a life of easy listening instead of acid rock. While other mothers are home awakening their daughters, I am in India, holding a semi-automatic weapon, knowing that any moment a determined group of criminals could burst through the door and assassinate us both.

Over the muffled sounds of the morning, I hear the elevator doors open down the hall. Nearly ten minutes have passed since the Director's call. It could be the rescue team, but it could also be a group of assassins. Once more, my body tenses as I rest my left arm on the back of the couch and cradle my weapon. Once more, my right index finger is poised on the trigger. The footsteps become louder as they approach. Although no one is talking, I can tell there is more than one person. This time, they stop right outside the door. A second passes, but feels much longer, as if time has stopped. A firm knock on the door—one, two, three raps. "Who is it?" I shout in the strongest most resolute voice I can muster.

"Yastrzemski," comes the reply.

Relief floods my body all at once, like when your car spins 360 and then stops, narrowly avoiding a collision. But I must remain vigilant. What if they had tapped into our communications? "I am going to unlock the door with my weapon pointed at the entrance," I tell whoever is there. "Walk in slowly, one-by-one, with your arms raised over your heads. I am here with my daughter and will not hesitate to shoot."

I know they can shoot through the door, so I stand as far as possible to the side, just able to reach and undo the lock. "Okay," I command. "Open the door and walk in slowly."

The first guy to enter must be six-foot-five and 240-pounds. Hands raised high above his head, he looks like an all-American football player and has a big, wide, confident, shit-eating grin. It's love at first sight, as I put down my weapon, and he gives me the sweetest bear hug I could ever imagine. One thing about the Bureau. They are far from perfect, and they have made some bad-ass mistakes, but they take care of their own.

"I have to wake up my daughter and pack all our stuff," I tell them. "It will take a few minutes."

"Sorry, Agent Crawford. Our orders are to move right out. One of the men will pack everything up and send it ahead. Just take your purse and your ID. Cars are waiting. This is a coordinated operation. If we're not downstairs in ten minutes they will send up a swat team."

I wake Keri gently but firmly and tell her we need to go right away. I help her get dressed and ready, grab my pocketbook, make sure the passports are inside, and tell the guys we're ready. My gun is still on the table, and I ask if I can take it.

"Absolutely, you'll be on one of our planes," one of them replies.

Minutes later we're in an SUV with blacked-out windows speeding toward the airport. I finally have an opportunity to ask what happened. "Were you able to sweep up the suspects?"

"Everyone had gone," they tell me. "The only people who were still there were the hospital administrators. We didn't even find Anish."

How did they know about Anish? I'm thinking. Were they tailing me? Did they have someone on the inside? "What about the transplant? Do the hospital people still expect to do the transplant?"

"No, they had taken it off their schedule. They told us that the person acting as liaison called to say the kidney donor had changed her mind. She no longer was willing to undergo the operation. No one seemed surprised. I guess it's not uncommon."

"Where do we go from here?"

"In a few minutes, you and your daughter will be on an agency plane back to the States. They have made several arrests in the Boston area and you're needed to take part in the interrogation. I hope you can get some sleep on the plane, 'cause it sounds like you're going to be busy when you get back home."

Chapter 31

Martin

The drive from downtown Boston to Quincy is short, but you gotta take the dreaded southeast expressway. Sometimes you sit there like you're on hold with the registry of motor vehicles. Tonight, I'm lucky. I drive past the Dorchester gas tank and exit at Neponset where the old drive-in theater used to be. My mind flashes back to sweaty summer nights with the metal speaker hooked on to the car window. My younger self, a clumsy teenager, trying to cop a feel while some horror movie played on the screen. Seems like another life. I turn on to Quincy Shore Drive and pass one of the remainin' clam shacks. I remember when places like these had carhops; teenage girls in fire red short-shorts who would strut over to your car and take your order. Now we have squawk boxes and drive-up windows at Mickey D's. Nostalgia is the temptation of hard times.

I enter Blake Jensen's neighborhood with the old, wood-frame two-families looking run-down and in need of repair. Parked cars are old and mottled with dents and scratches. Down the street, a crowd of on-lookers surrounds a half dozen squad cars. The curiosity for human tragedy is indifferent to the time of day. I park the Taurus two doors away from where Blake Jensen spent his final hours. Quincy police have cordoned off the house. I flash my badge, and they let me through.

Inside, the body of Blake Jensen lies dormant on the living room rug, deader than mackerel on a fish pier and smellin' nearly as bad. Broken glass litters the floor, chairs are tipped over, plates of old food lie upended on a coffee table. Clearly, there was a struggle. But, as I peer through the mess, I realize somethin' the Quincy police don't know. Blake Jensen had re-decorated the house. The leather couch is new, as is the recliner and livin' room rug. The flat screen TV that was there before is now connected to a home theater system. Beer cans, leftover fast-food containers, and half-full glasses with cigarette butts are still scattered about the room, but despite the mess, Jensen had spent some serious money.

I locate the officer in charge of the crime scene who was expectin' my visit and who greets me as if I'm not an additional burden. "Any signs of a break-in?" I ask.

"None at all. The guy has a security system, but it wasn't triggered. The windows and doors are all alarmed. He has a deadbolt and chain for both doors, but when we got here, the front door was unlocked."

"You think he let someone in?"

"He was a drug dealer. You'd think he'd be careful about letting people in. It must have been somebody he knew, like a known customer or another dealer."

"Mind if I take a quick look around?"

"Better not. I need to preserve the scene until forensics is finished. Looks like there was quite a struggle. We may be able to get blood or hair samples, and there could be prints all around the place. Hope you don't mind."

In fact, I don't mind the rebuff at all. On TV, every detective is like Sherlock Holmes, discoverin' a key piece of evidence that everyone else has overlooked. In real life, that rarely happens, and it's forensics that usually finds the evidence. I'm content to let the Quincy police do their job. Especially today when my mind is closer to New Delhi than Quincy. Checkin' my phone, I make sure I haven't missed a call from the Chief.

"Find anythin' of interest?" I ask.

"Yeah, kind of. He had a stash of drugs in a bureau drawer and a healthy amount of paraphernalia. You know, needles, rubber belts, spoons, couple of lighters, the usual stuff. Not surprising since he was a user. Guy's arm looks like the Milky Way. What did surprise us was the amount of cash. We found about $10,000. He's got the reputation on the street of being a small-time dealer."

"Where did you find it?"

"Sitting right in with the drugs. We were careful not to disturb the crime scene, but we could see it in the drawer. Guess he wasn't too worried about security."

"So, no signs of a robbery?"

"No. Place was a mess. Fucking guy lived like a pig. Sink full of dishes. Half-eaten pizza and leftovers from Taco Bell. Bedroom with laundry all over the floor; smelled like a high school locker room. Bathtub had so much hair, you'd think he had a pet gorilla. But that was just the way the asshole lived. Nothing pulled apart. No drawers opened or upturned. Whoever whacked him wasn't looking for drugs."

"Don't suppose you found the murder weapon?"

"No, but by the looks of the stab wounds, it wasn't just a knife some guy grabbed in the kitchen. Wounds looked like they came from a double-edge blade; could have been a Gerber. Makes you think it was pre-meditated. Forensics will have a better idea."

"Thanks, appreciate your help. I'd like to see the report when it comes up from forensics."

"No problem, but why are you guys interested? Was he dealing in Boston?"

I hesitate to answer. Don't want to explain why I'm here. I already screwed up by givin' the case to the Bureau. The last thing we need on this case is another city police department. Problem is, everybody's gonna know that Blake's father was recently murdered. Neal Jenson's murder was front page, and if the Quincy police haven't figured it out yet, they'll read about it in tomorrow's paper. I look up at him, and he's smilin'. He's no dummy. Knows I don't want to tell him.

"Guy's father was murdered a short time ago. Then, a little while later, someone did his father's girlfriend. You must have read about it in the papers. That's why I'm on the case. Blake Jensen's death probably got nothin' to do with those murders. He was just a low life shitkicker who probably moved into the wrong territory. Even so, we need to check it out. Unfortunately, when the reporters get hold of this, they'll try to tie the murders together. Makes great press."

"Any idea why he had so much cash?"

"Mighta inherited some money from his father's death. Maybe used it to do some deals. Guess we'll have to figure that out. Nothin' more for me to do here. Might as well head back to the office. Thanks for all your help."

I get back in the Taurus thinkin' about Blake Jensen. Sure, the money for redecoratin' coulda come from his inheritance. Shit! I suddenly realize. I'm gonna have to speak with Sheila Jensen. Thought makes me cringe. I can hardly imagine havin' to do that again. First, she loses her husband, then her son.

Back on Quincy Shore Drive, I see the sign for the clam shack I passed earlier and make a quick turn into the parkin' lot. The smell of fried food wafts through my open window. Used to be a time I couldn't eat after viewin' a murder scene. Somehow, you get used to it.

I order the whole belly fried clams, French fries, and a sixteen-ounce Diet Coke. I get it "to go," because a cop eatin' in his car is like a snail curled up in his shell. After a while you get a system. You spread a newspaper over your lap and put the plate on top of it. Any dips, like the ketchup and tartar sauce go on the console. The Coke goes on the dashboard along with the cell phone. The first clam is heavenly. The soft belly encased by deep-fried batter. No sooner do I reach for the Coke than the phone rings. Cassandra is my only thought as I grab for the phone, tippin' over the large Coke. Tryin' to catch it, I upend the plate of clams. The whole plate falls in my lap floatin' in a puddle of

Coke. But it don't matter. The voice on the other end of the line is the Chief. Cassandra is safe and on a military flight back home.

Chapter 32

Cassandra

Fortunately, I was able to catch a few hours of sleep on the flight. For as soon as I de-plane, a black limo is waiting on the tarmac. The driver is an agent I have worked with before. The plan is to stop briefly at my house, change clothes, and put my tired baby to bed. I already called ahead and arranged for a sitter.

"The lawyers will have Stone, Cohnheim, and Landis out of custody by tomorrow," the driver tells me. "No matter how high they set the bail, Stone will put up the bond. We want you to interrogate them now, before they can coordinate with their lawyers and corroborate their stories. We've already had a go at them, but they're well counseled and refused to answer anything of substance. Maybe you can get something out of them."

"I'll try my best. What can I offer them?"

"That's over my head. You can dangle reduced sentences or immunity, but you can't make any promises. Not without the Director."

"What's coming down? The shit must have been flying when everyone in India got away."

"Don't know. Donaldson's hard to read. He'll probably want a thorough de-briefing, but there's no time to do that before those three get out. After that, I think you're in for a long session. Wish you luck, Cat."

"Thanks, I'm going to need it."

An hour and a half later, I arrive at the detention center. I decide to start with Susan Landis. Standard operating procedure is to break down the little guys; promise immunity to the peons in order to get the big kahuna. The last time I saw Landis, I gave her a big hug, feigning tears, thanking her profusely, and promising to keep our conversation secret. I feel like such a rat.

An attendant brings Landis into the interrogation room. She looks downcast and frail. I was prepared for her to act insolent because of the subterfuge, but she looks cowed from being in custody. She sits across from me and says nothing, and I hope the silence will un-nerve her. I sit quietly, watching Landis fidget, kneading her hands, avoiding eye contact. The poor woman could hardly be more nervous.

"Ms. Landis," I finally begin, "I have just returned from New Delhi where my life was in danger. I was sent there through your recommendation. Who encouraged you to give me that information?"

"I'm sorry. My attorney has advised me not to answer any questions."

"Ms. Landis, if I may, let me describe your predicament. You are part of an international conspiracy to trade in illegal human organs. There is no doubt about your guilt or innocence since you approached me directly and provided the contact information in writing. The illegal organization, of which you are a part, is suspected of committing at least three murders. You could be prosecuted under the RICO act for conspiring in this illegal transaction, and you may well be charged as an accessory to murder. You have a choice. You can cooperate with law enforcement, in which case we can promise at least a reduced sentence or possibly complete immunity from prosecution; or you can remain silent and face most of your remaining life behind bars. Let me repeat. There is no question about your guilt. No lawyer on earth can make the note you gave me go away. Your future depends on whether you side with the good guys or the bad guys. I would strongly advise you to make the right choice. Do you understand?"

"Yes," Susan Landis replies as tears streak down her cheeks. Her hands shake like a meth addict. She wipes her eyes with a damp tissue.

"Now, who directed you to put me in contact with Herman Poleskey?"

"What can you offer me?" She asks in a tremulous voice.

"That depends upon what you tell us and your role in the organization. If you were simply a conduit for information, we can request full immunity."

"How will I know? Why should I believe you?"

"The FBI wants to prosecute the leaders of this international ring. If you were simply a conduit, it would be well worthwhile for us to let you go free in exchange for your testimony."

"What if I am endangered by my testimony?"

"Do you have reason to believe that may be the case?"

"I don't know."

"We can offer you witness protection. Criminals rarely take the risk of intimidating FBI witnesses."

"I'm scared. I don't know what to do. I want to consult my lawyer."

"That's perfectly reasonable. However, I would be careful. Bradley Stone may offer to pay your legal expenses, but his attorneys have his interests in mind, not yours."

"I would like some privacy to call my own lawyer."

I retrieve Landis's cell phone and leave her in the interrogation room to make her call. I'm pleased with the first interrogation. It was easier than I expected, but it probably means that Landis has little knowledge about the whole affair. Even if she is just a messenger, however, her testimony about who sent her will be important. The next interrogation probably will not be as easy.

Bradley Stone glares at me when he is led into the room. I introduce myself and explain that I am the woman who his contacts sent to New Delhi to buy an illegal kidney for my daughter.

"I know nothing about that, Ms. Crawford."

"You are not aware, Mr. Stone, that one of your technicians gave me the telephone number of a kidney broker?"

"On the advice of counsel, I refuse to answer any questions."

"Are you not aware, Mr. Stone, that Neal Jensen received an illegal kidney from a contact he made through one of your technicians?"

"On the advice of counsel, I refuse to answer any questions."

"Three murders have been committed, sir. Don't you think you have any responsibility to assist this investigation?"

"On the advice of counsel, I refuse to answer any questions."

I know that Stone already lied to me, since I'm aware of the taped conversations with Roni Cohnheim. However, I prefer to keep that secret, because if he lies under oath in his deposition, we can use it against him. I continue to ask him a series of questions, all of which he refuses to answer. Eventually, I realize any more time spent with Stone will be wasted and decide to move on to Cohnheim.

"I know who you are, Ms. Crawford. It makes little sense for me to pretend otherwise. However, our attorneys have told us not to answer any questions unless we are required to do so under oath. I am sorry to be so uncooperative, but I will follow their advice."

"Ms. Cohnheim, I probably don't need to explain how much you have to lose. You face serious criminal charges. In addition to being part of an international conspiracy to illegally distribute human organs, you may well be indicted as an accessory to murder. Even in the unlikely chance that your lawyers get you off with a reduced sentence, you will be deported and lose your business. I suggest you will be far better off if you cooperate with this investigation."

"On the advice of counsel, I will refuse to answer any questions."

"Ms. Cohnheim, Neal Jensen is dead. Cynthia Fleming is dead. Miguel Sanchez is dead. All of them were murdered. I may have narrowly escaped New Delhi with my life. If you face being charged as an accessory, don't you think it may be in your interest to respond to my questions?"

"With all due respect, Ms. Crawford, you are wasting your time. I have been here before and will not be intimidated by your threats. I will not answer any questions, but I will tell you one thing. Graduates of the Nattai Institute have prolonged the lives of thousands of kidney patients. I am proud of the work I do. I have no regrets or misgivings, unlike you, Ms. Crawford, who unfortunately made the wrong choice. The tragedy here is not the threat to my future. The tragedy is a little girl who was denied the possibility of living a normal life."

It feels like a knife twisting in my gut. I've never lost it during an interrogation, but I can feel the tears welling up in my eyes. I was staring at this woman, trying to intimidate her, but she hurt me in a place I have no defenses. I'm totally humiliated by my weakness and have to look away. I know I'm being observed by another agent and am mortified that I cannot hold it together. "If you don't cooperate Ms. Cohnheim, that statement will be used against you in a criminal prosecution," I tell her, but we both know she has got the better of this encounter.

Chapter 33

Martin

Once again, I'm drivin' by the million-dollar mansions on Jerusalem Road on my way to see Sheila Jensen. First, I had to question her after the murder of her husband, and now, again, after the murder of her son. It's like goin' back to the dentist for a second root canal. There are now four murders. If I knew nothin' else, I would think the odds that these murders are related are close to 100 percent. I park the Taurus in front of the Jensen house, and just as I'm gettin' out, a police cruiser drives by. The cop slows down and gives the Taurus a long look. Given the neighborhood, it makes me feel like I'm drivin' while black. Strange, what it's like to be on the other side.

Sheila Jensen is expectin' me and meets me at the door. Poor woman looks like she's been run over by a bus. Her eyes and nose have red splotches from cryin'. "I'm so sorry Ms. Jensen," I blurt out. "It's hard to believe this happened twice. You have my sincere condolences."

"Thank you, Detective. Come in. Can I offer you a cup of coffee?"

"No thank you," I reply, rememberin' how I spilled the last one all over her rug.

"Have you made any progress on my husband's case?"

"Confidentially, Ms. Jensen, I believe we have. We have recently detained several suspects for questionin' but have not yet brought any formal charges. The case is ongoin' and very active, so I can't give you any further details."

"I told you that slut was involved. She knew too much and they got rid of her so she couldn't talk."

"As I said, I can't comment on that, but I'll keep you informed when we have somethin' definite. Meanwhile, I need to ask you a few questions and will try to be as brief as possible. I can't imagine how difficult this has been for you. Do you remember the last time you spoke to your son?"

"A few days ago. It was just a routine call."

"Did he give you any indication that he was in danger or that somethin' was wrong?"

"No, not at all."

"I'm sorry to bring this up, but do you know if he was takin' or dealin' drugs?"

"Blake had a drug problem. I assume it had not gone away."

"You think his death was related to the drug trade?"

"I have no idea, Detective. That's your job."

"I know Blake needed money, but I noticed he had just redecorated his house and had quite a few expensive new items."

"Really? I didn't know."

"I assume he must have received some money from your husband's estate."

"No, he wouldn't have had time. The proceeds were just released."

"We also discovered a large amount of cash. You have any idea how he may have had a large sum of money?"

"No. Sorry. I have no idea."

We talk longer, but nothin' else of substance comes from our conversation, and I got an appointment on the other side of the city. "We'll continue our investigation, Ms. Jensen. Thank you, again, for answerin' my questions. If you think of anythin' that might have bearin' on the case, please don't hesitate to call."

Back in the Taurus, I drive toward the city of Chelsea, which is just north of downtown Boston. The drive takes me through the roadways of the recently completed "Big Dig." I gotta read the highway signs so

I don't get lost in the city I've lived in all my life. It's hard to imagine the scope of this project. It includes a web of tunnels and off-ramps that are buried under Boston Harbor and underneath the skyscrapers in the city center. They tell me the twenty-four-billion-dollar road project was the most expensive city construction project in the history of the world.

Leavin' the tunnels, I drive on to the Mystic River Bridge and exit at Route One toward Chelsea. A world away from Jerusalem Road, it's like goin' from the QE-II to the Staten Island Ferry. In 1991, Chelsea was the most crime-ridden city in Massachusetts. The city's criminals included four former mayors who were all indicted for various crimes. City had to declare bankruptcy and was taken over by the state. Since then, Chelsea has begun to recover, but parts are still run down and full of crime and drugs. It's here that I arranged to meet a character nicknamed "The Gator." Since the Fenway case, he's been an occasional informant. He may be a drug dealer, but he's my drug dealer, and it's understood that I don't ask too many questions. It's not a perfect world.

The Gator slinks into the Taurus like a snake slitherin' beneath a rock. "At least this don't look like a cop car," he says. "How come you drivin' a shitbox like this, Goldberg?"

"I guess I'm not scorin' the big bucks like you."

"Yeah, I'm big-time all right. I'll be no-time if the wrong person sees me with you."

"Listen, Gator, what do you know about Blake Jensen?"

"The guy who got popped the other day? Small-time. I dunno who did it."

"He had over ten grand stashed in the house."

"Jensen? No way he could score that much money. That muthafucker used more than he sold. He was lucky to sell enough to support his habit."

"Maybe he was movin' into bigger time."

"Fuck no. He got his stuff from the blood man. I'd know if he was movin' up."

"The blood man. Who's that?"

"You ask too many questions Goldberg. I told ya, I don't know who did it, but this guy was purely small time."

"Who is this blood man?"

"I shouldna said nothin'. If I say, you gonna owe me. You know what I'm talkin' about?"

"Who is it, Gator?"

"He bought from Moreno or one of his pals. They call him the blood man 'cause he tries to look legit by workin' as a dialysis tech. Wouldn't trust that son of a bitch to stick no needle in my body."

"Moreno is in jail down in Mexico."

"Not any more. He got outta there, no sweat."

"Could it of been Moreno that did Blake?"

"Doubt it. Moreno wouldn't risk time for that little shit."

"Gator, you ever hear of a kid named Miguel Sanchez?"

"Nope, never heard the name. Honest. Didn't I give you enough? Hey, drop me off up at the Box District. Town is comin' back, Goldberg. Gentri'cation. All these young tech guys movin' in. Good for business. Y'know, Horatio Alger was born in Chelsea."

"Yeah, I know. So was Albert DeSalvo—the Boston Strangler."

Chapter 34

Cassandra

Yesterday, I barely made it through the day. My internal clock was nine hours behind and wouldn't catch up. In the mirror, I looked like a shaggy dog who had just come out of a muddy pond. How I managed to conduct three interrogations was a mystery. By this morning, however, some measure of humanity had returned thanks to ten hours of sleep in my own bed. It was Sunday, and I took Keri for a ride to Crane's Beach on Boston's north shore. We walked on the long beach, and I tried to boost my daughter's spirits. On our trip to India, I had told Keri that we were going to secretly check things out. We were going to pretend we wanted a kidney to see if it was a good place to get a transplant. "Don't get your hopes up," I had told my daughter. "Even if it looks real, this is going to be a trial run. We are just going to gather information." Nevertheless, when Keri saw all the doctors, she began to hope it was for real. Of course, her hopes were dashed, and she has been in a funk since we returned. I felt like such a horrible mother, but Keri was too young to be told the truth.

After a pleasant day spent with my daughter, I started to feel a little better. I had a late afternoon appointment with my hairdresser and even had my nails done. I said good riddance to my Sandra Ford persona and dressed in black, straight-leg capri pants and a V-necked blouse with cuffed sleeves. I wanted to look and feel like myself for a dinner with Martin celebrating my safe return.

I arrive at Spadaro's ten minutes early because Martin always gets there before me. But there he is, sitting in his usual booth. I am about to complain that he always gets there first, but before opening my mouth to speak, I am overcome with the pleasure of seeing him and I bury my head in his warm hug. When I look up, Martin's eyes are watery, and he's trying to hold back tears.

"Thought I'd never see you again, Cat. Could've never forgiven myself, gettin' you involved in this, lettin' you go over there with that precious little girl. It wasn't right. I should never have let it happen."

"Martin, I don't work for you, remember? It wasn't you who sent me. Anyway, it's over. I'm back safely, and I can't tell you how good it is to see you."

"How is Keri?"

"She's upset. Disappointed. How can I blame her? She'll be okay. She'll get through this like everything else she has overcome. But it isn't fair. She deserves to have a normal life. And this time the fault is mine. I should never have done this to her."

"Like you said, it's done. You can't go on blamin' yourself. Your intentions were good. You tried to do the right thing."

Martin doesn't know about my intentions. He doesn't know what I went through in New Delhi. Doesn't know the decision I had to face. And I am not ready to talk about it. Maybe someday, but I can't bring myself to discuss it now. Fortunately, our conversation is interrupted by the waitress who brings over a Grey Goose Martini. Martin probably ordered it an hour ago.

"Cat, tell me all about it. I only heard a quick summary from the Chief. Musta been pretty hairy."

I tell Martin the story but leave out my decision about whether or not to deceive the FBI. I tell him about Anish and the Apollo Medical Center, and describe how scared I was, crouching behind the couch with my gun, afraid that both Keri and I would be killed.

"I'm glad it's over," Martin says. "The hospital and doctors sound so good you must have been tempted."

"You just can't imagine what a relief it is to be back home safely with Keri," I answer, avoiding the topic. "But I've been out of touch with your end of the investigation. Anything new, Martin?"

"Cat, I got important news. Could tie things together. You heard that Blake Jensen was murdered. Looked like just an unrelated drug murder, but I had naggin' doubts. A double murder of a father and son had to be connected, but what was the connection between drugs and kidneys? How did the pieces fit together? Couldn't get it outta my mind, so I went to see one of my informers on the street. In fact, someone you know about."

"Me? I only know one of your informers. It must have been the Gator from the Fenway case."

"You got it. Turns out Blake got his drugs from Jose Moreno, the guy who was friendly with Miguel Sanchez."

"The guy who is in prison in Mexico?"

"Not anymore. Gator said they let him go."

"You think Moreno killed Blake?"

"I don't know. What if Blake was doin' a deal with Moreno and his father found out? Say his father threatened to go to the police if Blake did the deal. Moreno could have killed both Jensens. Could have even killed the girl if he thought she knew somethin'."

"I don't know. Sounds like a reach. Moreno and Blake Jensen are involved with drugs, but we have no evidence linking them to the kidney trade. We know AKLC is behind the kidney trade, and I think I may get some corroborating evidence from Susan Landis."

"Landis—the nurse who gave you the contact, right?"

"Yes, but she hardly seems like the type to be involved with international organ traders. I think the poor woman was innocent and naïve. Someone put her up to it. She had no idea how she was exposing herself by passing contact information to patients."

"You thinkin' Stone or Cohnheim put her up to it? Would she testify against 'em?"

"I'm hoping. When I told her the charges she could face, she was scared shit. She met with her attorney, and she might make a deal to turn state's evidence."

"That'd be great, Cat. Could be the break we've been lookin' for. Meanwhile, I'm gonna track down Jose Moreno."

Chapter 35

Martin

The next mornin', I meet with D'Angelo to talk about detainin' Moreno. A tip from a confidential informant ain't enough to arrest Moreno on a drug charge, but I want some excuse to bring him in for questionin'. We decide to detain him about the death of Miguel Sanchez. Given warnings from the Gator about Moreno, we proceed carefully. First, we put his house under surveillance. The next mornin', accompanied by two squad cars with heavily armed cops, we leave to arrest him at his house.

If Moreno is a big-time dealer, you'd never know it from the outside of his house. He lives on the second floor of an old, wood-frame two-family on a street like Miguel's. It reminds me of arrests I made in Southie. The kids that come from these poor neighborhoods can be tougher than titanium, but the community and the families are close. Even the ones who make it big are reluctant to move, and they often settle just a street or two away from their parents.

At 6:00 a.m., D'Angelo and I follow a team of police up the wooden staircase. They knock on Moreno's door loud enough to wake him out of a coma. "Police Moreno! Open the door slowly and put your hands up. Don't try anything stupid. There's a lot of us and we're armed."

"I'm comin'." A half-awake Moreno opens the door wearin' boxer shorts and a Red Sox tee shirt. "What the fuck is this about?" he says. "It's the fuckin middle a the night."

"We're takin' you in for questioning about the death of Miguel Sanchez. You have the right to remain silent. Anythin' you say can and will be used against you in a court of law. You have the right to an attorney. If you cannot afford an attorney, one will be provided for you. Do you understand the rights I have just read to you?"

"Aw shit! I answered all your questions in Mexico. I don't know nuthin."

"Do you understand the rights I just read to you?"

"Fuckin' A, yes. Can I get dressed?"

"Yeah, but one of us stays with you."

An hour later, I enter the interrogation room where Moreno has been waitin' impatiently. "This is a fuckin' joke," he complains. "You clowns questioned me when I was in Mexico. Miguel was my friend. I grew up with him. I had nuthin' to do with what happened."

"Your friend needed money. He was desperate to get money for his father's operation. Maybe he came to you, Jose."

"He never told me what he was doin'. I didn't even know he was goin' to Mexico."

"No? Let's think about it. Miguel needed to make a score. How does a poor kid make a score these days? He tries to sell drugs. He's an amateur. He goes to Mexico and gets himself killed. Just so happens his best friend is a dealer and gets imprisoned in Mexico on drug charges at the exact same time. Just a coincidence, Jose?"

"I ain't no dealer. I went to school to be a dialysis technician. That's what I do. The police in Mexico were mixed up. They had the wrong guy. That's why they let me go."

"You quit your dialysis job."

"I got a new one. Different place. You better stop fuckin with me."

"You tell us about Miguel. We'll leave you alone."

"I told 'em in Mexico. Miguel worked for AKLC. I worked there and know what goes on. They send their patients to these guys that sell kidneys for 200 grand. They gotta buy these kidneys from someone, right? I don't know what the fuck Miguel was doin', but I heard they found him without his kidneys. Does that sound like a fuckin drug deal? I got outta AKLC. Those are dangerous muthafuckers."

"Okay Jose," D'Angelo says. "That's your story. How about Blake Jensen?"

"Who?"

"Blake Jensen."

"Don't know the guy."

"C'mon Moreno. You know what's happenin' on the street. You want to walk outta here with no charges? You tell us what you know about Jensen."

"Okay, I heard of him. He was a user. A small-time addict."

"You know he was murdered."

"Yeah, I heard."

"Who would want him dead?"

"Look, this got nuthin' to do with me. All I heard about this guy was that he was a small-time little shit. Wasn't big enough for anybody to bother with."

"Then how come we found ten grand under his mattress?"

"Fuck do I know. Maybe he robbed a bank."

"Sure, Moreno, and maybe I'm the Sundance Kid. This ain't Dodge City. Hasn't been a bank robbery around here in years."

"How the fuck should I know? Maybe he was a B&E man. Maybe he hit the fuckin' lottery or got lucky at Foxwoods. Maybe he tried to extort the wrong muthafucker. Ain't got nuthin' to do with me. Draggin' me here to this shithole at six in the mornin.' I ain't puttin' up with this shit!"

D'Angelo points his finger at Moreno's chest. "Are you threatenin' us, Moreno?"

"Take it any way you want."

Chapter 36

Cassandra

Susan Landis may have been naïve, but she had a good lawyer. He realized how badly the FBI wanted her testimony, and he was prepared to drive a hard bargain. It wasn't necessary. Nobody thought this confused young woman was part of an international cartel of human organ traders. Provided she had evidence that could implicate any of the suspects, and she was willing to testify under oath, she was granted complete immunity from prosecution.

I joined a videotaped session with FBI personnel and attorneys from both sides. I listened and took notes as our lawyers asked questions and Landis told her story.

"How did you come to work for AKLC?" the lawyer asked.

"I was enrolled in a certification program for dialysis technicians at the Nattai Institute. They had an excellent placement service, and the demand for dialysis techs was strong. Before graduating, I had interviewed at several companies including AKLC. Around the time I received my certification, AKLC offered me a position."

"Prior to your work at AKLC, did anyone ever speak to you about people seeking or receiving illegal kidneys?"

"Well, of course it was mentioned in the literature that we studied, but no one ever spoke to me personally until my final placement interview?"

"Who in AKLC was present at that interview?"

"No, it was the final placement office interview at Nattai. I met with the President, Roni Cohnheim."

"Can you describe that meeting, Ms. Landis? Please give us as much detail as you can remember."

"She talked about the position at AKLC and what I could expect. Then, she offered me some advice that she said I didn't hear in class. She said that some of my patients would be desperate to find kidneys; people who had been on waiting lists for years. Some who were running out of time and afraid of dying. Some of them would be so desperate, they would go to criminals in third world countries to buy illegal organs. They might ask me where they could buy a kidney. I remember being surprised and said to her, 'Really? How would I know anything about that?'"

"How did she respond?"

"She said 'of course you wouldn't,' but she told me that a number of AKLC patients had gone that route. Some had died or been grievously injured; good people who you never thought would consider risking their lives with criminal dealers. People, even smart people, she said, will take extraordinary risks if they fear death. I assumed she was about to tell me how to discourage those people so they wouldn't be harmed."

"And is that what she did, Ms. Landis?"

"No, she described how she worked in dialysis in Israel. She said that unlike in the U.S., Israeli health insurance would often pay for transplants that occur in other countries. She met people who coordinated these transplants, and the outcomes were good. A lot of lives were saved. I didn't know why she was telling me this, or what it had to do with me."

"Did you ever ask her if the procedures were illegal?"

"No. I guess I was a little intimidated being in the President's office. I didn't know what she was getting at, or why she was telling me this."

"Go on. Sorry to interrupt."

"She told me if I ever had a patient who indicated that they might risk the black market, I should report it to her or to the director of the center. She had seen too many people get harmed and she wanted to prevent any further tragedies."

"Ms. Landis, did she ever suggest that she or anyone connected with her or with the dialysis center could help any of these people find a kidney?"

"No. The whole conversation sounded reasonable. Some patients were getting harmed by trying to get black market kidneys, and she wanted to prevent that from happening."

"Why did you suppose she told you about Israel?"

"I don't know. Perhaps it was a criticism of the U.S. I guess I never gave it any thought."

"Is that everything you can remember about the interview?"

"Yes. Nothing stood out as being very unusual."

"Okay, thank you Ms. Landis. Now you started work at AKLC. Did anyone there ever mention this warning about black market kidneys?"

"No, never. I think I would remember if they did."

"Did you ever have a situation in which you reported a patient who asked about the black market?"

"Not until Ms. Ford. She had repeatedly asked about it for her little girl. She asked a lot of questions about China and seemed desperate to find a kidney. I remembered the conversation, and I contacted Ms. Cohnheim."

One of the lawyers interrupted. "Did you mention this to anyone else in the dialysis center, or did anyone else speak with you about it?"

"No. President Cohnheim had told me it was confidential patient information that was private and should not be shared."

"Go on," the attorney said. "Then what happened?"

"She asked me a number of questions about the little girl and her mother. I remember exactly what she told me: 'Susan,' she said, 'you could do this woman a favor that might save her child from harm. Give her this telephone number and make sure she never tells anyone where she got it. She will get expert advice. You will be doing a good deed.'"

"Do you have that telephone number, Ms. Landis?"

"No, I never made a copy, but I gave it to Ms. Ford."

After getting a written statement from Susan Landis, I use it to get a search warrant for Roni Cohnheim's business and residence. From the taped phone conversations, I know Stone told her to destroy anything incriminating, but I'm hoping for a break; something she overlooked. Something that might lead to the people who are buying the kidneys and arranging the surgeries. So far, there is no actionable intelligence from the hospital in New Delhi.

Along with a team of agents, I arrive at Roni Cohnheim's house at 6:00 a.m. Opening the door, Cohnheim looks at me like I'm a roach that just crawled out of her morning bowl of cereal. "You're under arrest," I tell her, and I recite the Miranda warnings. "We have a warrant to search your house." Roni Cohnheim rarely loses her composure, but this time she is livid. Her complexion changes from olive to red. "What is it this time?" she asks. "You already arrested me before. The judge set me free on bail."

"Sorry Ms. Cohnheim. We have new evidence. We're bringing you in on different charges."

"What are they? I want to call my lawyer. I want to know what the hell is going on."

"You'll have plenty of time for that. Get what you need to take with you."

A team of investigators begins to comb through her belongings. They fill up boxes with paperwork; bills, receipts, bank statements, calendars, notepads, even recipes stuck to the refrigerator. They search for fingerprints, footprints, hair samples. They look for semen stains on sheets and pillowcases. They open the dishwasher and search for lipstick stains on coffee cups. They carefully collect her laptop computer and any external hard drives, disks, and thumb drives. Those will go to the lab for examination. Roni Cohnheim may have already destroyed anything that was incriminating, but we are hoping for a break.

At 10:00 a.m., I begin to interrogate her for the second time in a week. Last time, she ignored any threats, knowing Stone would bail her out. This time, she cannot get out so easily. I need to make her believe she is in serious trouble; the kind of trouble that could make her consider a plea bargain. “Ms. Cohnheim, I have here a copy of a written statement given to us by one of your employees; a woman by the name of Susan Landis. The statement reveals that you induced her to help an AKLC patient buy an illegal kidney. You have conspired with international organ traders who arrange illegal kidney transplants costing hundreds of thousands of dollars. You participated in this arrangement by encouraging your technician to supply contact information for an illegal kidney broker. If I may say so, Ms. Cohnheim, you face a near certain conviction.”

“I told you before, I’ve done nothing wrong,” Cohnheim answers, unperturbed. “I’m proud of what I do. I spent years as a nurse in the nephrology unit. I watched many people suffer and die because they could not find kidney donors. You are so self-righteous, upholding your noble view of the law, thinking you have all the right answers. Well, let me tell you something, Agent Crawford. A sentence of death can bend the moral compass.”

“You conspired with international criminals, Ms. Cohnheim. You referred innocent people to black-market organ dealers. Susan Landis has given us sworn statements.”

“I simply gave a telephone number to a desperate person to keep her from harm’s way; to save some desperate patient from going to some soulless, illegal organ dealer that could cost that person their life. Susan Landis didn’t tell you anything you didn’t already know. You’re not naïve, Ms. Crawford. Surely, you never thought Susan Landis gave you that telephone number on her own."

"Surely, you did not risk colluding with these criminals without any payback. We will subpoena your books, Ms. Cohnheim. The Nattai Institute seems to be very well funded. Maybe some of the funding comes from referral fees."

"Neither myself nor the institute ever accepted a penny for helping desperate people get a healthy kidney."

"Then where did funding come from that enabled you to open so many schools?"

"On the advice of counsel, I respectfully decline to answer any more questions."

"You know Herman Poleskey. Maybe he can corroborate your story. Do you have his contact information?"

"I refuse to answer."

"I don't think you realize the seriousness of these charges. We now have a sworn, written statement from your own employee. We have so much evidence, including my own testimony, that your conviction is a foregone conclusion. At a minimum, you will be found guilty of trafficking in illegal organs. There is little doubt you will spend years in an American prison. Yet, you possess information that could substantially reduce your exposure. The Bureau is more interested in the international traders than the number of years one Israeli spends in jail. If I were in your position, I would want my lawyer to negotiate a deal. Notice, I'm saying *your* lawyer, not Mr. Stone's, who has other considerations. Don't you realize that you may be indicted for conspiracy to commit murder?"

"That is ridiculous. Nobody was murdered. Scaring me will not work."

"What about Neal Jensen? Wasn't he murdered to keep him silent?"

"Neal Jensen? You don't get it. Mr. Jensen's kidney transplant was unsuccessful despite the efforts of his medical team. Transplants simply do not work 100 percent of the time. He was disappointed and angry, but he came to realize that organ transplants are not foolproof. My understanding was that he hoped to get another transplant. That was the only hope he had to live out a decent life. Nobody else was going to do anything for him. Do you think he was about to cut off his only chance for survival?"

"I think your only chance of survival—at least out of prison—is to cooperate with us. We have enough evidence to keep you here, Ms. Cohnheim. We will tell the judge that you are a flight risk. You are an Israeli citizen who could possibly return to your home country and be out of our reach. This time, it won't be easy to get out on bail. I suggest you have a long talk with your attorney."

"You enjoy threatening me, Ms. Crawford. You are so sanctimonious. I suggest you have a talk with your daughter. Tell her you could have got her a new kidney. Tell her you could have saved her life but decided not to. Tell her you couldn't get off your high horse enough to have a little empathy for your own child. Watch her getting weaker. Watch her skin start to turn yellow. Watch her die slowly, Ms. Crawford, as her kidneys fail. You suggest I have a long talk with my attorney? I suggest you have a long talk with your conscience."

Back in my office, I close the door so no one can hear me cry. Roni Cohnheim is cruel, and she knew just where to twist the knife. I am angry at myself for letting her get to me a second time. My emotions have been on edge for several weeks. Every time I look at Keri, I have self-doubts. Every time I take her to dialysis, I think I could have spared her the ordeal. She could be healthy. She could be normal. What kind of mother? What kind of person am I? Roni Cohnheim knew just how to hurt me. The woman actually seems mean enough to be involved in organ trading and murder. But what if it's the other way around? Is it possible that she is right and I am wrong? Wrong not only about my daughter, but about Cohnheim. What if Martin's investigation shows that the murders were about drugs? That Jose Moreno killed all three of those people. What if that cold-hearted bitch was telling the truth?

Chapter 37

Martin

I think that Yana, my Russian dental hygienist, musta gone to the Stalinist School of Dentistry. She sticks her metal pick between two of my bottom teeth and probes downward into my gums like the roto-rooter man diggin' for sludge. "Is sensitive?" she asks, as if she cannot see my body stiffen and my hands grip the chair like a rock climber on El Capitan. "Yrrrghh," I attempt to answer despite the black tube suctionin' my tongue. I suspect her grandparents took part in the pogroms. Mercifully, she straightens up and steps on the foot pedal, raisin' my chair from the helpless supine position. "Rinse," she commands, and I spit a combination of blood and mucous into the little white bowl, but a long sticky strand still hangs from my mouth like a turd that has not yet fallen into the toilet. I swipe it with the blue paper bib as she waits with her stainless-steel pick, poised to inflict her therapy on the next tooth. At my second bicuspid, she encounters a sensitive area that she immediately probes with the hooked end of her scaler.

"Arrgh!" I cry, and she smiles like she has just discovered long-lost treasure from the Andrea Doria. "Is a problem here, Mr. Goldberg. We have Dr. Berman take a look. You need maybe a root canal."

I leave the dental office beaten up and knowin' I'm about to be a thousand dollars poorer; and that's with dental insurance. It's almost 1:00, and my stomach's grumblin'. After the dental ordeal, I figure I deserve a treat. The dental office is less than a mile from Rubin's, my favorite Deli. I plan to order my usual, "The Manhattan;" and because I'm hungry I'll pay an extra two dollars to get it "overstuffed."

Just before entering the deli, my cell phone rings. "Martin," comes Cassandra's familier voice. "We just got a break. One of our I.T. technicians was working on Roni Cohnheim's computer. She had wiped her hard drive, but he was able to recover some of the data. I had asked him to do a search for Herman Poleskey. The last name, Poleskey, didn't come up, but Herman did. There was an entry for a Herman Seidelman with an Israeli telephone number as well as an American cell phone number. It must be our man. We tried to track his phone and initially found it had been turned off, but just a minute ago, he switched it on to make a call. He is somewhere in the Coolidge Corner area of Brookline."

"Coolidge Corner? I'm here right now goin' to Rubin's deli."

"Hold tight. I'm leaving in a minute and bringing backup."

I kinda remember one photograph of Herman Poleskey that Cassandra secretly snapped with her phone. Regardless, this hunt now belongs to the Bureau, and I know they don't want a Boston detective to interfere. But the fact that he may be close by makes me feel tense and on alert. Seidelman could be armed and dangerous, and he may not be alone. I cannot help lookin' around for the portly man in that half-forgotten photo. If I happen to spot him, I can at least follow him until Cassandra arrives.

Seein' no one like him on the sidewalk, I walk into Rubin's, but not before I retrieve my service revolver from the glove compartment. Suddenly, I freeze, as I spot someone in a booth who fits Seidelman's description. But then, I look around and sees others who fit the same description, as if a portly Jewish man would stand out in a kosher deli. Still, I gotta strange sense of danger. My pulse is beatin' fast and the hairs on the back of my neck are standin' up. I always make fun of people who believe in that kinda stuff, but I can't shake the feelin'.

"Excuse me!" someone barks, and I realize I'm still standin' just inside the front door and blockin' the entrance. I walk over to the deli counter where I'm third in line. I keep glancin' from one table to the next, lookin' for Herman, eliminatin' most of the possibilities. The woman at the front of the line must be orderin' a half-pound of every meat at the deli counter: corned beef, tongue, turkey, roast beef, pastrami. I look back at the door, hopin' to see Cassandra, but she has not yet arrived. The woman orders pickled herring, smoked whitefish salad, nova lox. The slightly overweight man behind her shifts his feet impatiently. Finally, she pays for her order, pickin' out pennies for the exact change one-by-one from her little black purse. By now, my attention is driftin', when I hear the clerk say, "I have your order Mr. Seidelman."

My heart rate spikes. I resist the temptation to stare at the man, and it's a good thing since Seidelman turns as if to see if anyone has heard. I look down at the ground but can see him outta the corner of my eye, glancin' around the room like a bird on a feeder checkin' for hawks. He fits my fuzzy recollection of Herman Poleskey's photo.

I only got seconds to decide what to do. I got my service revolver but don't want to risk a shootout in the middle of Rubin's deli. Better to wait outside the front door where the man has to exit. Can I arrest him? Can I detain him until Crawford and her agents arrive? Seidelman is talkin' to the clerk. Several people are now in line behind me, and I quietly slip outta the line and go out the front door. Lookin' left and right on Harvard Street, I'm hopin' to see Cassandra or her colleagues, but the sidewalk is full of lunchtime strollers, none lookin' like FBI agents.

I got seconds to consider my predicament. I got no backup. Seidelman may be armed, or he may have an armed bodyguard nearby, possibly waitin' in one of the parked cars. What should I do? I can surprise him when he walks out; tell him he's under arrest. What if he reaches for a weapon? Then, I gotta be prepared to shoot him on the crowded sidewalk. What if a bodyguard is watchin'? I would be standin' on the sidewalk, exposed and in danger. There could be a fire fight. Collateral damage is a possibility. What if I simply follow him? That could also be dangerous, especially if he has backup. I gotta decide. Crouchin', so nobody can see, I slip my revolver from my waistband, remove the safety, and tuck it back in.

Through the window, I see Seidelman hand cash to the clerk. No surprise he don't pay with a credit card. He takes his bag of purchases from the counter and begins to walk toward the door. Once more, I look up and down the street, hopin' to see agents who can provide backup; hopin' not to see anyone watchin' the door from behind a parked car.

An elderly couple is walkin' in as Seidelman approaches the door. He holds the door open for them and lets them pass. "Thank you," the man says to him. "My pleasure," he remarks, and just from those two words, I can hear his Israeli accent. Seidelman steps out onto the sidewalk, and I approach him from the side.

"Boston Police, Mr. Seidelman. You're under arrest." In my left hand, my wallet is open, badge facin' out. My right hand grips my revolver. Seidelman, clearly taken by surprise, wheels around to face me, and just as he does, a shot rings out. Then another. Next thing I know, I'm lyin' face down on the sidewalk and Seidelman has fallen on top of me. Actin' instinctively, I pull free and reach for my revolver. Holdin' it in front of me with two hands, I pan left and right, desperately lookin' for the shooter. In the background, people are screamin', some lyin' on the ground coverin' their heads. For all they know, this is the first Al Qaeda attack on a Jewish delicatessen.

The shooter is nowhere in sight, but I could still be a target. I'm an easy mark on the sidewalk with no cover. The shooter could be hidin' behind a car. I consider runnin' back inside the deli, but after a seemingly long pause, one that probably lasted only a few seconds, I figure if I haven't been shot by now, the perp must have fled.

For the first time since the shots were fired, I'm aware of a painful cry. Herman Seidelman lies curled on the ground moanin' in pain. Blood pools on the sidewalk, mixed in with a spilled container of chicken noodle soup. Floating in the pool are soggy, half-sour pickles and a dozen knishes. Despite my level of anxiety, I can't help thinkin' it's a waste of good deli.

Seconds later, sirens are screamin' down Harvard Street. Dressed in civilian clothes and holdin' a gun over a wounded victim, I do not want to become a target of the Brookline police, who, in this wealthy town, are more used to rescuin' stray cats than seein' a shooting. I tuck my revolver back into my waistband and stand up holdin' out my wallet and badge. The first police to arrive come outta their car crouched down with guns pointin' at my chest. "Boston police detective," I call out, nervously displayin' my badge. Fortunately, no one panics. An ambulance arrives and a team of EMT's attends to Seidelman. They check his vital signs, move him carefully on to a stretcher, and load him into the van. I warn them that the man is a criminal and could be armed and dangerous, despite the fact that he appears barely conscious.

Minutes later, Cassandra and the FBI arrive. By now, it seems like the entire Brookline police force is here. With the contingent of police and FBI, the scene resembles a law enforcement convention. A crowd of thirty or forty curiosity seekers closes in like ants around a lump of sugar. The Brookline police push back the crowd to give them space and preserve the crime scene. Cassandra comes up by my side.

"Martin, are you okay?"

"One a the bullets musta grazed my arm," I answer, noticin' the pain for the first time and seein' some blood oozing through my shirt. "Nothin' serious."

"Did you see who did it?" she asks.

"No, never saw no one. Had no cover. He could easily have killed me but musta run after the first shots."

"Maybe he already made his hit. Who do you think was the target?"

"Don't know."

"It could have been someone protecting Seidelman, or someone from the organization who was afraid to see Seidelman arrested. It also could have been someone who had been tracking you, afraid the investigation was getting too close. I suppose we can't rule out Jose Moreno."

"If they were after me, they could easily have shot me on the sidewalk."

"Not necessarily. After seeing both of you down, they might have figured they made their hit; or they may have been scared and fled the scene. No one wants to stick around for a murder charge."

"I dunno, Cat. If Seidelman lives, maybe we'll find out."

"Meanwhile, Martin, you better be careful. If someone is after you, they might not give up after one attempt."

"You too, Cat. If they're after me, you might also be a target."

Chapter 38

Cassandra

I roll up Martin's shirt sleeve to look at his wound. It appears superficial, but it's oozing blood, and I insist on driving him to the emergency room to get it cleaned and disinfected. I think he's more embarrassed at the condition of his car than he is about being wounded. The car has the feeling of a city bus, littered with dog-eared newspapers, empty coffee cups, and the odor of leftover fried food.

Hospitals don't make wounded cops wait for treatment, so Martin is seen right away. Turns out the bullet barely penetrated his skin, but the doctor cleans the wound and closes it with five stitches. Martin wants me to take him home, but I refuse. No way I'm going to let him shop and cook dinner for himself after being shot. Since I'm driving his car, he doesn't have much of a choice.

One beneficiary of his misfortune is Keri. She is delighted to see her "Uncle Martin" walking through the front door. She runs up to greet him, and despite his sore arm, he lifts her up and gives her a big hug. They have grown fond of each other ever since Martin and I have become friends. The two of them have little games they play like thumb wrestling and stone-scissors-and-paper. I begin organizing things for dinner, knowing they will amuse themselves while I am busy.

I take out some sirloin steaks from the freezer and defrost them in the microwave. Because of her medical condition, Keri needs high protein in her diet. We frequently have beef and pork, and we have to avoid foods high in salt and potassium. Someday, if Keri gets a new kidney, she will be able to eat like a normal person. I put the steaks in the broiler and set the table. When I glance in the living room, I see the two of them playing a game of Chutes and Ladders.

"Okay, you little smarty pants, I'm gonna catch you now," I hear Martin say. "Anything but a three. Oh noooo!"

"Down the chute, down the chute, Uncle Martin," she cries, with that high-pitched little giggle that sends a cupid's arrow right through my heart.

Keri sits next to Martin for dinner, and he keeps sneaking extra vegetables onto her plate when she isn't looking. But sometimes, he lets her catch him, even while denying being the guilty culprit. It almost feels like a family dinner, and I can't help wondering whether the same thought has occurred to Martin. I let Keri have some ice cream for dessert, and Martin can't resist, even though he tells me he's on a diet. "Your uncle is a *freser,*" I tell Keri. "Can you say *freser?*"

"Freser, Uncle Freser!" she says. She'll be the only daughter of a black, female, FBI agent who can speak Yiddish. Overcoming her protests, I take my little girl up to bed. When I come back downstairs, Martin is putting away the dishes in all the wrong places.

"Martin, you need to relax. You got shot today, remember. Out of my kitchen. I think you need a drink."

"Gin and tonic?" he asks.

I mix a gin and tonic for Martin and pour myself a glass of Malbec from a previously opened bottle. We sit together on the sofa with the first opportunity to unwind after an intense day. "How are you feeling, Martin? Any pain from the wound?"

"Kinda dull ache, but nothin' too bad."

"I'm worried about you. Whoever fired those shots could try again."

"I'm worried about you too, Cat. If they came after me, they might come after you too."

"People rarely risk targeting FBI agents. If it was about Moreno and drugs, they wouldn't be coming after me. If it was about kidneys, they may have been trying to silence Seidelman."

"I'm worried just the same, Cat. Sometimes I wish I had a normal life. Leave all this crime and violence behind. Be able to sit here with you, spend some time together and not worry about work. You ever feel that way?"

I'm surprised by Martin's comment. Is he asking if we could ever have a relationship outside of work? I'm fond of Martin, but I'm not sure I'll ever have a normal relationship with him or any other man. How many times have I talked about it with my shrink? After my father died and my husband walked out on me, I've developed a suit of armor protecting my emotions. Instead of a real relationship, I go for guys like Leon. I get my intimacy, if you can call it that, without the risk. At least that's what my shrink tells me, and she's probably right.

Perhaps I should be looking for someone like Martin; just a nice guy who wants a quiet, family life. But I'm never attracted to guys like that. It's hard to imagine going at it with Martin like I do with Leon. Deep down, I know it would never work. Besides, Martin might not even be interested. I may have misinterpreted what he meant. Martin with a black woman? A lapsed southern Baptist? That may be a non-starter. He may not think of me that way at all.

"Cat, you still with me?"

"Sorry, Martin. I drifted off thinking about what you said. It would be nice to spend some time together and to leave all the daily crap we deal with behind. I'd enjoy that."

"Me too, Cat. Meanwhile, it's gettin' late. I gotta head back home."

"You're welcome to stay here, Martin. The sofa is a queen convertible. You're wounded and you had a long day. I can cook breakfast for you in the morning."

"Thanks Cat, but I don't have a change of clothes or nothin'. I best be headin' out."

I walk Martin to the door with my arm on his shoulder. I give him the usual peck on the cheek to say goodbye, but Martin draws his head back and looks me in the eye. “Thanks for takin’ care of me, Cat. You’re a treasure.” He gives me a quick kiss on the lips, leaving me startled, and hurries out the door like an embarrassed teenager.

Chapter 39

Martin

A noise downstairs wakes me from a deep sleep. My mind is fuzzy. I'm not sure whether it was a real sound or a dream. But then I hear it again. The room is dark. Must still be before sunrise. My puzzlement turns to anxiety as I remember bein' shot yesterday. They could be comin' back for me. My service revolver is in the night-table drawer. Openin' it quietly, I remove the gun and take off the safety. At the top of the stairway, I listen but hear nothin'. "Hello!" I call out. "Who's there?" Silence. Could be my nerves, just havin' had a close call, but I'm sure there was a sound. The stairway has twelve steps, and I'm hesitant to walk down 'cause there's no cover. Could call the police, but after all, I am the police, and if it turns out to be a false alarm, I'd look foolish.

Holdin' my weapon in front of me, I descend the stairway, slowly, one step at a time. The house is old and no matter how carefully I tread, each stair creaks like an old box spring. I'm not gonna surprise no one. And dressed in pajama bottoms and tee shirt, I probably wouldn't scare a nervous old lady.

A faint scrapin' sound comes from the kitchen, like somethin' has moved on the countertop. "Who's there?" I call out again but get no answer. I need to turn the corner into the kitchen. Flashin' through my mind are those grainy television videos from Iraq. Marines kickin' down a door, aimin' their weapons left and right as they burst into a room, not knowin' whether someone is waitin' to blow their heads off. Holdin' my revolver stiff-armed and chin-high, I round the corner prepared to shoot.

Despite the dark, I can tell the room is empty. Of course, anyone in the room would have heard me comin'. The kitchen has another doorway leadin' to the dinin' room. Someone could be just outside the kitchen waitin' for me to walk in with no cover. Another scrapin' noise. I recoil at the sound. And then I see it. The kitchen window is wide open. Dirty dishes, glasses, and cups from the last two days are piled up on the counter. The wind's been pushin' the window shade into the room, topplin' things on the counter. A coffee mug lies broken on the floor; probably the sound that woke me up.

I exhale, lettin' the tension escape my chest. This case has been doin' a job on me. I gotta get a grip. I turn on the lights. Clock on the stove reads 5:30. No way I'm fallin' back asleep, so I put up a pot of coffee. Newspaper won't arrive for another hour, so I turn on the TV for local news, curious about the coverage of the Brookline shooting. By 6:30, I'm hungry, but there isn't much in the fridge. Sounds kinda gross, but I take out two leftover pieces of frozen pizza and heat 'em in the microwave.

By 7:30, I'm sittin' at my desk checkin' messages. Shortly afterward, D'Angelo comes in with the forensic report on Herman Seidelman. The bullets came from an unknown rifle—one that had no matches in the database. He reports that Seidelman was shot in the chest and right side. The doctors operated on him overnight, and he's in the ICU listed in critical condition. No way we're gonna get to question him today, if ever.

The two of us discuss where we are in the case. We review the evidence that seems to have so many loose ends. We keep lookin' for the missing piece that will tie the murders together. If Cohnheim was tellin' the truth, Neal Jensen needed AKLC. If they were his only hope for a new kidney, he wouldn't a been a threat to 'em, and they wouldn't a had a reason to kill him. If Moreno and Gator were tellin' the truth, Blake Jensen was a small-time addict, and Moreno wouldn't a risked killin' him. If Sheila Jensen was tellin' the truth, Blake wouldn't a been next in line to inherit, so he didn't have motive to kill his father. It's still unclear how he came into so much money. Sheila Jensen and her boyfriend, Derrick Hanson, coulda killed Jensen for his inheritance, but she wouldn't a killed her own son. Clayton Thurmond is a wild card who coulda killed Jensen and Fleming outta jealousy. Plus, if Jensen had changed his will, Thurmond could possibly inherit the estate. Miguel Sanchez coulda been selling a kidney through contacts he made at AKLC, but he also coulda been in Mexico for a drug deal, possibly at the bequest of Moreno. Finally, someone shot Herman Seidelman, but we don't know whether he or I was the target. What a spiderweb of people and motives. Four and possibly five unsolved murders are on our plate, and if we don't come up with some answers, the Chief sure as hell is gonna be on our backs. We're interrupted by a knock on the door from the coroner, Charley Fredricks.

"Good to see you both," Fredricks says. "Martin, I heard you dodged a bullet."

"I'll have to dodge one from the Chief unless we make some progress on these murders. What's up Charley?"

"Remember when Cynthia Fleming was murdered, and you found a medical record in her copier? I decided to examine it. I remembered you were bothered by the fact it was left behind."

"Yeah, we found out the medical record was for someone who moved to another dialysis center. At first, I assumed it was incriminatin' evidence, 'cause it proved Fleming had taken the T through Z files home, and her killer musta taken them. Thought it was odd that the killer missed it after such a thorough search of the apartment. Then, I thought he could have planted it there. Made it look like Fleming was killed 'cause she was copyin' AKLC medical records. But I discounted that possibility because it ran counter to the thrust of the investigation. Just the same, it stuck in my mind."

"Your instincts were good, Martin. I examined the medical record for DNA. Some of the DNA on the medical record matches the DNA from the money they found in Blake Jensen's house."

"Are you saying Blake Jensen killed the Fleming girl?" D'Angelo asks.

"No. Blake Jensen is not a match. But whoever gave Blake Jensen this money probably killed Cynthia Fleming."

"How do you get DNA off paper money?" D'Angelo asks. "Gotta be a lotta different people who handle dollar bills."

"Used to be we couldn't do it, but we're not talking about fingerprints on an ink pad. We now have touch DNA. When people handle money, they can leave a residue of skin cells, especially if they're squeezing it between their thumb and forefinger to count it out. We use an electrostatic detection device to procure a sample. It can take as little as seven or eight microscopic cells for us to get a DNA profile. Everyone's DNA contains genetic markers, and analysts use thirteen of those markers for comparisons. Although people may have several markers in common, no cases have ever been found in which people share all thirteen markers, except identical twins. Hence, each person has their own unique profile. The process became well known from the Jon Benet Ramsey case in 1966. You remember the six-year-old girl who was murdered? They suspected her parents, but they were able to take touch DNA from her underwear, and it didn't match the DNA of her parents."

"So how did you discover the match?"

"Whoever gave Jensen the money must have been counting it from a stack of bills. Like any right-handed person who counts money, he was holding the stack down with his left thumb as he removed each bill from the stack with his right thumb; just like you would deal from a deck of cards. The same print appears on each bill at about the same place. Jensen also counted the stack, so we have a similar set of his

DNA prints. On a lark, I decided to compare the DNA on the medical record with those on the money. I came up with a matching profile, and it wasn't Jensen's."

"Great work, Charley, but we still don't know who gave Jensen the money. The Gator said Jensen was too small to do such a big drug deal. Moreno said the same thing. Of course, Moreno mighta done a drug deal with Blake and coulda been coverin' up his own crime."

"It could be Moreno," D'Angelo says. "Say Neil Jensen needs $200,000 for the kidney. He looks flush, but he don't got that much cash. He knows Blake deals and he's got enough cash to back a good size deal."

"I see where you're goin', Tony. Let's play this out. Suppose the Jensen's plan a drug deal with Moreno, who sends Miguel Sanchez to Mexico to make the buy. Sanchez is an amateur and somehow fucks up and gets himself killed. Moreno has to rescue the deal. He gets caught but bribes himself out. It ends up costin' more than he figured, and the Jensen's get the short end. Neal Jensen threatens Moreno. Maybe he tells Moreno he'll be an anonymous informer and has hidden a letter that will implicate Moreno if anything happens to him—like something he saw on TV. He thinks he can intimidate Moreno, but Jensen is naïve. He's used to dealin' with businessmen and knows nothin' about street violence. Moreno feels threatened and snuffs him out without a second thought."

"Could happen," D'Angelo says. Moreno might think Fleming knows, or she might have the letter. He goes to search her place and ends up killin' her. But why take the medical records?"

"Good question, Tony. Let's think about that. Moreno is a dialysis tech who worked at AKLC. He knows it's illegal for those medical records to be taken outta the office, and he also knows about Jensen's failed transplant. It wouldn't take a brain surgeon to figure out that Fleming was trying to investigate AKLC for killin' her fiancé. He figures that the presence of the medical records makes it look like AKLC killed Fleming. But if they did, they would never leave the incriminatin' evidence. So, Moreno takes the records, but places one under the cover of the copier, knowin' the police will find it and think the killer overlooked it."

"It sounds possible," Fredricks interjects. "But if Blake got his share of the drug money, why was he killed?"

"Blake must have suspected that Moreno knocked off his old man," D'Angelo says. "Maybe he blackmails Moreno, thinkin' he can protect himself. Moreno comes up with one or more payments before a good opportunity to kill Jensen. Blake is such a low life that everyone believes it was just another drug murder."

"Everybody except my friend Martin," Fredricks says. "He interrogates Moreno and scares the shit outta him. Moreno worries that Martin has the goods on him. He tails Martin to the deli and waits from a distance with a high-powered rifle."

"Right," D'Angelo says. "But he misses. Or maybe he figures he made the hit since both of 'em were down on the sidewalk."

"And get this," I tell them. "Moreno has no idea how lucky it is that he hits Herman Seidelman, again makin' the crime seem like it was associated with AKLC. It's totally speculative, but it all fits together. There's a ton of hunches and no hard evidence, but it's the only scenario that ties in every one of the murders. If Moreno made a payment to Blake and left his fingerprints on the money, we got our man. It's enough for us to get a search warrant, arrest Moreno again, and bring him in."

Chapter 40

Martin

The next mornin', the sun is barely up when I crank up the Taurus. I meet D'Angelo in the station parking lot, and we drive to Moreno's house in Fall River. Two squad cars accompany us for backup. Few people are out at this hour, and the neighborhood is quiet. Must be garbage day as barrels line the sidewalk, half of 'em overflowin'. Fall River don't got those trucks with mechanical arms that pick up the barrels, so people still have the old steel trash cans dented and rusty with age. I park the Taurus in front of Moreno's two-family and make a mental note to have my guys search his trash.

We walk up the old wooden steps and knock loudly on the door. "Police, Moreno! We got a warrant for your arrest. Open the door, and don't try anythin' stupid." We got our Glocks drawn and safeties off. We stand to the sides of the door, avoidin' any direct line of fire. There's no answer and we try again, not knowin' if Moreno is away or just pretendin'. "Whaddya think, Tony? Should we break down the door?"

"He could be armed, waiting for us to come in. Let's call downstairs for backup."

Four backup cops join us outside the door. "We got a search warrant, Moreno," I yell through the closed door. "We got backup, and we're comin' in. Don't get yourself hurt."

The door is bolt locked, and we need crowbars to break it down. If Moreno is armed, he could fire through the door, but even Moreno must know that shootin' cops is not a great idea. When the door splinters open, we go in with guns drawn. It ain't a big place, and we been here once before. We fan out, each takin' different rooms and quickly realize the place is empty. I notice a red light on the kitchen stove. Burners are off, but the stove is hot and the stovetop warnin' light is still on. Moreno musta left minutes before we got here. Maybe he heard us comin'. D'Angelo calls from the other room. "Martin, he left his laptop on. I moved the mouse and the screen had Google Map directions: 49 Whistler Drive in Cohasset."

"Shit, Tony, that's Neil Jensen's house. We were right. Moreno was somehow involved with the Jensens. Sheila Jensen could be in trouble. Maybe she knew too much. May have known more than she told us. If that's where he's headin', we better get over there fast. He ain't goin' there to make a condolence call. Moreno has been on a spree, disposin' of anyone who could expose him. The stove is still hot, so he's only minutes ahead of us."

I tell the backup team to stay while investigators arrive to search the apartment. Can't be positive where Moreno went, and he could be comin' back. I'm hopin' the forensic team will find somethin' that places Moreno at the scene of one a the murders. "Make sure they search those trash barrels before they're picked up," I yell through the car window as we drive off toward Cohasset.

It's an hour's drive without traffic, but already the mornin' rush has started. Route 24 north is slow approachin' the junction of 93. A short distance down 93, the highway splits, the left fork leadin' to downtown Boston and the right to the south shore. By now, the fork to Boston is backed up, so Boston drivers, famous for their nastiness, drive up the ride side intendin' to cut in to the left fork at the last second. As a result, the right fork to the south shore and Cohasset is jammed, even though few drivers are goin' there. Fortunately, we have emergency lights strapped to the roof.

A half hour later, we turn into Jensen's street. A car is parked in front. Don't know if it belongs to Moreno. "Good we got here fast," Tony says. "Hope we're not too late."

I'm filled with a sense of dread as I get outta the car. I recall my previous interviews with Sheila Jensen. Never liked her. She was bitter about her husband's affair with Cynthia Fleming, convinced that Fleming was after Neal's money and plied him with sex to sucker him into payin' $200,000 for his kidney. I'm confident Shiela Jensen was wrong. Never thought Fleming was that kinda woman. Regardless, nobody deserves to be murdered, and I got an awful fear that I'm about to find Sheila Jensen's dead body sprawled on her expensive carpet; possibly where I spilled my coffee.

"I'm gonna call for backup, Tony, but we can't wait. I'll take the front a the house. You take the back. If Moreno's in there, we don't want him to escape. I'll ring the doorbell. If no one answers, I'll try callin' him out. If he still don't answer, we gotta break in. Be careful. This is one dangerous son-of-a-bitch."

I hold my service revolver in my right hand and ring the doorbell with my left. Nobody answers, and I try again. Silence. Car is still out front, so the chances of a confrontation are real. I step back and yell into the house. "Moreno, we know you're in there. We don't want a confrontation. Come out with your hands up. You won't get hurt. We got backup on their way. You don't got a chance once the sharpshooters get here. Don't be stupid. You're a young guy. You don't want to get yourself killed."

Nothin'. We can't wait outside for backup while Moreno could be in there with Sheila. It could already be too late. Of course, he could use her as a hostage. What would I do if Moreno threatened to kill her? But there is no time to dither. "Moreno, I'm comin' in," I yell through an open window. "Don't do anythin' stupid."

Neighbors are beginnin' to step outside to see what's goin' on. I grasp the front door handle, and it turns in my hand. House is unlocked. I step inside holdin' my gun straight out in front a me. There's a hall closet. I yank the door open and dodge to the side. Nothin'. Just coats.

Then I hear a sound from the back. A scrapin' noise. A door movin'. I duck behind the closet door. "Who's there? Police! Put your hands up."

"It's me, Martin, don't shoot," D'Angelo says. "The back door to the kitchen was unlocked. No one's in the kitchen."

"Guess people in this town don't have to lock their doors. Let's check out the resta the downstairs."

Edgin' around corners, we go in opposite directions, searchin' the livin' room, dinin' room, and den. House is eerily quiet. "Maybe no one's here," D'Angelo says. "They coulda left in another car."

"Don't know. Gotta look upstairs. Could be a sittin' duck on the stairway. I'll start up, Tony. Cover me from behind."

There are maybe a dozen stairs to the second floor. Every step gives more exposure. What would Moreno do if he is waitin' upstairs? Would he risk a shootout on the stairway? He'd probably rather hide and wait 'til he was behind us. Then, he could shoot us in the back. I start cautiously up the stairs. When I reach the top, I signal D'Angelo to follow. "Tony, check out the rooms on the left. I'll go right."

Door to the first room on the right is open. A bedroom. Don't see anyone inside. Moreno could be crouched behind the bed or hidin' in the closet. If he was behind the bed, he could already have gotten off the first shot. I enter with my gun pointed forward and check behind and under the bed. No one there. I jerk open the closet door, steppin' to the side, pinnin' myself against the wall. No sound. No movement. I peek around the open door into the closet. Blouses, pants, skirts, neatly on hangers. Nobody there.

There's a double door at the end of the hallway. Probably the master bedroom. That's where I want to go, but on the way, there's an open door to a bathroom. Appears empty, but the shower curtain is drawn. I picture all the movies where a dead body lies bleedin' in the bathtub. I picture Sheila Jensen's body crumpled in the tub and shove the shower curtain aside. Nothin'.

"Nada on that side," D'Angelo says, as he joins me, and we approach the double-door at the end of the hall.

"You hear that?" I ask. I motion D'Angelo to be quiet, lean closer to the door, and hear the sound again. A muffled voice. What's it mean? Moreno wouldn't make any noise. It could be Sheila being held hostage, possibly gagged, or maybe lettin' out a dyin' breath.

"Come out Moreno! Hands Up. We know you're in there."

Nothin'.

"Last chance Moreno. We're comin' in. You got thirty seconds to make yourself known. Don't be stupid."

The time passes. I motion to D'Angelo with my leg, suggestin' we both kick open the double-doors, him on the right, me on the left. Guns ready, we give each other one last look and kick hard at the doors. Left door flies open. Right door hits somethin' and stops halfway. I can see from my side that a body is stoppin' the door. My heart sinks. We were too slow. We're too late. I'm prepared to see Sheila Jensen lyin' dead, sprawled on the bedroom rug.

But it's not Sheila. It's a male, and it takes only a second to recognize Jose Moreno. And behind Moreno, Sheila Jensen, gagged and tied to a chair. Thank God alive.

D'Angelo checks Moreno. His eyes are turned up in his head, very dead. I remove the gag from Sheila Jensen. Her face is swollen and got several bruises. She recognizes me and starts to wail. "He killed my son. He killed Blake. I was such a fool," she wails and breaks down sobbin'.

I kneel beside her chair, unfasten the ties and try to talk to her, but she's hysterical. "Please, Mrs. Jensen, can you tell us who you are talkin' about?"

"Derrick. Derrick Hanson. He killed Blake. After you told me about Blake's money, I found large amounts missing from my accounts. He denied having anything to do with Blake or the money.

Told me Blake got killed in a bad drug deal. He demanded to know how I knew about Blake's money. Who told me? I told him you were here questioning me. He killed my son. It's my fault. Ooooooh, I thought he loved me. I was such a fool."

Sheila Jensen is sobbing. It's difficult to get her to talk. "Was it Derrick who shot this man and tied you up? Please Mrs. Jensen. Time is critical."

"Yes, Derrick said someone was coming to talk to him. He said it was private business and asked me to stay downstairs in the den. I heard the person come in and go upstairs with Derrick. Then, I heard a loud noise. I ran upstairs fearing Derrick had been harmed, but Derrick came out with a wild look on his face. He hit me and tied me up. He never cared about me. He was just after my money. I was an idiot."

"Do you have any idea where Derrick went?"

"He said he was leaving the country. Told me I would never see him again. I was terrified; tied to the chair next to a dead body. I pleaded with him to let me go, but he said he couldn't. He gagged me. Said someone would rescue me. That was bullshit. He didn't care."

"Do you know what kinda car Derrick was drivin'?"

"A Toyota Rav 4—red. I saw him drive up to the house."

"You know the license plate number by any chance?"

"No, sorry."

"That's okay. Tony, put out an all points for a red Toyota Rav 4, headin' outta Cohasset, probably on the way to Logan airport."

"On it, Martin."

Sirens scream outside as the Cohasset police arrive at the house. Although we called for backup, we're in plain clothes and don't want to be mistaken for assailants. I run to the top of the stairs and call down just as the police barge in. "Boston Detectives, we're upstairs. Everythin's under control. One person down."

Several officers climb the stairway, guns in hand despite the reassurances. This might be the biggest crime they've ever seen in Cohasset, and I try to calm them down. "Detective Goldberg, Boston Police, and my partner Tony D'Angelo. We got a homicide, and the perp has fled. The homeowner was tied and gagged but is okay. We know the identity of both the victim and the killer and have an all-points with the state police. It's your jurisdiction, but I think you better secure the scene for forensics."

"Thanks detective," the officer replies. "We'll take a look. You guys okay?"

"Yeah, but we got to get outta here and help find the son-of-a-bitch. Thanks for gettin' here so fast."

We begin the drive from Cohasset, but I remember the traffic jam we passed comin' the other way. Now it's the heart of rush hour and traffic is worse. D'Angelo checks his traffic app and finds out there is a monumental tie-up on the southeast expressway. An 18-wheeler from the Stop and Shop warehouse jackknifed and tipped over. Apples, oranges, and watermelons lie strewn across all four lanes of highway. Traffic is stopped waitin' for the road to be cleared, and for the trailer to be righted and towed away.

Instead of takin' the highway, we turn toward route 3A. The old road is called the Southern Artery 'cause it used to be the most direct way to commute from Boston's south shore before the expressway. Traffic is light as we cross the Fore River Bridge between the towns of Weymouth and Quincy. Instead of chancin' the traffic in downtown Quincy, we turn on to Quincy Shore Drive and drive along Wollaston Beach, just a stone's throw from Blake Jensen's former residence. From there, we take Morrissey Boulevard into the city. As we approach the Expo center, D'Angelo says we're past the truck accident and can get back on the expressway.

Meanwhile, we've been listenin' to police radio. Two helicopters have been deployed over the expressway. With every inch of the expressway jammed solid for miles, there isn't much the police can do but surveil from above. Hanson may already be in the city tunnels, but because we detoured around the accident, we're probably close behind.

The police have set up a checkpoint at the far exit of the Williams tunnel, the one that connects to the airport. They will pull over any red Toyota SUV. Police will also monitor cars comin' outta the other tunnel exits such as route 1A goin' to the north shore. If one a those red cars belongs to Hanson, he won't be able to exit the tunnels without bein' stopped. Incredibly, just as we approach the entrance to the tunnel, the portal lights turn red and two patrolmen halt all incomin' traffic.

We got our emergency lights on the car roof, and the patrolman comes over to my side window. "Tunnel is temporarily closed," he says.

Through the open window, I show him my identification. "Boston Police Detective Goldberg. We were the ones that called this in. We're pursuing the fugitive. Let us through."

He pauses and checks with his partner. They decide to let us through. "We were just notified that a red Toyota is stopped in the tunnel 1.3 miles from this entrance," he tells us. "That would be around Dewey Square. The driver was seen running from the car. We're emptying the inbound side of the tunnel, letting all the cars that are in it pass through and stopping everyone else from entering. Once it's empty police will be able to drive from the north, the wrong way on the empty side, where he left the Toyota. Good luck."

We enter the tunnel and D'Angelo asks, "How do they know where he's at?"

"They gave me a tour once," I tell him. "The Big Dig tunnels got the most sophisticated traffic control center in the world. They got over 400 closed circuit TV cameras that send live video to the Operations

Control Center. The center has a wall with a ninety-inch TV and over fifty video monitors. You go in that fuckin room and you think you're in Mission Control in Houston."

"Why would he abandon his car?" D'Angelo asks.

"He must have been listenin' to the police band on his smartphone and heard the police were checkin' cars at every tunnel exit. Remember, Hanson worked construction on the Big Dig. He knows the tunnels have miles of vent shafts, storm drains, and emergency stairways. The son of a bitch is armed and dangerous, and he knows the territory. That must be why he stopped at Dewey Square."

"Why is that?"

I got less than a minute to explain it to Tony. "Picture this," I say. "Imagine a four-decker sandwich. The bottom layer, 120 feet underneath the ground, is the four-lane highway we're on right now. To build this highway, they tunneled underneath an existin' eighty-for-year-old subway line. Not an old abandoned subway, but the MBTA Red Line, which was carryin' thousands of people every day and was roarin' through the tunnel just over their heads. Then, they built a third subway tunnel, the Silver Line, thirty-six inches above the Red Line tunnel. Finally, they constructed a transit station at ground level above the roof of the third tunnel. Besides that, this highway runs right underneath Dewey Square, tunnelin' directly underneath city skyscrapers and the busiest intersection in the city of Boston. So, there's a maze of stairways, vent shafts, and passageways, and Hanson knows them all."

"Holy shit, what a mess. I hope there's police comin' behind us."

"Not right away, Tony. We were the last car in before the tunnel was closed. The traffic's backed up at the entrance and will totally clog the highway, delayin' police who could otherwise follow us. The only other way for the police to get in fast would be to come from the north, driving the wrong way on the northbound side of the tunnel. But they can't do that until the remainin' traffic gets through and the tunnel empties."

Just as I finish the explainin', we reach the abandoned Toyota. Clearly, we're the first ones there. The tunnel is empty and eerie with no other cars. I pull up next to the Toyota and tell D'Angelo to move out. "Hurry, check all the doors and vents on the walkway. You take the left side; I'll take the right. Have your gun ready."

I run down the elevated walkway on the side of the road, checkin' every door and vent. In the distance, I hear police sirens at the other end. Suddenly, I come to a door that's slightly ajar. Hanson could be waitin' on the other side. I reach out with one leg and kick the door open, quickly movin' back and pinnin' myself against the tunnel wall with my Glock ready. When no one appears, I know I must enter the room.

Chapter 41

Cassandra

After Martin left the night before last, I tossed and turned in bed with conflicting emotions. It was well into the morning before I finally fell asleep. Somehow, I managed to get Keri to school on time, and then I left immediately for the hospital. I spent the entire day there, mostly in the surgical waiting room, leafing through outdated magazines and watching distraught family members worrying about their loved ones. The room was filled with anxiety and tension. Few places could have been less pleasant to spend my day. Nevertheless, I was not going to pass up any possibility, no matter how remote, of talking to Herman Seidelman. If he died, I would lose my most valuable witness. He could be the key to prosecute AKLC and the entire ring of international kidney traders.

After pressing my FBI credentials, the surgeon in charge of the case agreed to speak with me. "It was a difficult operation," he said, "but he is likely to pull through. One of the bullets damaged his lung and lodged close to his heart. The surgery was delicate, but I'm optimistic that he will recover. We have moved him to the surgical ICU. You won't be able to see him until he gains some strength. Very likely, that won't be until tomorrow. I suggest you go home and get some sleep and come back tomorrow morning."

Despite his advice, I waited at the hospital until well after midnight. I was unable to see Seidelman and finally took the surgeon's suggestion and drove home. I returned to the hospital by 8:30 the next morning, having only managed about three hours of sleep. I'm fortunate to have a babysitter who can pick Keri up after school.

I spent the morning and early afternoon sitting near the ICU, and it was an arduous wait. One of the patients in the ICU had passed away. His wife was in the waiting room alone and was overcome with grief. Seeing there was no one else to offer comfort, I went over and sat with her. The woman had been married for fort-two years, and her husband was stricken with a brain aneurism. Her two grown children lived out of state and had hoped to see their father before he passed, but they hadn't made it in time. I held her and comforted her for more than an hour until one of her children arrived. Thc ordeal left me exhausted and emotionally drained. Nevertheless, I was not going anywhere until I could speak with Herman Seidelman.

Now, I am still waiting, pacing back and forth through the long corridors of the Massachusetts General Hospital. The General, as it is called, has the busiest level one trauma center in the state, treating an average of 2,500 patients per year. With 950 beds, it is the largest hospital in New England and the main teaching hospital of the Harvard University Medical School. *U.S. News and World Report* has rated the hospital number one in the entire country. If Herman Seidelman has any chance to survive, he has landed in the right place.

After a seemingly interminable wait, a nurse finally approaches me in the hallway. "Mr. Seidelman is awake and reasonably alert," she says. "I know you have been waiting a long time, but he has survived quite an ordeal and needs to conserve his strength. I will let you see him for five minutes. Please be considerate of his condition."

I walk down the hallway to where an armed policeman is standing guard. Given the prior attack, I had requested a security detail to guard the room. I show my identification and quietly enter the room. Seidelman is propped up in bed hooked up to monitors and intravenous tubes. His face is drawn, his skin pasty and pale, but he appears conscious and aware. I approach Seidelman's bedside and bend over to speak to him. "Hello, Herman. Do you know who I am?"

"Yes, of course, Ms. Ford. I tried to help your daughter, but you lied to me and caused much trouble."

"I work for the FBI, Herman. I was doing my job."

"Your daughter would have a new kidney if you had not deceived us."

"I also could have been killed."

"I do not work with killers, Ms. Ford. My work saves lives."

"I'm sure you believe that, Herman, but the law does not see it that way. I'm here to help you. If you cooperate with the FBI, you can get out of this predicament much easier."

"Sorry, Ms. Ford. I am not interested."

"Herman, we have more than enough evidence to convict you of illegally selling organs. You are not an old man. You have many years ahead of you. You don't want to sit in an American jail after you recover. The FBI would rather break an international ring of organ traders than have you rotting in jail. You can make a deal and go back to Israel. We want to know who you work with, who tipped you off to the sting. We need to know if we have a mole inside the FBI."

"You are wasting your time, Ms. Ford. I will not inform on the people I work with. They are not bad people. They have saved many lives. Your laws are outdated. Perhaps even cruel. If I must, I will take my punishment, but I will not rat on my associates."

"Don't be a fool, Herman. Do you think those people you call your associates would serve jail time for you? Do you think they would even hesitate to..."

"Ms. Ford, your time is up. Mr. Seidelman needs his rest. You will have to see him another time."

"Think it over, Herman. I don't think you're a bad person. You can do the right thing and save your butt at the same time. Don't be a *schmuck*."

Chapter 42

Martin

Whaddya think goes through your mind when you gotta burst into a dangerous room? Is there a serial killer waitin' with a gun pointed at the door? Will you take one step and be struck by a hail of bullets? Before you see anything, before you hear anything, before you even get a glimpse of the killer—will your life be over? You will have no second chance. You will have nothin'. Darkness. Forever. You will never see your daughter Meredith, your friend Cassandra, your colleagues on the force. They will come to your funeral. They will make speeches. A few may shed tears. They will say you were a good man. A brave man. One that died in the line of duty. It will not comfort you, for you will be only a memory.

But your mind doesn't work that way. You may have those thoughts when you lie awake at night, unable to sleep. You might daydream them alone at your desk on a dull afternoon. But durin' a confrontation—a firefight—you got no stray thoughts. Your adrenalin is coursin'. Your heart is pumpin'. Every nerve endin' on alert. Every sense on edge. Fear is somethin' you think about afterward. To an onlooker, you look fearless and brave. But you're on automatic pilot. Your trainin' kicks in; your sense of self-preservation; your fight or flight response. You ain't got the time or the luxury to stop and think.

That's my state as I gotta enter the room. Holdin' my Glock chin high, straight-armed in front of me, I step into the doorway rotatin' my gun right to left, checkin' the corners, the ceilin', the floor, lookin' for other doors. I see nothin'. Hear nothin'. No one's shot at me. The room is empty. I exhale. It's simply a bare, unused room.

I hurry back out to the tunnel. Police still haven't arrived. Along the sides of the tunnel there's wall vents. Fresh air gotta be constantly pumped into the tunnels to maintain the air quality. Huge fans pump the air down giant ducts and out through the smaller vents. Suddenly, I see a piece of paper blowin' outta one a the vents. It's torn, but I examine it and see it's part of a boarding pass with today's date. I call back to D'Angelo. "I'm goin' in this vent. Wait here and bring help when they arrive."

The vent's narrow, and I'm big. I know all the small wall vents are connected to larger ducts, but I can barely squeeze through. I hold my revolver in front of me and shimmy forward in the dark usin' my elbows and feet to push through. It feels like the "low-crawl" from army basic trainin'. I gotta keep my gun aimin' forward. Hanson could be waitin' where the vent connects to a larger duct. If I see any movement at the end, I gotta shoot first. Otherwise, I may never live to get off a shot.

There must be lights in the larger duct, 'cause there's some faint glow in the distance. My pants snag on a sharp piece of metal, and I hear them rip as I crawl forward. I feel blood runnin' down my leg, but I can't worry about it. The light is closer now, perhaps twenty feet away, when I hear the echo of distant footsteps. Hanson is bigger than me and must have had trouble gettin' through the vent, so I'm not far behind. The footsteps mean he musta reached the larger duct where he can stand and run. The clap of his shoes echo as he runs down the air supply duct.

Squeezin' through, I finally reach the larger duct. I hold my gun out and peek around the corner to see if Hanson is in sight. The duct curves, however, and I can't see him. Then, a new sound reaches my ears. Steppin' into the larger duct the wind hits me in the face. There are over 200 giant fans that blow air into the Big Dig tunnels, and one must sit at the end of this duct. The system to vent the tunnels is no less sophisticated than the rest a this giant project. As the traffic builds toward rush hour, and the exhaust accumulates, the output of the fans automatically increases to vent the tunnels and keep enough fresh air. Runnin' down the duct toward the fan, a twenty mile per hour headwind slows my progress. I got no idea what waits for me at the end. If there is no way out, Hanson may be crouchin' at the end, aimin' his gun, waitin' for me to appear. But as I round the last curve, no one's in sight.

Just before the end of the duct, the fan blows my hair straight back and nearly tears the clothes from my body. I see a metal door and approach with caution, aware that Hanson knows the territory and I don't. I'm like a blind man chasin' someone with perfect sight. Once again, I kick a door open and retreat against the wall. No shots. Nothin' happens. Inside the door is a steel staircase. Hanson's footsteps echo on the stairs high above. The stairway winds upwards, turnin' at 90-degree angles, with landin's every eight steps. I pause. Is it safe to go up? I consider my predicament. If we are directly beneath each other, Hanson can't shoot down through several grates of metal stairs. The bullets will get deflected. But if I'm goin' up on the opposite side, he might be able to get a clear shot.

For the first time, I consider givin' up the chase and waitin' for help. I don't know what lies at the top a the stairs, but I know Hanson could be lookin' down, waitin' for me to become an easy target. Then again, the stairway must lead somewhere, and Hanson could escape and be a mortal threat to anyone he encounters. He could take hostages or simply dispose of anyone in his way. I decide to climb the first few levels and pursue him as best I can.

Startin' from 120 feet below the ground, it's like climbin' an eight-story buildin'. I take the first two tiers, quickly runnin' up the stairs and then waitin' on each landin', pressed flush against the wall. I'm overweight. I'm outta shape. I'm pantin'. I remember meetin' Hanson at Carson Beach. Guy was in great shape. Lives at the gym. Probably not even winded. I listen for his movements over my raspy breathin', but hear nothin'. As I run toward the third tier, two shots ring out. The bullets ricochet, tat-tat-tat, off the steel staircase and concrete walls soundin' like machine gun fire. Fearin' I'm in Hanson's sight, I climb to the fourth tier, hopin' to be directly below him, protected by the steel stair grates. A bullet whizzes by my neck and another grazes my ankle, probably from a ricochet. I get no chance to fire off a shot.

Pressed against the wall on the fourth tier, all is still. Again, I assess my situation. I'm not far below Hanson, but if I try to go up any further, I'm bound to be exposed. For similar reasons, Hanson can't come down. I wait for him to make the next move. A few seconds pass and I hear a scrapin' sound, like a steel door openin', that echoes down the stairway. And then, I hear the roar. A subway train is hurtlin' through the tunnel not far above my head. My God, I realize, there must be an entrance to the red-line tracks.

Cautiously, I climb the stairway, knowin' Hanson might still be waitin' at the top. More likely, however, he has fled through the door. He must expect reinforcements are comin', and his only chance is to get away. Just the same, I can't take any chances. I climb to each landin' as fast I can, then rest, pressed against the wall, tryin' to avoid any sight line from above. With only two or three landin's to go, I miss a step and fall face first on the metal stairs, my forehead bangin' against the steel grate. Blood runs from my forehead, but all I can think of is my own death. Sprawled on the steps, I'm such an easy target, a ten-year-old could kill me with a .22. Sadly, my last thoughts are not about the life I've lived or the people I've loved. I don't see my life flash before me. Instead, I'm pissed at myself for bein' such a big, clumsy, oaf.

Seconds pass. My teeth unclench. My shoulders ease. I breathe. I lower my arms that were coverin' my head. I am still alive. Luckily, Hanson must have already fled through the door. Blood is oozin' from my forehead, drippin' into my right eye. But I got no time to spare. I press my hand against the wound and continue up the stairs.

The steel door is partially open, the third doorway I must negotiate. This one can't be kicked open. It's too big. With my back pressed against the door, I slither toward the openin' until I can see the subway tunnel and the tracks runnin' off to my right into the distance. I see no one. Lookin' down to the left is more difficult. Slowly, I creep to the end of the door, where I can lean my head around and follow the tracks leadin' left. No one in sight there either.

This is not a station. There is no platform to stand on. A narrow ribbon of walkway, little more than a ledge, runs parallel alongside and above the tracks. The ledge is not wide enough to protect me from an oncomin' train, but every thirty feet, the wall of the tunnel has a person-size indentation built to protect transit workers in case of emergency.

Not knowin' which way to go, I listen and hear footsteps to my right. With my gun aimed forward, I begin walkin' down the narrow ledge, listenin' for Hanson's footsteps, but all I can hear is the faint sound of wind blowin' through the tunnel. As the sound gets louder, I suddenly realize it's not only wind. It's wind forced forward by an oncomin' train. Now, I'm too far to get back to the doorway. The next indent is fifteen feet down the walkway, and I run for my life. If I slip off the edge, I'll be carnage beneath the tracks. The blood from my forehead seeps into my right eye. The train pushes the air through the tunnel, howlin' like a storm against my back. The wheels of the old trolley cars screech against the rails. The sound reverberates through the tunnel reaching a crescendo as the train slaps the tail end of my jacket just as I squeeze into the indentation. I am still alive.

The back of the train passes drawing air, whooshing behind it. The noise fades into the distance. I peek out, watchin' the lights of the rear car disappear down the tunnel. A shot rings out, shatterin' the concrete just past my indent. I press my back against the wall, and try to suck in my stomach so it doesn't stick out into the open. All is quiet. I stick my head barely out of the indent, just for an instant, and quickly bring it back in, but I see nothin'. I wait, listenin' intently, and then, peekin' out again, I see Hanson's arm move out from his indent with his gun. I fire. The shot misses. The arm retracts. It feels like World War I with vertical trenches.

Neither of us can safely move, but I got the advantage. We both know help is on the way. Hanson can't stay where he is. A series of shots whizzes by, forcin' me against the back a the indent. Hanson is out of his indent and runnin'. He runs and fires at the same time, tryin' to keep me pinned until he can reach the next indent. I get off a coupla shots, but duckin' in and out, tryin' not to expose myself, I can't get a steady aim. Now, I am ninety feet behind, and I hear the wind and then the distant sound of another train. The cars roar past, inches from my belly. As the first car approaches Hanson, he needs to back against his indent, givin' me the opportunity to run to the next one. The last car passes Hanson, and I still got ten feet to go. I fire continuously, forcin' Hanson to stay protected inside his indent, even as he fires off a couple of errant shots.

Again, it's eerily quiet. The light from the staircase is well behind us, and the tunnel is nearly dark, lit only by the faint glow of a green traffic signal further down the track. A dampness fills the air, and the near century-old concrete walls smell of age and decay. Seconds pass. The silence is broken by a large rat, scamperin' between the tracks, huntin' for the occasional morsel of garbage thrown from a train. Then, another sound. The clankin' of boots on the steel staircase back in the distance. D'Angelo has sent help.

I carefully lean outta my indent just before Hanson does the same. I fire a shot and hear Hanson curse. It mighta hit his arm or shoulder. The wind picks up, indicatin' another train in the distance, the third in a short time. It must be a busy hour or else the hopelessly incompetent

MBTA has suddenly improved its service. Hanson knows he gotta keep going. He repeats his last move, firin' back at me, forcin' me to take cover, as he runs toward the next indent. Hanson must figure he's pretty safe, 'cause he can hear the train comin' and knows I will only have seconds before havin' to squeeze back into my indent. Ahead of the train, the wind gusts through the tunnel. The old cars screech against the metal rails. Then, just above the din, I hear an agonizin' scream. I peek out and see Hanson has fallen off the ledge onto the tracks. The noise intensifies. The train is bearin' down. Reachin' out from my indent, I frantically wave my arms, hopin' the conductor can see, but within seconds the train is upon me and I huddle back against the tunnel wall. The train passes, only inches away from my gut, which I am suckin' in with all my strength. The conductor spots Hanson who I can now see wavin' wildly on the tracks. He hits the emergency brakes. The sudden shriek of brakes is like an ice pick penetratin' my eardrums. As the train screeches and skids to a stop, I can see the passengers in the rear car thrown from their seats and tumblin' to the floor. Screams echo from inside the car. Up ahead, the conductor jumps from the train on to the ledge and peers down under the car. But it is too late. The train was too close. It could not possibly have stopped in time. Someone will have the grisly work of retrievin' all the body parts that will be torn, crushed, blood-soaked, shattered, and strewn haphazardly between the rails.

Chapter 43

Martin

I emerge from the tunnels bone-weary tired. My pants are damp and filthy. My shirt sweaty, blood-stained, and stuck to my back. My shoes wet and muddy. The bullet that grazed my ankle has left my sock damp with blood. A jagged cut from the metal stairway runs across my forehead, and the dried blood has coagulated above my right eye. Bruises show on my arms and face. If I sat next to you in a bar, you would slide down a couple of seats. After the adrenaline rush, after the life-threatenin' encounter, I am totally spent and would love to be able to rest.

But I can't. Cassandra left a message that she was waitin' to question Seidelman at the hospital. No matter how tired, I'm doggedly determined to see the resta the case through. I drive directly to the Mass General Hospital and asks the woman at the reception desk for Seidelman's room number. She hesitates, lookin' at me like I'm some kinda vermin that's just risen out of a swamp. "Are you immediate family?" she asks, doubtfully. I show her my badge, and she rolls her eyes before reluctantly divulgin' the information.

I arrive at Herman Seidelman's room just as Cassandra's walkin' out. She looks nearly as tired as me. Says she's been awake for most of the last twenty-four hours. Her face is puffy, eyes red, hair matted. Her clothes are wrinkled and a coffee stain shows on her blouse.

"Holy shit, Martin. What happened to you? Are you alright?"

"Just a little banged up. Long story. You go first. Did you see Seidelman?"

"Yes. He's out of surgery and his prognosis is good. I just spoke with him, but the nurse would only give me a few minutes."

"What'd he say?"

"He's not ready to talk. I told him he was facing prosecution. I held out the possibility of letting him off and sending him back to Israel if he identified his associates. The guy is still in shock, but he is not stupid. No way he wants to spend most of his remaining years in an American jail. I think he'll come around, but not right away. It has to sink in."

"You ask how they found out about the sting?"

"Yes, but I didn't get anything. I can't explain it, but I have a positive feeling about him. I think he is basically a decent person, and he doesn't want to rat on the others. In the end, though, he will make the right decision—for him and for us. I intend to see him again tomorrow. Meanwhile, you look like shit, Martin. Tell me what happened."

"It was Derrick Hanson, Cat. He killed all of 'em. It was all about money, not kidneys. He even killed Jose Moreno."

"Is he in custody?"

"God's custody, or Satan's." I describe the chase through the vent pipes and tunnels. "He fell off the ledge right in front of an oncomin' train; a grisly demise."

"Not one he didn't deserve. He was Sheila Jensen's lover. Is that why he killed Neal Jensen?"

"It wasn't outta love. He was after her money all along. In the beginnin', he figured Neal didn't have long to live. Sheila would inherit the estate, and he would be on easy street. But Neal came back lookin' healthy with a new kidney, and he was threatenin' to disinherit his wife. Hanson decided not to wait."

"So, with Neal out of the way, why did he kill Fleming?"

"Blake Jensen was afraid that his father had written him and his mother outta the will and left everything to Fleming. Blake figured Fleming had the will, but his father probably wouldn't register it until after the divorce. Blake expressed his fear to his mother who later told Hanson. He ransacked Fleming's condo lookin' for the will. Whether he intended to kill her or was surprised by her comin' home, we'll never know."

"But Blake knew, didn't he Martin?"

"Right, and that's where Blake's money came from. He tried to blackmail Hanson, which was a fatal mistake. Hanson took money from Sheila's accounts and musta made a payment before he had a good opportunity to kill Blake."

"The guy turned into a serial killer. I guess after the first one, the others come easier. But Martin, how did Moreno get involved?"

"Moreno was Blake's friendly drug dealer, and Blake had a big mouth. Not only had he complained to his mother and Moreno about his father's will. He also told Moreno how Hanson was after his mother's money. Moreno realized all three murders couldn't be a coincidence. He wasn't sidetracked like us, worryin' about kidneys. There was only one person who could benefit, and that was Derrick Hanson."

"You're going to tell me that Moreno, the drug dealer, was not an upstanding citizen who immediately reported it to the police."

"Right again. He tried to make a deal with Hanson for a piece a Sheila's inheritance. He went to see Hanson at the Cohasset house. Musta underestimated how dangerous the guy was. Hanson shot him, tied Sheila to a chair and tried to fly outta the country with Sheila's money."

"Okay, Martin, but who fired the shots at the deli?"

"Musta been Hanson. Sheila had confronted him about money missin' from her account. She told him that I knew about Blake's money and had asked her where it came from. We'll know for sure if they find the weapon."

"Well, Martin, my theory about the case was all wrong. I was convinced that the kidney people had committed the murders. I wasn't sure about Blake. That looked like a drug killing. But Neil Jensen, Cynthia Fleming, and Miguel Sanchez were all tied into the kidney trade, and the deli shooting looked like an attempt to silence Herman Seidelman."

"I was wrong too, Cat. When Charley Fredricks discovered the DNA evidence that tied Blake and Fleming's murders together, we made up a scenario where Jose Moreno committed all the murders. Ironically, if we hadn't mistakenly got a warrant to search Moreno's apartment, Derrick Hanson would have escaped to Europe. Moreno figured it out before we did. Don't say much for our investigative skills."

"Shit no, Martin, but we still have work to do. We don't know who killed Miguel Sanchez, and whether it was connected to kidneys or drugs. Bradley Stone, Rony Cohnheim, Susan Landis, and Herman Seidelman have all been charged with conspiracy to sell human organs. We have direct evidence on Seidelman, so his case is straightforward. Unless he cooperates, he will go from the hospital to prison. The other cases will not be easy to prosecute. We need to work with the D.A. to build the evidentiary case. Hopefully, we can also identify and prosecute their associates on the other end."

Chapter 44

Cassandra

I have been dreading the debriefing since boarding the military jet back home. I worked until midnight last night preparing my notes for the meeting. Given the failure of the sting, everyone will be looking to pinpoint the blame. No one wants to be responsible for the failure. Least of all, me.

Of course, I have other concerns. How much do they know? Are they aware that the surgery schedule could have been changed? Do they have any suspicions about the decision I made? My presentation has to be accurate and believable in every detail. It cannot raise any doubts. There are still those in the Bureau who would like to see me fail. I have decided to report the offer to move up the scheduled surgery. I will tell them I declined because it was safer to stick to the original operational plan and not risk any changes in the timeline. Appearing composed and confident is important. I have handled many of these debriefings in the past, and this one should be no different.

The meeting is scheduled for 11:00 a.m. in Donaldson's office. I arrive five minutes early and check in with his new secretary. Donaldson goes through secretaries like the Italians go through prime ministers. I have heard some ugly rumors and don't doubt they are true. I sit in the waiting area outside his office, surprised that no one else is there. After a ten-minute wait, I am told to go in.

Looking around as I enter, I wonder why Donaldson is the only one in the room. The debriefings are generally in the Director's office, but a number of planners, analysts, and participants from the operation are normally present. "Good morning, sir. Am I early?"

"Good morning to you, Cassandra," he says, putting his arm on my shoulder, leading me to sit down. I want to swipe it off but try not to react. I ought to be used to it by now.

"I'll be doing the debriefing myself today," Donaldson explains. "So many of the others are tied up, we gave up trying to schedule a team. I am familiar with the details of the case, but I want you to start from the beginning and provide a chronological review of the entire operation."

Having done this many times previously and rehearsed this one at home, I am well prepared. I begin with our first conversation, when Donaldson called me in to his office and asked me to work undercover. Wanting to sound thorough and sincere, I admit to being conflicted, worried about involving my daughter in the operation. I describe the dialysis center and everything I learned about Stone, Cohnheim, and AKLC. I tell him about the meetings with Herman "Poleskey" and the financial arrangements for the kidney transplant. Occasionally, Donaldson interrupts with a question.

"Did Poleskey ever mention the names of anyone in India—like someone to contact if you had a problem?"

"No, everything seemed very compartmentalized," I answer.

I provide a lengthy description of the Apollo Transplant Institute and all the people I met in India. I explain that the clinical process went exactly as planned, which wasn't surprising given the efficiency of the whole operation. Then, I describe how the doctor offered to move up the time of the surgery. "I knew immediately that I didn't want to change the schedule," I tell Donaldson. "The team had done extensive planning, and any change could inject unforeseen elements. Besides, I couldn't be absolutely sure of their readiness to respond earlier than scheduled. At the same time, I realized that most people would probably seize the opportunity to get the transplant over with as soon as possible and be done with all the anxiety. So, I purposely hesitated, pretending I was uncertain, trying to make up my mind. Then, I politely declined the offer."

"So, you had no further contact with the doctor, is that correct?"

"That's right. After he left, I had a short consultation with the anesthesiologist and then took Keri back to the flat. I picked up some take-out for dinner, read her a story, and put her to bed. I went to sleep a couple of hours later. I was having a cup of coffee the next morning when I received your call. I knew I might be in danger and assumed a defensive position with my weapon. Thankfully, the back-up team arrived about ten minutes later. I think you know the rest better than I do. Do you want me to continue?"

"Cassandra, is that the whole story? Are you sure you didn't leave anything out?"

The comment alarms me. A seemingly unnecessary question delivered in an ominous manner. What's going on? I look directly into Donaldson's eyes, trying to discern any clue. "No sir," I tell him. "I made detailed notes. I am quite sure I've covered everything."

"Quite sure, you say. What about the calls from your phone at 7:01 and 7:40?"

"My God, did I leave those out?" I answer. My mind is racing. I have been trained to think fast. In my job, a couple of seconds could mean life or death. How does he know about those calls? How much does he know? I can feel his eyes boring in to me and have to come up with something fast.

"Sorry, Sir, those were so routine, I didn't think they were relevant. I had called Anish to confirm the time he was to pick me up. Keri was scheduled to undergo a couple of tests before the final pre-op. Anish wanted to confirm the times with the hospital and said he would call me right back. When he hadn't called forty minutes later, I called him back. I'm sorry. I should have included those calls in my notes, but since nothing changed, they hardly seemed significant."

"What did Anish say when you called him back, Cassandra?"

"I never reached him. There was something wrong with the phone."

"Something wrong? Your phone was okay when I called. What was the problem?"

"Not my phone—his. I got a recorded message saying his phone was no longer in service."

"No longer in service? That should have set off all kinds of alarms. You must have known immediately that something had gone wrong. How could you forget that?"

I'm fucked, is my immediate reaction. The son of a bitch knows. With every explanation, with every attempt to cover it up, I'm digging myself deeper. Shouldn't I know by now? You can't outfox the fox. "I can't explain it, sir. I was so afraid for my daughter—it's like traumatic stress. It's never happened to me before. It was such a frightful experience; my mind must have just wiped the details."

"Come clean, Cassandra," he says, with just the slightest grin on his face. I stare at him and realize I am in trouble, but I stick with my explanation.

"I told you my story, sir. I reported on every detail, but my memory failed me about the two telephone calls. In any event, they were insignificant. I have nothing more to add."

"Let me try to help with your memory failure. You see, we plan these operations very carefully. We leave nothing to chance. That is why we have recordings of all your telephone conversations. That is why your chief contact, Anish, was also being monitored."

"What? You spied on me! You didn't trust your own agent."

"We leave nothing to chance, Cassandra."

"You put me in an impossible position. You made me choose between my daughter's life and my investigation. You set me up to fail, and then you recorded my failure."

"Don't you think I knew that from the beginning?"

"Of course. Then why did you do it?"

"Thoroughness, Cassandra. Fail-safe planning. I consulted privately with several psychologists who perform occasional work for the Bureau. We were well aware that you might have to choose between your daughter and your mission. Given your predicament, and the fact that you were a single mother, the psychologists concluded that if the opportunity somehow arose, you would betray the Bureau and get your daughter the kidney."

"If you thought that, why did you go ahead?"

"Simple," he says, with that condescending look on his face. "Knowing what you were likely to do, we planned accordingly. You behaved exactly as expected. Everything was in place to execute the sting whether or not you agreed to get the transplant."

I am stunned. I am not usually surprised by anything the Bureau does, but this is way beyond my expectations. I feel demeaned and used. No matter what I decided, Keri was not going to get a kidney. All these men had decided how a woman would react. How a "mere" woman, a single mother, might sacrifice her career for the health of her daughter. I am speechless. I am Livid. I light into him.

"You bastard. You played me. After all my work for the Bureau. After all these years, you backstabbed me. I guess you got what you wanted."

"Not yet, Cassandra. You double-crossed the FBI. You betrayed your fellow agents. You cooperated with international criminals. Don't you think you have to pay a price?"

"You set me up, Donaldson. You got what you wanted. I will tender my resignation immediately."

"Cassandra, I will require you to submit a detailed, written report of what occurred in New Delhi. I don't think you understand the seriousness of what you've done. What if other agents behave the same way and simply have to resign? Merely get a slap on the wrist? What kind of precedent would that set? I'm afraid you are subject to criminal charges."

"Criminal charges? Keri's operation never happened. You can't convict me for thoughts that were never carried out. I did not commit any criminal acts."

"You keep leaving out important details, Cassandra. After your 7:01 conversation with Anish, you immediately wired the final $50,000. Taxpayer money, by the way, that confirmed your oral agreement."

"You wouldn't bring charges. Not after the service I have given to the Bureau."

"Oh yes I would, Cassandra. I certainly would. But fortunately for you, I have thought of a possible alternative."

"I offered my resignation. What more do you want from me?"

"Cassandra, I'm a very private man. Not many people know about my personal life. I happen to have a little cabin in New Hampshire. It's quite a nice place. In the woods, very secluded, right on a freshwater lake. I think you would like to visit me there. Perhaps over a weekend. I suspect, just between the two of us, we can come to a little private arrangement."

I am shocked. Outraged. Flabbergasted. It's all I can do not to scream. "You're propositioning me? You perverted son of a bitch. If you think for one second that I would even consider…"

But he interrupts. "Keep your voice down, Cassandra. Think of your little girl. If charges are brought against you, it is certain you will go to prison. You know that. The evidence against you is solid. Little Keri will not have either parent. I know you have no close relatives. She will be placed in an orphanage or some seedy foster home. Quite possibly abused. Unlikely to ever get a kidney transplant. She will die an early death. Is that what you want for your daughter?"

"You can't do this. You…"

"Sshhh. Yes I can. And so can you. I know some of the things you had to do when you came up in this organization. When you had to work under cover ingratiating yourself to your own people. I think you can manage this arrangement quite well."

I feel nauseous. The bile rises from my stomach to the back of my throat. It's all I can do not to puke. Pictures of my rape as a teenager run through my head, and I start to tremble. I take a deep breath trying to gain control. Donaldson gets up from behind his desk, indicating that the discussion is over. He guides me to the door with one hand gently resting on my buttocks and gives a little squeeze. "Yes, Cassandra," he says. "I think we can make a mutually beneficial arrangement."

After the "debriefing" with Donaldson, I can barely manage to compose myself enough to drive home. The entire scene was so shocking that I have difficulty processing what has just transpired. Having worked in the Bureau for such a long time, I know about things that have gone down and have heard plenty of rumors. Now I know that some of those rumors are true.

James Donaldson is a vindictive man. If I defy him, there is little doubt that he will follow through on his threats. Of course, the obvious course of action is to report him; to file a sexual harassment claim with the Inspector General. At first glance, it seems quite straightforward. But I know that is not the case. If there is an investigation, I cannot be confident about the outcome. It would be his word against mine, a "he said-she said" confrontation. Except, in this case, he is the Director of Operations for the Boston office of the FBI, and I am an agent who tried to deceive the Bureau and undermine a criminal investigation.

I can imagine his testimony. He will describe how I secretly colluded with international criminals to foil an FBI operation and to purchase an illegal kidney; to betray my colleagues in the field, acting essentially as a double agent. And to pay for the kidney with taxpayer's dollars—200,000 of them.

The prosecution would describe how my criminal intent was discovered by my colleagues and how I reacted. When confronted with the evidence, I faced a near certain criminal conviction. Desperate, I devised an audacious plan to accuse my boss of sexual harassment. I concocted a bizarre story against a man who has given his entire adult life to serve the FBI, and who never has suffered the slightest blot on his reputation.

Who would the judge believe? Even if it was a toss-up, I cannot take the chance. I know if I lost, Keri would become an orphan just as Donaldson said. At best, she would be put in some foster home. With no one advocating for her, the chances of her ever getting a kidney would be slim, and she might well die within a few years. I simply cannot let that happen to my only daughter. Capitulating to Donaldson would be degrading, humiliating, as well as disgusting. The man is sick—a misogynist. If it wasn't for Keri, and it was just a matter of my going to jail, I would never give in. But the fact is, it comes down to this and only this: either I submit to Donaldson or my daughter's future and very life will be endangered.

Is there a moral answer to such a dilemma? Can an otherwise immoral act be the right thing to do if it saves an innocent person's life? How dissimilar is it to the decision I had to make in New Delhi? If the facts are really what they appear to be—with no other possibilities—either I acquiesce or my daughter becomes an orphan. There are no other alternatives. I must choose one or the other.

Chapter 45

Martin - 10 Months Later

March winds make it feel like it's still winter as I walk up the steps of the Suffolk County Courthouse. "JUSTICE FOR ALL" is carved above the entrance to the old, twenty-four-story building whose walls have heard the grisly details of Boston's most infamous crimes. Today will be the second day of Bradley Stone's trial.

Cassandra is already seated inside, and I take the seat next to her directly behind the prosecutors. Earlier, both of us provided testimony, but it's possible we could be called again. "Mornin' Cat. Thanks for savin' my seat. Get Keri off to school okay?"

"Yes, book report and all. She's doing great, Martin. Ever since she got the new kidney, she's like a different girl. Hanging out with new friends, never having to leave right after school for dialysis. The kidney has given her a new life. She asks about you all the time. We need to have you over for dinner. Maybe next ..."

"ALL RISE," the bailiff interrupts Cassandra as the judge enters the courtroom. "The Superior Court of Suffolk County is now in session, the Honorable Judge Haverford presiding." I look around the courtroom which is packed with onlookers and reporters from both the local and national press. Nothin' like a case involving murder, sex, and illegal kidneys to whip up a media frenzy. Crowds got here three hours early to line up for seats. Morbid curiosity draws the public's attention like flies to feces.

Prosecution lawyers have several more witnesses to call, and the judge asks them to proceed. Just after noon, the prosecution rests its case. "I know a quiet place where we can get lunch," I tell Cassandra. "We can get back in plenty of time for the defense."

Two blocks away, three steps beneath the sidewalk, is a little hole-in-the-wall with low-lighting, a bar, and tables. We find a quiet booth in the corner where we can talk. I order a bacon cheeseburger and fries. Cassandra gets a chicken Caesar salad.

"Howdya think it went, Cat?"

"I thought the DA had a strong case. The jurors probably knew nothing about the illegal trade in kidneys, and the prosecutor painted them a stark picture. She described how desperate people sell their kidneys to survive; how they are exploited by black market dealers who pay them a pittance and then sell their organs for hundreds of thousands of dollars; how many of the people are left with debilitating complications. What did you think, Martin?"

"I thought the description of the Sanchez murder really grabbed the jury's attention. A twenty-year-old kid who was kidnapped and kept prisoner until they had buyers for his organs. How they cut him open and harvested his liver, kidneys, and even his corneas. The jurors were shocked to see the photographs. Then, they were told not to believe for one minute that Stone was helpin' people. Without people like Stone to find buyers, she argued, the black market could not exist, and kids like Miguel Sanchez would still be alive."

"Martin, they never called Colonel Harris. I remember how excited you were after he agreed to turn state's evidence. I thought he would be a key prosecution witness."

"There was a long discussion about that among the prosecutors. They decided not to call him. The defense would've had a field day on cross. Harris would've admitted that the kidney saved his life. Without it, his wife would've been widowed. He wouldn't have seen his grandchildren marry. He never would've seen his great grandchildren. The jurors would melt. The defense would ask if he regretted gettin' the life-savin' operation. What could he say? They never included him on the witness list, so they didn't have to reveal him in discovery."

"It's ironic, Martin. After Cynthia Fleming's dangerous search for other kidney sales, you finally found what you were looking for, and then you couldn't use it. Sometimes truth is not the precursor of justice."

"Speakin' of truth, Cat, we have some talkin' to do. Not now. We gotta get back to the courtroom. I think there's part of this story you haven't told me."

Chapter 46

Cassandra – Back 10 Months Earlier

Nine days after my "debriefing," I drop Keri off at school. "It's just for a weekend, honeybun," I tell her. "I have to be away for work, but I'll be back on Sunday." I give Keri a goodbye kiss and tell her to be a good girl and mind the babysitter. I watch as the young girl scampers toward the school building, already calling out to friends. The tears drip down my cheeks.

Anyone who ever knew me would have difficulty believing what I'm about to do. I have become an accomplished, professional woman. Independent. Strong-willed, having overcome formidable obstacles throughout my life. I am not the kind of person who could easily be intimidated; to succumb to the threats of my devious boss or any other man. Over time, I have built up a healthy measure of confidence and self-respect. I am not a woman who would ever debase myself to another person, particularly to an individual I loathe.

Yet, the unbelievable has come to pass, and I have never felt more conflicted. Leaving my daughter with a baby sitter to spend the weekend submitting to a depraved man who sickens me, but doing it out of desperate concern for my daughter's future, I have considered every alternative and concluded that there is simply a stark choice. Either I submit, or my daughter becomes an orphan. I am suffering the consequences of breaking the law and my oath of office in order to get my daughter a kidney; not the legal consequences, but submission to blackmail. Is there no justice? Haven't I only wanted to be a good mother? Doing what any loving mother would have done to save her child's life?

On Friday afternoon, I begin the two-hour drive to Wolfeboro, New Hampshire. I am dreading what might happen. I have so many conflicting emotions, it is hard to disentangle them. But the one that dominates is fear. My mind keeps flashing back to high school, where I was raped as a teenager—a trauma that years of therapy have attempted but failed to completely dispel. I start to tremble uncontrollably and have to pull off the highway. Then, feeling the bile rise up in my throat, I am barely able to open the car door before puking on the pavement. The past, which I thought was behind me, which I thought I had mostly overcome, reclaims me like an old addiction. Feelings of guilt and insecurity flood back from the days I felt dirty and used and worthless.

I push myself to drive on. I have to go through with this; have to get control of my emotions if only for my daughter's sake. Taking deep breaths, I try to calm myself. Ever so gradually, I am able to draw on some of the resources I have worked so hard to acquire. I tell myself that I am not the humiliated girl that tried to be popular by sleeping with the football hero. I am no longer the teenager driven to depression and self-loathing; no longer the young person who fled from her past with no self-respect. I have tried to confront my demons. I have worked through years of pain. I understand that some of my trauma will never go away. But all those years of therapy have helped me accept what happened—to gradually build self-confidence and grow in to the woman I have become.

I know my defenses have not come without a cost. I had to protect myself. I had to build walls. Those defenses stunted some of my emotions and affected my relationships. I made myself safe from storms without, but less able to let the warmth and sunlight in.

By the time I cross the Merrimack River into New Hampshire, I am determined to confront this new atrocity. I have been in life threatening situations as an FBI agent. I have resources that other women don't have. I am smart. Somehow, in some way, I will figure out how to thwart James Donaldson. I do not yet see my way through the darkness, but I remember the quote from Camus that a friend gave me during my months of depression:

"In the depth of winter, I finally learned that there was in me an invincible summer."

After an hour more of driving, I leave the highway and drive on to a quiet country road. My GPS says to turn right on to an unpaved lane that narrows as it winds through dense woods. My anxiety heightens as I realize the road is totally secluded with no other houses in sight. My fear level rises again. Donaldson must be a sick man to force me into this. What is he capable of? What might he do to me? I think of characters from fiction: Christian Grey, Lisbeth Salander. What kind of weird things might he be into? There will be no one to answer my calls for help.

"Your destination is on the right," says the mild voice of the GPS. I turn down a long driveway that descends steeply toward a lake. The "little cabin" that Donaldson mentioned looks rustic but quite substantial. His black BMW sedan is parked on a gravel bed to the right. Aware of my potential peril, I back into the adjacent space, allowing for the possibility of an urgent getaway. After a short pause to steel myself, I take my carry-on from the back seat and approach the front door.

James Donaldson answers the door looking pleased. Dressed in khaki trousers, Izod Lacoste shirt and top siders, he looks as if he just stepped out of the yacht club. He seems to have a naturally condescending look. "Welcome to New Hampshire, Cassandra. How was the drive?"

"No problems, Sir."

"James, Cassandra, please. We're hardly here for official business, are we?"

Asshole, I think, but do not answer.

"You can freshen up in the bedroom and shower upstairs. First door on the right. But first, we have to exercise some precautions. I know you are not foolish enough to carry a weapon or wear a wire, but I would be derelict not to check."

Donaldson tells me to open my suitcase. He searches it thoroughly, feeling for anything in the linings. "I'm afraid I'll need the keys to your car, unless you have other things you need to bring inside."

I smile derisively and hand him the keys. "I'm afraid we have to do a brief body search, Cassandra. Even your tight little cavities. We've both been in this business a long time. I'm sure you realize it's standard operating procedure."

I submit to the humiliating procedure that I have witnessed countless times from the other side. I take my carry bag upstairs to the first room on the right, which is obviously Donaldson's bedroom. A king-size bed dominates the wood-paneled room. Oak night tables are on both sides of the bed and a matching bureau sits on the opposite wall topped by a lengthy mirror. A brown and beige carpet with tones matching the furniture covers the floor. It is woodsy, tastefully decorated, and has a masculine feel. It is also immaculate. Not a thing out of place. I have always suspected Donaldson of being compulsive, possibly explaining the unusual intimation for me to shower.

Showering suits me fine. It will allow some time to snoop around while I am alone. Donaldson is smart, so it may be difficult to find anything incriminating. But I have plotted my strategy. Donaldson has a big ego, but like most men, he will have his insecurities, especially sexual. He will worry about his performance, and I will pretend to be seduced. Men are gullible. Women have been faking orgasms since the beginning of time, and men always want to believe in their potency and masculinity. I want him to feel confident, let down his guard, so I can have space to look for anything incriminating. For what, I am not sure.

Anything that may compromise him: pictures, letters, pornography, old phone or credit card receipts—anything that might indicate sexual perversion, illegal activity, embezzlement, or use of government property.

I close the door, undress, and turn on the shower. Using the noise as cover, I search the night table drawers. One side is empty. The top drawer on the other side has condoms and KY Jelly as well as a comb, nail clippers, reading glasses, and other personal care items. The bottom drawer has a Glock. I am not surprised, having my own in a locked bedroom drawer. I search the bureau drawers, take a quick look in the closet, and an even quicker shower, not wanting to arouse suspicion. I dress casually in Jeans and a quarter-zip pullover and return downstairs.

Donaldson has put a vase of cut flowers centered on the coffee table in front of the couch. "Can I make you a drink, Cassandra?" He asks. I would love a drink, perhaps even need one, but I don't trust him. He's a spy. No telling what he might put in my drink. I ask if I can mix one myself. Donaldson smiles. "There is no need to drug you, Cassandra," he replies smugly.

Donaldson sits on the couch and beckons me to sit next to him. "I have some good news for you," he says. "I have accepted your report in full. I have absolved you of any responsibility for the failure of the New Delhi mission. Just as a precaution, however, I have appended a note to keep the file open in case any new evidence happens to emerge. I trust you will ensure that never happens. I have also requested that you be appointed for the new directorship. How does that suit you?"

I look at him knowing that he revels in exercising his power over me. "I appreciate that Sir."

"James."

"Yes…. James."

"I think there are ways to express your thanks, Cassandra." He stands and moves the vase of flowers to the end of the table. Then, standing in front of my face as I am seated on the couch, and without any preliminaries, he takes down his pants. He is already erect. "I think you know what to do, Cassandra."

"I must do this," I say to myself. I have had extensive training as an undercover agent and have learned to compartmentalize—disassociate myself from a task that I loathe. I try to go away in my mind; try to focus on my plan. But the act is so repulsive, so perverted, that I can only partially shield my emotions. It's all I can do not to be sick.

I manage to get through most of the weekend, submitting to him and pretending to enjoy it. Donaldson is fastidious, super orderly, and definitely compulsive. Pens and pencils on his desk are lined up perfectly parallel. Kitchen implements are carefully sorted into separate cubbies. The man always has to be in control. Fortunately, it means he is also clean; uses a condom, washes up afterwards. Perhaps, he is a germaphobe. Thankfully, he is not into anything too kinky, although he did tie and restrain my arms the night before.

I think it is power that drives him, and sex is a means to exercise it. For him, the two are so entwined it is difficult to separate them. He needs to be dominant. Maybe it's the only way he can get off. I play into it, indulging his needs, hoping to lull him into a false sense of mastery. I have had some success. He has ignored me while having a lengthy telephone conversation and has left me alone to take several showers. They provided time for me to search through cabinets and closets, photo albums, and files. Once he left his iPad, and I raced through his contacts and browsing history, wishing he hadn't sequestered my iPhone camera.

On Sunday morning, we have breakfast together. I have submitted to his abuse all weekend but have found nothing to incriminate him. Where will this end? I can't endure another weekend like this, but I have not thought of an alternative. The one thing I know for sure is that I can't risk going to jail and leaving my daughter an orphan. Donaldson, dressed in a blue velour robe, finishes his second cup of coffee. "I'm going upstairs to clean up, shave, and get dressed," he tells me. "Do take care of the dishes."

The night before, I had searched the room he uses as a study. There were two locked drawers in his desk. I found some pins and kitchen tools I could use to jimmy the locks—a skill I developed years ago working undercover. Last night, I had no time to open the drawers. As soon as he goes upstairs, I stash the dishes in the washer without rinsing them and work on the drawers. The bottom one opens easily and is filled with hang files. They are all labeled, and I scan through them as quickly as possible.

I find a file with credit card statements and put it on the desk. I am totally focused, looking through the charges, and do not hear him noiselessly sneaking down the stairway. "What do you think you're doing, Cassandra?" the voice comes from behind me. I am caught. There is no plausible excuse. There is nothing I can say, as I turn and stare open-mouthed at Donaldson. He is still dressed in his bathrobe and has a venomous look on his face.

"You're a bad girl, Cassandra, and bad girls deserve to be punished. Go in the living room, strip off your clothes and get on the couch. I want you on your hands and knees, doggie style."

I am sickened, imagining what he intends to do. What if I refuse? Will he force me? Physically abuse me? He towers over me and can easily overwhelm any resistance. I hesitate for just a moment, but Donaldson grabs me and pushes me toward the living room. I do as instructed, and he comes up behind me and slaps my bare buttocks, meting out punishment and humiliation at the same time. The violence arouses him, and I can see his erection emerge through the slit in his bathrobe. He takes a condom from his bathrobe pocket, slips it on, and pushes the vase of flowers to the end of the table.

"Naughty girl, Cassandra," he says after the act. "I am going upstairs to clean up. I trust you won't try anything like that again."

I am mortified. I feel filthy, and the tears are streaking down my cheeks. Nevertheless, my determination has not wavered, and my mind has never stopped working. I have been trained to detect any inconsistency and to discern any action that does not fit a logical pattern of behavior. Despite being at the apex of my fear and anxiety, I noticed Donaldson moving the flowers. It didn't make sense. Being compulsive, he had always placed the vase of flowers at the exact middle of the table. Why would he move them? Especially at that moment. Right in the midst of his sexual excitement. It should have been the last thing on his mind. And it wasn't the first time it happened. He did the same thing the first time he commanded a sexual act on the couch. I noticed it then but didn't give it much credence, thinking, perhaps, he did not want them to get knocked over. But, if anything, he had moved them closer. There had to be a reason.

He has gone upstairs to "clean up." I move the vase of flowers back to the middle of the table. I assume my former position on the couch. Then, I slide the flowers to the side and sight through the spot where they had been. Were the flowers blocking something he wanted to see? No, stupid, it was the other way around. The flowers were blocking the view of the sexual act. There must be a camera. The sicko has been recording his abuse.

I peer along the sight line where the flowers had been until I see it. It is concealed as part of a track light. The Bureau has often used the same type for espionage, and I am familiar with the apparatus. It must be triggered either by movement or a switch. I have to think fast. At most, I have maybe ten minutes until Donaldson returns.

It couldn't be an internet connected camera. I know all about those from previous surveillance. He couldn't take the chance that his ISP (internet service provider) might see the footage. Even if he had a VPN (virtual private network), there would be a risk of discovery. Instead, the device will have an SD memory card, the tiny piece of plastic inserted in the camera's card slot. It is not easily accessible because this is a surveillance instrument. God knows what is in that memory card. I certainly could not be the first woman Donaldson has abused. No telling what he would do if he catches me, but this is the opportunity I've been waiting for, and I have to take the chance.

I cannot reach the light, but I quickly drag over a chair to stand on. The device is held together with Phillips-head screws. There are tools in the kitchen drawer that I had discovered previously, and I run to get them. I climb back up on the chair, still in discomfort, having the repulsive feeling that Donaldson is still inside me. Standing on the chair, trying to unscrew the light, I find the screwdriver too big. I rush to the drawer and find one that is smaller. Back on the chair, I remove the four screws holding the latch. Sure enough, the tiny camera has an SD slot. I release the catch and put the tiny card in my pocket.

I have to make an instant decision. Should I try to re-attach the panel before he returns to cover up what I have done? Or, should I flee the house now, as fast as I can? Then, I hear him coming down the steps. I jump off the chair, run to the front door and slam it behind me. Donaldson must have seen the chair underneath the camera light and immediately realized what has occurred. Dressed only with a bath towel wrapped around his waist, he opens the front door and runs toward my car. This is not the first time in my life that I have had to make a quick escape. Donaldson took my car keys, but I keep a spare key attached to the rocker panel under the driver-side door. I reach for the key as Donaldson bolts out the door. It is difficult to run in the tightly wrapped towel and he rips it off, running naked toward the car.

I pull the door open, jump in the car, and turn the electronic key in the ignition just as Donaldson reaches the car. He grabs me by my upper left arm trying to yank me out of the car. My head is halfway out, but keeping my grip on the steering wheel, I can still reach the gas pedal. I stomp the pedal to the floor, the tires spin on the gravel, gain purchase, and the car lurches forward, causing the open door to slam shut into Donaldson's naked body. He lies sprawled on the ground, crumpled and bleeding, as I pull myself back to a sitting position and drive away.

Chapter 47

Cassandra – 10 Months Later

On the third day of the trial, the defense presents its case. Martin and I sit together in the row behind the prosecutors. When the judge declares a break for lunch, we go to the same restaurant we had frequented the day before.

"What do you think, Martin?" I ask as we sit in a booth waiting for our order. "The prosecution looked awfully strong yesterday. After the jury saw those pictures of Miguel Sanchez, they were visibly upset. Do you think the defense was able to win them back?"

"Hard to say, Cat. You're right about yesterday, but the defense was surprisingly good. Stone was impressive. He told the story about his son, strugglin' for years, hopin' to get a kidney from the waitin' list. Stone told the jurors that thousands of people are willin' to sell their organs to save other people's lives, but the government won't let 'em. He explained how people die each year needlessly, while they could be given perfectly good organs. Then, he described how he watched his only son die, knowin' he coulda saved him, and how the guilt has eaten away at him ever since."

"You're right. Stone's testimony was heart-wrenching."

"The resta his defense was also good. The lawyer brought in those character witnesses. People who got a second chance at life 'cause of a kidney transplant. He brought in former patients who had good outcomes. He described how Stone's centers helped 'em survive until they got a new kidney. I know he connected with some a the jurors. A couple of 'em were even in tears."

"I agree, Martin. He did get to them, but the D.A. came right back on cross. She made Stone admit that some clients were given telephone numbers for black market kidney brokers. Then, she forced Stone to admit to his extra-marital affair with Cohnheim. That sullied his image with the jurors."

"That's true. Hard to guess how it will come down. If it was up to the judge, he'd find Stone guilty of breakin' the law. Wouldn't let the ends justify the means. But the jury is different. They may be sympathetic to Stone and his story."

"Could be. It only takes one juror to acquit. If Stone and Cohnheim walk, we won't have gotten any of them. That will be the end of the story."

"You're probably right, Cat, but what about your story? Remember what I asked you yesterday? I think there is more of your story that you haven't told me."

Something I haven't told him? Does Martin know about my decision in New Delhi? My report to the Bureau is secret. How could he possibly have found out? "I think I've told you everything, Martin. What do you think I left out?"

"Cat, we're close friends. We confide in each other. Whatever you tell me will never be repeated. You know that."

I stare at Martin across the table. I have been afraid to tell him about my decision in New Delhi. He is my dear friend, but he doesn't recognize the gulf between us. Martin grew up in a different world. The people around him gave him support. He could succeed by following the rules. He thinks I should be the same way: polite, less rough, more cooperative. Perhaps, a little more "white." He thinks he understands me because we both grew up relatively poor. But he really has no clue what it was like to be a young, black woman in Birmingham and Boston. I learned to fight for everything I got. Fight hard for myself and fight even harder for my daughter. If I had been a nice little girl, I would still be in rural Alabama, living with my mother, helping to clean other people's toilets. I didn't get here by following Martin's rules. I had to do some ugly things to work my way up the FBI hierarchy. Someday, I might be able to tell Martin about the decisions I made in this case, but no way will he ever hear the entire story.

"Martin. I don't know what you're getting at."

"I listened to your testimony in court. You made a telephone call to Anish at 7:00 Tuesday morning, and another call around 7:40. Why would you call Anish at that hour?"

"You heard my testimony. I wasn't sure of the clinical schedule. I had a lot of things going through my head. I was nervous about Keri. I didn't want to take any chance of making a mistake and screwing the whole thing up."

"C'mon Cat. You had the whole schedule in your cell phone. Don't you remember readin' it to me in the restaurant before you left? You just had to check your phone. There was no need to call Anish at that hour. And why two calls? Minutes before the Director called you. Somethin' was goin' on. What would make you lie under oath? What were you coverin' up?"

I realize the gig is up. I can't bullshit my way through this one. I will have to tell him about my decision in New Delhi, but there's no way I will ever tell him the rest. I describe how the surgeon offered to move up the schedule. How I realized I could get Keri a kidney, and how I stayed up all night trying to decide what to do.

"The schedule change gave me an opportunity I hadn't expected. I had to choose, Martin. I had to choose between myself and my daughter. I had to choose whether to get her a life-saving transplant—one with a live kidney that would last twice as long as one she might get from the waiting list. And what if her name never reached the top of the list? What if I had to watch her die? I could never live with myself. The Bureau messed with me. They never should have put me in that position. So, I did what my heart told me. What my mother would have done. What I've done all my life. I decided to take care of my own, and I knew I could take anything they could throw at me."

"You decided to sabotage the operation. You called Anish to arrange the transplant?"

"Yes, I did, and when he didn't call me back, I tried him again forty minutes later. I got a recording saying his phone service had been discontinued. Minutes later, Donaldson called to tell me the sting had been compromised."

"You're goddamn lucky the sting was thwarted. Keri would have gotten a new kidney, but you would have sacrificed yourself. They would have sent you to prison."

"I knew that, Martin, but it was Keri's life."

"Somethin' still doesn't fit. You double-crossed them. The whole operation got screwed up, and they ended up givin' you a promotion. I think you still have more to tell me."

"You're right, I haven't told you the worst of it. They knew all along. The planning team for the operation included psychologists. They knew I might have to choose between my daughter and my career. Given the opportunity, they concluded, I would sacrifice myself to get a kidney for my daughter. I was furious. 'You bastard,' I told Donaldson. 'You knew you were setting me up. How could you do that to me?'"

"What'd he say?"

"The bastard was so smug. He said they already decided what I would do. I behaved exactly as they expected. They had everything in place to execute the sting whether or not I agreed to get the transplant. No matter what I decided, Keri was not going to get a kidney. It sucked, Martin. They didn't care. They just used me. All these men had decided how a woman would react. I was stunned. I asked him why they couldn't discuss it with me in advance. He said it would be a rather unusual practice to have to counsel senior personnel about not becoming double agents."

"How did you find out they knew?"

"Donaldson told me at my debriefing. He told me they tapped my phone and planted listening devices. They also bugged Anish and had him under surveillance. They listened to my 7:00 a.m. call."

"That S.O.B! He set you up. After all you've done. You musta been pissed when you found out."

"At first, I was shocked. That quickly turned to anger. I couldn't believe the organization could do that to me, one of its own people."

"What did Donaldson do? He couldn't tolerate an agent who betrayed the Bureau and undermined his operation."

There is no way on earth I can tell Martin the whole truth. He could never understand. He would never be able to see me in the same light. Our relationship would never be the same. Even if he doubts what I am going to tell him, he won't guess what I actually did with Donaldson. Martin cares about me. He thinks he understands me. He'll believe what he wants to believe about me. People don't easily abandon their beliefs. Besides, there's no predicting what he might do if I tell him the truth. I can't control his reaction. He might be so upset, he could go to the I.G., which would eventually reveal my later decision. This story cannot see the light of day. It would expose the whole plan I formulated; everything I did. What am I going to tell him?

"Donaldson didn't see it that way, Martin. According to him, I carried out the mission the exact way they had planned. I met all of their expectations. He rationalized putting me in such an untenable position. He compared it to agents who undertake operations knowing it could end in their deaths. 'You knew the risks of going undercover in India,' he said. 'You and your daughter could have been killed.' Then, he congratulated me and offered me the Directorship. I never had so many conflicting emotions at the same time."

"Maybe I'm wrong, Cat, but it don't make much sense to me. I can't pretend to know how the Bureau operates. I still think Donaldson's an asshole who wouldn't hesitate to throw you under the bus. His big operation fails, and he gives you a promotion. What am I missing, Cat?"

"I don't like Donaldson either, Martin, but I did what he asked, even at the price of involving my daughter. Despite everything, he kept his word about the promotion. I'm just glad it's over."

Martin stares into my eyes. I know he wants to believe me, but there must be details in his mind that don't fit together. He doesn't say anything, but I can tell that he is not convinced by my story.

Chapter 48

Cassandra – Back 10 Months Earlier

As I drive away from Donaldson's cottage, I think about how I got here. All my life, I have been willing to take chances. I left my home and my mother in Alabama. I attended college in New England despite fearing that I wouldn't fit in. I joined the FBI as a lone black woman. I risked working undercover. I can't imagine how my life would have been if I had stayed in Alabama. I would have been a sunrise eclipsed by clouds, hating myself for not living up to my potential.

The chance I took in New Delhi was a mistake. I knew the kind of people I worked for. I should have figured the Bureau would be keeping me under surveillance. Now, because of that mistake, I have taken a bigger chance. I have staked my future on what might be in a tiny SD memory card. If nothing is there, I will have left myself defenseless against retaliation. Donaldson is a powerful and vindictive man and will do anything to save himself, perhaps even resort to violence. But I was desperate. I grasped at this possibility because it seemed like the only way out. I could not wimp out and go through another episode like this past weekend—not without sacrificing any remaining vestige of self-respect.

Donaldson must already be planning some kind of retaliation. I need to construct a detailed plan of action. Security is paramount. Donaldson might follow me. He might go to my house. If he is desperate enough, he might be a threat to my daughter. I can't chance going home. I keep a burner phone in the glove compartment, and I call my long-time babysitter who knows my occupation. "Caroline, this is an emergency. Pack a small bag for Keri and meet me at the Airport

Hilton in ninety minutes. Wait outside in the car, and I will call you on your cell."

What if Donaldson put a tracker on my car. I must secure the evidence (if there is any evidence) by making copies of the memory card and sending them to reliable places. On the way to Logan airport, I stop at a Staples and buy a camera and two USB thumb drives. Inside my car, I load the SD card into the camera, connect it to my laptop, and download the data. I then save copies to the thumb drives. Staples has Federal Express. I fill in my personal account number and mail two copies: one to myself at a private mailbox store, and one to my mother who will not know what to do with a USB drive.

When I get to Logan Airport, I park in the garage and check in to the Hilton under an alias. I then call Caroline, meet her outside, and take Keri through a side entrance and up to the room. As anxious as I am to see the content of the SD card, I first order room service, and then spend several hours with Keri before putting her to bed.

As soon as Keri is down, I boot up my laptop. My pulse quickens as I see the files are large—a good sign that there are videos. It takes only minutes to see what I have. The main file is a compendium of three years of sex acts with various women. There are long blank shots and videos of an empty couch. Donaldson must edit these on other media and put the same SD card back in the camera. I recognize two agents: one presently employed and one who has since left the agency. I remember that both had disciplinary issues, and both managed to survive them and advance in the organization. Donaldson must have blackmailed them just as he did with me. He cannot afford to let these get out. It would not only end his career but would lead to disgrace and criminal prosecution.

Through all these years, I have learned to think like an FBI agent. I am now in a position of strength, and I have the opportunity to press my advantage. I know what I want more than anything in the world, and now I know how to get it. It doesn't take me long to construct my plan. I would love for Donaldson to get his due, but that is not my primary objective. What I have decided to do, many would find immoral and offensive. It is probably a more questionable moral decision than double crossing the Bureau or surrendering myself to Donaldson. But I am neither evil nor insensitive. I am aware of the moral consequences of my actions, and I am prepared to live with my decision.

I know Martin would never condone my plan. At some point, I might have to tell him. Not the whole story. Not the part about the weekend with Donaldson. I will never do that. Martin is a nice person with a good heart, and he still has a measure of innocence that I lost long ago. He thinks we're alike because we both grew up in relative poverty, but he doesn't have a clue how different we are, and I will not disillusion him. He may be shocked to hear what I intend to do, but he will believe it and never suspect that there was anything more.

When I wake early the next morning, Keri is still sleeping. There is no predicting what a threatened Donaldson might do, and I want to control the situation before he can act. I place a call to Donaldson on my burner phone and arrange to meet him that evening. It has to be in a public place for my own security, but it must provide privacy for our discussion. I reserve a private dining room at Elaine's on the Harbor.

When Donaldson arrives, I am already seated. He greets me graciously and is polite and professional. His years of training have taught him to conceal his emotions. He orders drinks and talks about the menu. One would never suspect that he is seething inside. I am sickened by his fraudulent façade, and by the necessity of being so close to him. I cut the small talk short.

"As you must realize, *James*, I have seen the videos. I was surprised that you never changed out the memory card. You are a sick man. I almost feel sorry for you and for what's going to happen…"

"Crawford, let's be reasonable about this," he interrupts. "We can make an arrangement. We both have reputations and careers to think about."

"Is that so? I believe your illustrious career is just about over."

"You won't do it Crawford. Think about it. You will ruin my career, but you will also go down. You will go to prison for acting as a double agent. What you did was treasonous. You may take some pleasure from revenge, but your daughter will still be without parents and will end up in some shitty foster home."

"No way, you pervert. No judge is going to put me in prison after seeing those videos; after hearing how you set me up and used the result to abuse me. Your degenerate ass is going behind bars in a place where your fellow inmates are not fond of FBI agents, especially ones that abused a sister. Perhaps, you'll get a taste of your own medicine."

"You're rolling the dice with your daughter's future, Crawford. But even if you're right, your career will be ruined. There's no way you can serve in the Bureau after you undermined an operation. No security organization will ever employ you."

Over the past hours, I have thought of that and many other things. Through this long ordeal that began with a snake bite over two years ago, I have had to consider how life is so unfair. How an innocent little girl's life can be ruined by chance in a split second. I have dealt with a medical system designed for fairness, but which favors the rich. I have worked in an organization that uses its people and denigrates its women. I have dealt with international criminals that prey on desperate people to sell their organs; with wealthy doctors who ignore the black-market trade for their own benefit; and with a perverted supervisor who channels his neuroses into sexual dominance over his powerless employees.

I have been forced to make moral judgements. Whether to involve my only daughter in an effort to arrest criminals. Whether a promotion and raise that would pay for my daughter's college justified risking her involvement. I had to lie to my daughter, shunting her to a new dialysis clinic; pretending we were going to India to look for a kidney. I had to make the most excruciating decision—whether to deceive the FBI and let criminals go free to get Keri an illegal kidney. I had to judge whether it was morally acceptable to debase myself and commit repulsive sexual acts to prevent my daughter from becoming an orphan. And now, I have made this final moral judgement; this plan that would permit a mentally disturbed, sexual deviant to walk free.

Donaldson sits staring at me, but I do not flinch from eye contact, and I give him my reply. "You are a sick, perverted son of a bitch, and you deserve to rot in prison, but I am going to give you an out. I loathe letting you walk. It's revolting to me, but I'm going to give you one chance for a deal. You listen carefully because you are going to do exactly what I ask. If you mess it up, those recordings will be front page in every newspaper in the country."

Chapter 49

Martin – 10 Months Later

The jury has spent two days in deliberation when the judge announces that the court will re-convene in thirty minutes. Cassandra and I have been sitting together on a bench near the courthouse. "Well, Cat, how do you think they'll come down?"

"I thought the closing arguments from the defense were effective," she answers. "He made Bradley Stone a sympathetic person; a man wounded by the death of his son, devoting his life to helping others avoid his fate. He pointed out that the prosecution never presented evidence that Stone profited in any way—probably because he didn't. The defense pleaded with the jurists not to convict a man who believed he was doing good. Besides, he never did anything more than passing a telephone number. It was a powerful emotional argument, and he only had to pull the heartstrings of one juror to acquit."

"I agree the defense was good, Cat, but I think the prosecutor was better. She made it clear to the jury that this case was not about whether it was right or wrong to buy a kidney. She told the jurists that there was no correct moral answer to that question. Who among them could decide what was right if their own child was dying? Perhaps only God could decide. But, she told them, it was not the duty of the jury to play God. It was not within their purview to even consider the moral question. The law is clear. They must simply apply the law, and they must do so even if they believe the law is unjust."

We return to the courtroom, crowded with onlookers and press, a scene of constant movement and noise until the judge enters and the room suddenly quiets down. "All rise," the bailiff intones. The judge looks over the assemblage from his raised dais and makes his announcement. The jurors were hopelessly deadlocked. They could not reach a decision. He declares a hung jury and a mistrial. The prosecutors will have to decide whether to re-try the case.

After the verdict, I sit across from Cassandra in the restaurant and think about our unlikely relationship. My father was murdered by two black men as I hid only several feet away. Guilt was probably the drivin' force that propelled me into law enforcement. The Boston police force, when I first got my badge, was a haven for the Irish and Italians. Back then, I never had any black colleagues or friends.

Then, I met Cassandra when we were workin' on the same case. She was attractive, stylish, cool—everythin' that I was not. She was black. I never assumed she would have any interest in me, but I was wrong. We became friends, and I got to appreciate her many qualities. She was smart, capable, reliable, and a great parent. After Florence died, she was there for me, and we became close friends. I even began to wonder if our friendship could be somethin' more.

Now, I look at her and suspect she hasn't told me the truth. Does she feel guilty about what she's done? Is she afraid of losin' my respect? Does she think there could be somethin' more between us, and she doesn't want to ruin the possibility? Sometimes I dare to consider that, despite knowin' our differences.

"We been friends for a long time," I tell Cassandra. "I think you should tell me the whole story."

"Martin, I told you what I did. I didn't want to admit that I was going to deceive the Bureau. What else can I say?"

"You can tell me the rest of the story, Cat."

"I have, Martin. What makes you think there is something else?"

"What about Herman Seidelman, Cat? The one thing that didn't make any sense was why the Bureau let Seidelman go. You let him go back to Israel. He was a person you coulda definitely convicted. You had all the evidence. At first, I figured you musta made a deal.

Seidelman musta named names; turned state's evidence. Trouble was, if Seidelman sung, his testimony would've been used against Cohnheim and Stone. But there was nothin' from Seidelman at the trial, so he didn't rat on his people, did he?"

"No, Martin, he didn't."

"But he was a criminal, as well as a valuable witness. And if he had to serve time, which was nearly certain, he might eventually have cracked and exposed the whole international ring. This was a person who Donaldson would never let go unless there was some kinda deal. So, I asked myself, what could Seidelman have had, besides his testimony, to buy his freedom?"

"Okay, Martin. I haven't told you the whole truth. I've been afraid to tell you, but here is the rest of the story. I knew Donaldson was vulnerable. He had conceived a plan that was unjust and discriminatory. He put a female employee in an untenable position. There's a boatload of gender discrimination in the Bureau, and it's the 'me too' era. Donaldson is smart. He sees CEOs going down like Hong Kong journalists. I knew he would not want to risk a black mark on his record. I threatened to go to the I.G. and expose the way he treated a single mother and her daughter."

"And you offered him a deal?"

"Yes, I did. I'm sorry, Martin. I should have told you from the beginning, but I was afraid of what you would think. I did what I had to do, and I hope you can understand. I knew that Herman Seidelman would do almost anything to get out of jail and go back to Israel. I had visited Seidelman in the hospital and studied his medical chart; knew his blood type was compatible to Keri's. Seidelman had something I desperately wanted. Something I wanted more than anything else in the world. So, I pressured Donaldson to contact Seidelman—to tell Seidelman that it was the only way he was ever going to get out of prison. And Seidelman agreed to the deal."

I stare into Cassandra's eyes across the table. Can you ever really know anyone? Even yourself? When fate intrudes upon your world and grinds you down, threatens what you love the most, how will you react? What are you capable of doing? What compromises are you willing to make? I like Cat. I respect her. I'm glad she finally told me the whole truth. But I know I could not have done what she did. And yet, who am I to make a moral judgement? What did Roni Cohnheim say? "A sentence of death can bend the moral compass."

Author's Note

This book is a work of fiction. Names, characters, and incidents are either the products of my imagination or are used fictitiously. Any resemblance to actual events or persons is entirely coincidental. Descriptions of places and locales, especially those of the Boston neighborhoods and the hospital in India, are accurate to the best of my knowledge, but any connection among those places to the kidney trade is fictitious. Although the descriptions of the Big Dig construction project are generally accurate, the scenario of the chase through the tunnels is entirely fictional and, in fact, is not possible.

Although this book is a fictional story, I feel responsible to be clear about several issues. I do not encourage anyone to seek an illegal kidney. Although I raise some critical issues about the current system of organ procurement in the U.S., I believe the organizations that manage procurement are well-meaning, professional, and reliable. There may be better ways to organize organ procurement, but they involve complex ethical, moral, and medical issues. I would be pleased if this book raises questions and stimulates discussion of these issues, but it is not my intention to advocate or provide any answers.

Nevertheless, the descriptions of kidney disease and its prevalence, the shortage of kidneys for transplant, the size of the black-market for kidneys, the process of dialysis, and the description of kidney transplants are accurate to the best of my knowledge at the time this book was researched.

The process of kidney allocation has undergone some changes since this book was researched. Deceased kidneys are now allocated within a 250-mile circle around donor centers instead of the previous donation service areas. Some problems have been alleviated, but many persist. Well-informed patients can still list in multiple areas. Because of the larger distribution areas, many more offers are made to transplant hospitals, more offers are refused, and more kidneys are being discarded. As a result, it is estimated that approximately 20 percent of kidneys are now placed "out of sequence," meaning they are not going to recipients at the top of the waiting list. This is a troubling development for fairness and equity.

For readers who would like to learn more about kidney disease and treatment, including prospective patients and their families, kidney donors, and charitable donors, a wealth of resources are available. The following five web sites are a reasonable place to start:

1. National Kidney Foundation, www.kidney.org
2. United Network for Organ Sharing, www.unos.org
3. Organ Procurement and Treatment Network (OPTN), htpps://optn.transplant.hrsa.gov
4. National Institute of Diabetes and Digestive and Kidney Diseases (NIDDK), www.niddk.nih.gov
5. American Kidney Fund, www.kidneyfund.org

Glossary of Yiddish Terms

Bulke	A baked roll
Farshtayst?	You understand?
Farshtunkener	Stinky, smelly
Freser	A person who overeats, devours
Goyim	Gentile, non-Jew
Mensch	A decent person
Meshugener	An insane person
Mitzvah (mitzvot, pl.)	A good deed
Rugelach	A pastry with filling inside a pocket of dough
Sachel	Good sense, street smarts
Schmuck	Fool, idiot
Shlemiel	A clumsy, inept person
Shtetl	Small town, village
Shtup	Sexual intercourse
Tsouris	Trouble
Yiddisha Kop	A smart person (literally a Jewish head)
Zaftig	Pleasantly plump
Zei Gezunt	Be healthy

Acknowledgments

Writing this novel has been a long process and attempting to market it even longer. So, after wallpapering my entire house with rejections, I now have an opportunity to thank the many people who helped me over the years and along the way.

I have been blessed with many friendships, most of which are much older than my picture in the book. They have enriched my life in numerous ways, including their availability as beta readers. My novel has benefited from their observations, suggestions, and criticisms, although I suspect they were far too sparing of the latter. I have tried to remember everyone, but my memory, which was never remarkable, has failed to improve with age. Hence, I apologize for anyone I have left out. In no particular order, I am grateful for the following readers:

Larry and Linda Katzman, Phyllis Rothberg, Frank and Vicki Solomon, Ruth and Tai Chang, Maureen Rubin, Kathy Dunham, Marge Stockford, Kim Holcomb, Mike Grogan, Rich Morassi, Mike and Patti Fontanarosa, Michael Snell, David Hark, Lilly Pelzman, Butch Lofchie, Leslie Worris, Billy and Diane Chesko, Andy Millen, Mick Watson, and Jack Mills.

I was fortunate to work with several different consultants whose suggestions required me to produce endless re-writes. Truthfully, they were helpful, wise, and professional, and my sincere thanks goes out to Anna Solomon, Laurie Harper, and Patricia Mulcahy. Charlotte Pierce from Pierce Press helped guide me through the publication process. Additionally, a note of thanks goes to Dr. Ted Steinman who reviewed much of my text on kidney transplants. Any errors in that regard are entirely my own.

I owe a debt of gratitude to two people who guided and influenced my career in health policy. My heartfelt thanks to Stuart Altman who started out as my boss at Brandeis University and became my close friend, mentor, colleague, collaborator and co-author of our book "Power, Politics, and Universal Healthcare: The Inside Story of a

Century-Long Battle." I would be remiss if I did not thank Joan Curhan from the Harvard Kennedy School who introduced me to Stuart.

The folks at BookLocker have been a pleasure to work with. Knowing more about not getting published then the actual art of publishing, they have made my journey easy, efficient, and professional.

Last and most important is my gratitude to my family. My son, Brian, was a beta reader, but more importantly, an inspiration. Often you dream that your kids will be better than you, and although some might say the bar was not that high, he has exceeded it in every respect, although I can still out-drive him on the golf course.

I can't possibly express all my thanks, love, and gratitude to my wife, Ellen. She has edited this novel so many times, I'm sure she has memorized it. As a result, any remaining mistakes in spelling, grammar, or syntax is entirely her fault, as I am used to blaming her for everything, and she still puts up with me. This book is partly a product of her suggestions and criticisms as well as her countless hours of editing every re-write. More importantly, she has given me encouragement and support through all the years of revisions and rejections. I love her dearly, and this book would not have been possible without her.

www.ingramcontent.com/pod-product-compliance
Lightning Source LLC
Chambersburg PA
CBHW071500110625
28057CB00023B/238/J
* 9 7 8 1 9 5 9 6 2 2 5 6 7 *